M. KOTSYUBINSKY
STORIES

M. KOTSYUBINSKY

CHRYSALIS

AND
OTHER STORIES

Fredonia Books
Amsterdam, The Netherlands

Chrysalis and Other Stories

by
Mikhail Mikhailovich Kotsyubinsky

ISBN: 1-58963-584-1

Fredonia Books
Amsterdam, The Netherlands
http://www.fredoniabooks.com

CONTENTS

OVEN BRIDE

Ion first noticed Gashitsa at a dance.

The Moldovaneska melody throbbing in his ears set his feet walking of themselves, unable to keep still even for a moment. Ion responded with every muscle, his face shining with elation and sweat, until he broke away from a group of his fellows, rent the circle of dancers asunder, caught up two maidens and was suddenly caught himself in a stare under delicate brows, a look that blazed with youth and the South.

"What witchcraft is this!" thought Ion with sidelong glances as he cut swift figures with his feet. "Can't remember that I ever saw her before...."

There was no time to think: the music and the dance demanded all his attention.

The musicians were three swarthy Gipsies sitting in a row on a bench near the circle. The fiddler, a frail homely boy in narrow rusty trousers and Moldavian shirt, bent his head, a shock of black hair instead of a cap, to the very sounding-board of his instrument as though listening with surprise to the sounds struck forth by his bow. His neighbour, the clarinet, was an elderly Gipsy and seemed to be playing in his sleep: rocking with closed eyes, his heavy bulk clad in padded black. In his moments of sweetest reverie, the instrument slipped from his lips and fell silent, but, as though caught red-handed, leapt back again and began to shrill like a creature possessed. The third, the trumpet, worked hardest of all. Perhaps it was the heat, perhaps his efforts, but he was wet with perspiration. His shirt lay pasted on his muscular body, and rivulets streamed down his broad dusky features; still he kept playing and playing with cheeks inflated like a full moon and his eyes popping until it seemed that they must fall out. "Turrum-turrum-tarra!" shouted the trumpet as though trying to waggle the walls of Jericho. Only when it gasped for breath could the scrape of the fiddle and the squeal of the clarinet be heard.

"Tarrara-rum-tarra!"

In the clouds of dust raised in the thunder of iron-shod boots one could glimpse young faces now and then. They were wet and flushed, but how earnest! Holding hands, lifting and lowering them evenly, stepping unhesitatingly and smoothly, and stamping firmly like good horses on the threshing-floor, the young folk seemed not so much to be dancing as performing some very serious business, a piece of work to be done unhurriedly and conscientiously.

"Tarra-tarra-turrum!" pierced the dust, rolling over the square, shattering against the little stone church, and scattering to the hazy mountains and the violet forests under the vault of the evening.

And the round-dancers kept pounding the rhythm, their hands rising and falling, white kerchiefs shimmering in maiden fingers. Warmed by the whirling, the faces shone with moisture and eyes stole mischievously more often from under lowered lashes to meet with one another, handclasps growing firmer and the breathing harder; while the dust, exploding under metal heels and scores of stamping boots, lept into the dance itself. It spun a dance of its own, nearly effacing the circle.

until divided again by the chain of coloured costumes and heated young faces.

It was warm.... The sun was slowly setting, getting bigger, brighter and hotter. The air was filled with light and heat, flinging a golden net over the dancers, musicians and motley spectators of all ages.

The din was terrific. Someone was drawing water from the well, and the tall rusty crane screeched mercilessly, while the hundred-throated crowd hummed like the driving rain of summer. The cries of the children, the laughter of the young folk, the thumping of strong feet, the scraping of the fiddle and piping of the clarinet, all merged into a strange but harmonious chorus ever dominated by the strident "turrum-turrum-tarra" rising over the dancers to break against the walls of the church and flutter away over the sun-drenched spaces.

But then the music stopped. The circle swung another round by sheer inertia and scattered, the girls deserting their young men to vanish in the crowd. Gashitsa, too, made to flit away, but was held by a firm hand. She turned with surprise on the laughing Ion, his face shining with moisture. His hand was firmly holding hers.

"Let go!" She tugged and blushed.

"What'll you give me if I do?" His grasp grew even firmer.

"What're you holding me for, when I don't even know you?" Gashitsa reddened with her efforts.

"I'm Ion, son of Kostaki.... And you? Who are you?"

As his grip relaxed, the girl suddenly tore free and sprang away so quickly that her starched skirt flapped like a flag in the wind.

"You may guess if you like!" she retorted, her dark eyes scorching him again.

Disappointed, the young man scratched his ear so

violently that his cap slipped over his nose. He moved towards his fellows lounging near by.

Their reception was comradely: one of them flung an arm about his neck and pulled so hard that he swayed; another squeezed his hand until the tears came. But Ion was not to be put out. Smiling all over his hairless, slightly pock-marked face, he looked now at the group of girls where Gashitsa stood, now at his newly bought braces which, crossing smartly over his deep chest, supported his wide-blown *sharovary* of green cloth split crimson over the boots. The blue braces were brand-new and their silver clasps had been drawing glances of envy from the young men and of approval from the girls—something that tickled the vanity of the owner of this most modish innovation. Ion, therefore, turned confidently to one of his fellows.

"Tell me brother! Who's that girl over there?" He pointed to Gashitsa.

"Which one? That wild goat in the white skirt?"

"Yes, yes."

"Why, that's Gashitsa, the daughter of Shtefanaki Mitsa who owns the windmill. Don't you know her?"

How could he have overlooked someone so pretty? thought Ion. Perhaps because she lived at the edge of the village and could not come to the dances often? The strains of a swift Bulgareska roused him from his thoughts. Several young fellows lunged to dance, drawing their girls with them. Ion eyed the group where Gashitsa stood, broke into the circle and caught her unawares by the belt she wore. With a lightness astonishing for one with such toil-tamed legs as his he danced away, slanting smiling glances at her. Conscious of his attention, Gashitsa blushed, her eyes downcast.

When the music stopped Ion stood beaming with streaming face, while Gashitsa, rosy and breathless, loosened a white handkerchief embroidered at the edges to wipe her brow. But on its way to her cheeks, the little cloth suddenly lept from her fingers, glittered once at its embroidered edge and fluttered into the hands of Ion.

"Oh!" she shrilled and caught at the free end of the handkerchief.

But Ion drew it to himself, and with it Gashitsa. The struggle was waged in silence and with equal stubbornness on both sides. The girl's features were touched with both annoyance and secret glee over the young man's obvious advances.

Victory, of course, went to the strongest. Freeing the handkerchief, Ion darted away wiping his face with it as he ran, closely pursued by Gashitsa.

"Give it back!" Her voice rang sharply, but her eyes danced.

Ion adroitly folded it slantwise and threw it around his neck, tying a knot at the chin.

"Give it back, I say!"

"And what'll you give me?" he teased, fending off her extended hand.

"Give it back to me straightaway!"

"And will you give me your lips?"

"Oh-ho! He's out of his mind!" Gashitsa's shining eyes belied her grumble. "That's my only care—to kiss you! Better keep the handkerchief!"

"Well said! You should have let it go at that long ago!" exulted Ion, coming nearer.

The minx had been waiting for just this chance to snatch the kerchief from his neck. Still, Ion was wary. Catching her hand as she snatched for the kerchief, he flung his other arm about her waist and drew her hand to him.

"Take your hand away!" she cried, struggling weakly.

The musicians struck up again and happy Ion strove away to the dance drawing Gashitsa with him.

To the very last dance, Ion would not leave Gashitsa, paying court according to all rules, while the bristling girl grew more and more amiable, soothing the soul of the young man with melting if mischievous looks.

The sun was about to vanish, as the spectators straggled to their homes and the young people too went their ways. The square grew larger and very still. The musicians took leave of the fainting day with some final strains. Only the dust floated lazily for a time against the reddening sky and then settled gently on the little church's shadow striking across the square to the very cottages.

The days passed and Ion could think only of Gashitsa. Wherever he might be and whatever he might be doing, he could see only that bluish spark in the dark eyes of the girl, the firm line of her brows and her luxurious waist. Again and again he clicked his tongue: "What a girl, what a girl! Maybe I ought to marry!" And how modest she was: the looks she had given him when he had been scampering about her! How vividly it all stood out in his mind: the whole dance! The melody of the Moldovaneska still rung in his ears; and he thought again of that little scene with the handkerchief. It was so real that he unwittingly clutched the kerchief about his neck, as though afraid that the girl's mischievous fingers might suddenly pluck it away.

He met her once—near the church before the service. She walked in holiday dress, starched all over, and very important. Her white jacket speckled with red was ever so slightly worn on the right side where her *cavaliers* had laid their hard toilers' hands during the dance. If the truth be told, it was this worn spot that now brought a host of sweet memories to Ion's mind. But out there in front of the church and the people it had been awkward to tell her what he felt, so that he just greeted her and spoke the rest with his eyes alone.

On another occasion it happened differently.

It was evening and the sun was dipping beyond the forest line when he and a group of his fellows were returning from the vineyards. Chatting with one another, they were descending unhurriedly into the valley when someone in their midst let out a cry that was neither cry nor laugh:

"Ho-ho-ho!"

"Hi-hi-hi!" shrilled the answer from below, and the young men looked down and saw a group of girls with huge woven vine baskets on their shoulders. They were striding rapidly down the dusty road.

"Ho-ho-ho!" bellowed the horde of young fellows as they ran down the hill to head them off.

"Hi-hi-hi!" came the devilish chorus of the girls fleeing from their pursuers.

It was an inarticulate outcry, caught up by the surrounding hills and flung against the sleepy quiet of the rosy evening.

Ion hardly knew how it came about, but in the chase he had caught Gashitsa, thrown his arm round her neck and pressed her to him. His breast was heaving from the run, and the feel of the young girl's body made him drunk. He happily embraced her in all the screaming and shouting and kept saying things that neither he nor she could comprehend. The noise abated, but it was only at the edge of the village that Gashitsa broke from his embrace and flittered away to an outlying cottage beyond the windmills on the hill.

"So that's where she lives!" thought Ion, eyeing the old, very ordinary Moldavian cottage, its overhanging thatch of rushes, latticed windows and whitewashed walls. The mound of a cellar could be seen beside it, and its yard was surrounded by sheds and the tall narrow

15

wicker silos. A brand-new crane hovered over the well in the road directly before the house, as though guarding the entrance. Two big dogs were growling and snapping at each other beyond the gate, but, noticing Ion, promptly joined forces and bit at his heels until he vanished around a bend.

As he reached the gate of his own home, Ion heard the stentorian voice of his father through the open doors. *"Nunte shi Bukovina!"** he stormed in his favourite malediction.

This brought a smile to the lips of his son.

"Father is going it!" thought Ion of his explosive, though not unkind parent.

The odour of hot maize tickled his nostrils as he crossed the threshold. His mother, scrawny Anika, had just drawn a pot of cooked maize from the oven and dumped the fragrant yellow mass on a plate on the three-legged table.

Kostaki senior was a burly Moldavian with a face as flushed as a red pepper and a neck even redder against the spotless white of his array; he wore a shirt gathered at the waist by a red belt, but reaching beneath the knees of his white trousers. He sat on the bench by the table stressing his words with shake of arm and shock of rusty-grey hair. His fuzzy chin bristling like a grey porcupine seemed to share the wrath of its owner and be ready to plunge into the fray with him.

"Nunte shi Bukovina!" thundered Kostaki. "He thinks he can insult me before all the world just because he's got a windmill and I haven't.... *Draku!*** Mosh Kostaki is not last among the Moldavians for all that! Eh?"

"Whom're you talking of? What's happened?" asked Ion.

---

* Literally: "Wedding and Bukovina!"—a malediction obscure even to Moldavians.
** Devil.

"Who? Why, of that Mitsa Shtefanaki, the one who lives behind the windmill at the end of the village...."

Ion listened curiously to the story of the quarrel his father had had with Gashitsa's father at the pot-house over a quart of wine.

"I won't let him get away with it!... What's that you say? What if he is rich! Our God Almighty is the same to all Moldavians.... I'll take him to court. To court with that miller of Hell! *Nunte shi Bukovina!*" Highly irritated, Kostaki senior reached for the tobacco-pouch at the back of his belt.

"Ye-ess! A lot you'll do to him!" Anika drawled. "A rich man will get what he wants even from the Devil, while a poor one won't even get his oxen home."

The end of this exchange was heard from the passage into which the mistress carried the table, smoking pot and all.

"Time for supper!" admonished Anika.

Kostaki senior returned the tobacco-pouch to his belt and began his supper. Ripping bits of the maize paste from the gruel, he rolled them into little balls, dipping them into a generously peppered bean sauce, catching up stray wisps of the peppers which he chewed as vigorously as if they were his enemies, his face as glowing as the evening sun. Finishing his meal with a draught of wine from a pitcher, he turned to his son.

"Drive the horses to the night pasture, because I'm going to ride to the volost tomorrow to lodge a complaint."

Anika only sighed.

Ion quickly did as he was bid: the pack was slung over the back of one of the horses and the metal hobbles jingled in his hands. He had only to mount with his customary leap and be off.

It was a soft still evening. The dust raised by the droves returned gently to earth. A star peeped here and there from the wan skies. Ion felt that he ought to ride by Gashitsa's cottage. It was not in his path, quite the other way indeed, but the temptation was strong. The familiar road was soon reached ... and there was the windmill slowly waving its wings like a great bird, and there the crane long-necked over the well and intent on snatching a pail of water out of the depths for someone. For whom was it straining so hard, even screeching?

Ion approached the well, looked and felt his heart leap. It was Gashitsa who was rapidly drawing up the bucket hand over hand. Her thin linen jacket held her young body compactly. He could see the strong young arms, curve of shoulders and high heaving bosom.

He had been too astonished to stop the horses, and drew them up with some difficulty only when he had passed. He dismounted and made for the well, drawing the startled animals after him.

"Good evening!"

"Good evening to you!" Gashitsa was struggling with the line and did not even glance at the young man; her eyes were fixed on the black depths of the well.

Ion stood watching.

"Won't you let me have a drink?"

Gashitsa offered him the bucket, but instead of bending to drink, Ion caught her by the hand.

"Shush, they'll see us!"

"There's no one around." Ion pressed the girl to him, and she did not resist.

"Why do you keep after me if you don't intend to wed?"

"And would you marry me?" he asked, bringing his big pock-marked face, now shining and hot, a little nearer.

The restless horses suddenly jerked at the reins, nearly pulling him from his feet.

"Whoa! Damn the devil's brood!" he cried, jerking at the rope wrapped around his hand.

"Gashitsa!" called someone from the cottage.

The girl grew flustered, snatched the bucket and hurried to the gate.

"I'll come again ... tonight!" she heard Ion say.

Ion lept on to his horse, lashing the "devil's brood" which had interrupted his tryst at the most delightful moment.

The horses shook their manes angrily and dashed up the road in a cloud of dust.

An entire colony of windmills arose beyond the hill and hemmed him in on all sides. Some stood dark and still, their ribbed wings suggestive of bats in the night. Others, shedding reddish light from open doors, swung their wings about and about unhaltingly, evenly, and seemed at the point of rising from their sites, away into the dark.

The horses broke into a gallop on the hillside. The slope was covered with broad maize fields filling the air with fragrance. Ion's heart warmed within him and he began the endless song in a melancholy voice.

The horses settled to a walk now, snorting because of the dust. The chain that held them together rustled as they moved, while the song floated over the great fields.

The road turned and descended into a wide, almost limitless valley darker than the gently sloping hills. A moist but pleasant chill caught up with Ion, making the horses neigh and raise their heads. The still surface of the lake glittered amid the rushes. Frogs spoke up somewhere beneath the vapours, tumbling lazily over the reeds, and the deepening skies ignited their stars.

There were grazing horses stirring on the pastures. The night herdsmen lay about a bonfire where Ion soon joined them. Talking about girls, wine and the latest army recruitings—ordinary man's talk—they hardly no-

2ᴸ

ticed the approach of midnight. Ion decided to go to the village. He asked the others to look after his horses, promising a quart of wine. The prospect of a drink brought ready response from several. Ion dropped his coat and set off for the village on the hill in his vest alone.

The cocks gave voice on all sides as he approached the windmills, and he shortened his stride.

The village was asleep. The grey silhouettes of the cottages merged indistinctly. There was something of the graveyard about it all, of funeral silence amid the looming crosses.

In the dead quiet Ion could hear his own heart and the thud of his boots muffled by the dust.

He came up to the crane and saw the shadow of the fence, then went nearer and looked over into the yard. It was dark. Only in the blacker shades of the cottage could he perceive something white. Perhaps the beds of the family? Ion put his chest against the fence and heaved himself over on his hands before he remembered the dogs that had pursued him down the road by day. He paused, undecided. Still, he had to make up his mind! Bending forward, he advanced as stealthily as a cat towards the swelling of earth on which the cottage stood. He was soon in the middle of the yard. . . . Just a little more and. . . . But what was this? A dog? No, it was only a block of wood. He moved on and nearly stepped on a dog curled up by the cottage. He reached the mound on which the cottage stood and paused again. He could feel the warmth under the jutting roof and heard the breathing of the sleeping family on their white outdoor bed. "Which is Gashitsa?" he thought, scanning the huddled figures. "Must be this one!" he decided and felt for the shape on the bed; he found an elbow, a shoulder and, suddenly, a curly prickly beard.

"Ah!" came a sleepy grumble.

Ion turned to stone, his hand hovering over the beard. His heart seemed to have stopped for a moment, but all was quiet.

Like a shadow, he slipped farther. Someone's little foot peeped from under a quilt. No, that could not be her either. It was only at the edge that he recognized Gashitsa by her black braids winding from under the quilt like two fat snakes.

"Gashitsa! Gashitsa!" he whispered, nudging her shoulder, but the girl slept very soundly.

"Gashitsa, wake up! It's me—Ion!"

The girl uneasily turned her head, then abruptly sat up and rubbed her eyes.

"Gashitsa," pleaded Ion, "let's go to the garden or somewhere!"

Gashitsa took her fists from her eyes and looked at him with fear.

"What are you doing here? Go away at once! They'll hear us!"

"No, they won't!" whispered the young man, drawing her round to a corner of the cottage. "I said I would come and I'm here!" he soothed, holding her hands and telling her how he had pricked his own on her father's beard.

The girl marvelled at his courage and laughed.

"I'm so thirsty, my heart's afire," said Ion. "Haven't you anything to drink?"

"There's water in the passage."

"Who cares for water? Perhaps there's a jug of wine left?"

"Wait a minute," Gashitsa mused. "I'll be back straightaway!" And she darted to the depths of the cottage.

Cautiously opening a door from the passage to the interior, she found a small closet, extracted a candle and matches, felt for the cellar key on the wall and stole back to Ion.

"Let's go!" she said, moving ahead.

One behind the other, their necks apprehensively turned, they passed the sleepers on tiptoe.

The dog growled in its sleep as they went by, but did not wake up.

Gashitsa opened the cellar door and the cold mustiness floated to meet them. Descending a few steps into the dark they lit the candle. The darkness shrank away, lurking in the corners.

Gashitsa dripped a bit of wax on one of the barrels and set the candle on it. There were nine such stout full barrels standing importantly around the cellar in a semicircle with smaller barrels and other vessels at their flanks. It was a gloomy cellar, however, even grim. The shadows danced on the walls with the flame of the thin yellow candle.

"Where's the white wine?" Ion broke the silence.

Gashitsa seized a jug and set it under one of the spigots. The transparent yellow liquid struck the bottom in hissing foam.

"That'll do!" he said when the jug was half full. He picked it up with both hands, blew away the foam and eagerly put it to his lips.

Gashitsa, leaning against a barrel, never took her eyes from her beloved, enjoying his pleasure.

"Good wine!" gasped Ion at last, wiping his mouth with his sleeve and setting the jug on the floor "Thanks," he added, embracing the girl. She did not think to resist, feeling far too well in the arms of her lover; she trembled at the touch of his muscular hands and the warmth of his young desirable body. There was a curious ringing in her ears and a mist in her mind, Ion's words came to her as from beyond a wall.

She would never be sorry for having loved him, he assured. Weren't all the fellows afraid of him? And why? Because he was the strongest, that's why! Who could compare with him for strength? No one! Only yesterday Petraki, a strong fellow too, had tried to wrestle with him, but he, Ion, had crashed him to earth, nearly knocking the soul out of him.... And how cunning he was too, that is, he, Ion! They would never whip him in the army where he had to go for a month. And why? Because he could speak Russtian. How? Very simple, listen: "Got safe dutsar! Kingdom come! Weetch!" It was pronounced weetch, he explained, and not weetch!

He was so carried away with these strange words, the symbols of the faith of the Russians, that he even released the girl.

The fitful light of the candle could barely take in the whole of Ion's figure, his dangling arms and pock-touched face wearing an expression of concentration as he moved his wide lips folding so strangely over these unintelligible words. Monotonously, he chanted syllable by syllable, while Gashitsa stood spellbound with folded hands.

"How clever he is!" she thought with a fresh rush of affection.

"Good?" concluded Ion.

"Very," she whispered, "only, I could not understand anything."

"Ah, well, even the fellows don't understand it, let alone the girls!" With this, Ion tossed off what was left of the wine. The warmth of it spread through his body and a new light appeared in his eyes. His heart grew weightless, his head clear and his arms and legs very strong and agile. Thrusting his thumbs into his vest pockets, Ion regarded Gashitsa with contented superiority.

"And do you know what the oath is?"

"No, I don't," said the girl sadly.

"You don't? Well, it's like this: 'I swear ... by God ... Christ ... the Saviour ... the faith ... the truth....'"

Sincerely impressed, Gashitsa shook her head and clicked her tongue. "How hard it is!"

"Why, there's nothing easier." Ion was rapidly losing hold of himself. "I know the whole exercise with the rifle. I'll show you if you like."

He turned about the cellar, seized a long broom in the corner and stood at attention raising his shoulders so high that his head nearly vanished between them. Forgetting about his precarious position in someone else's cellar, he thundered the command:

" 'Tention! Left right, left right!"

The whole figure of him with his shoulders high, his heated pocked face between them, the broom pressed to his side and his stiff rooster's stride, seemed so funny to Gashitsa that she could not help giggling, but Ion noticed nothing. He darted to and fro across the cellar stamping the floor and shouting: "Left right, left right!"

The dogs barked desperately above.

"Who's there?" a deep voice boomed.

Ion's knees gave way, and Gashitsa, at her father's cry, plunged to the candle and put it out. The cellar grew black and still; only the dogs could be heard in the yard above, and there were heavy footsteps.

"Who's there?" demanded the voice again.

Ion sat staring stupidly at the darkness, while Gashitsa shook with fear behind a barrel. But soon all was quiet above. The dog whined and barked no more and the footsteps retreated into the quiet.

"Gashitsa!" whispered Ion.

"What is it?"

"Where are you?"

"Here, behind the barrel...."

Ion felt his way through the dark and pressed himself beside her. They sat silently for some moments.

"Let's get away from here!" he pleaded at last.

"I'm afraid. Better wait!"

But they soon grew tired of sitting still and, supporting each other, they stumbled about the barrels and climbed out of the cellar.

"Let's go to the vineyard!" begged Ion.

Gashitsa urged him to go home, but could not quite resist the passionate plea of her lover and, hardly aware of how it happened, found herself behind the cottage on the path leading to the vineyard.

They found themselves a spot in the thick of the bushes where Ion gathered enough grass to soften the ground.

The soft soil exuded moisture, and the old spreading bushes thrust their strong branches high, like many hands. A star winked only here and there amid the broad black leaves. It was cold and rather frightening. Gashitsa pressed to Ion in spite of herself and then surrendered to his heated caresses.

Dawn was breaking when they parted—Ion gratified and happy and Gashitsa abashed, with her eyes on the ground; she was heavy-hearted and full of forebodings.

The young man and the girl met in the vineyard nearly every night.

Time passed and the spring gave way to a summer that was hot, dry and sultry.

The vines were covered with pale-green tassels, the corn stalks in the fields grew plaited and the barley yellow; it seemed that all that thriving land was growing threaded with grey.

The grass with which Ion had feathered their nest in the vineyard had dried and withered. And alas! Time had also withered the feelings in his heart for Gashitsa.

More and more rarely did he spring over the fence into the familiar vineyard by night, and more and more eagerly did he turn to look at the other girls. Gashitsa's reproaches and tears repelled him even more.

The ease with which he had won the heart of Gashitsa, who had so meakly given him all that a girl could, now quickly quenched the first flame of his love. The caresses so dear to her, lost all the charm of novelty for him. Gashitsa simply bored him now.

To desert her had never occurred to him at first. He had seduced her and must surely marry. What a row her parents would raise if he didn't—and what would people say? Ah! And how would his father look at it, the hot-headed but very just Mosh Kostaki?

But as his indifference to Gashitsa grew, this very same father, the irate Kostaki, seemed to him as a deliverer. Ion recalled the quarrel between his father and Gashitsa's parent, Mosh Shtefanaki, and seized upon their enmity as upon a life-buoy.

Would his father ever agree to such a daughter-in-law, the daughter of his enemy? No, never!

He, Ion, would have been very glad to marry Gashitsa, but how could he when the fathers were at loggerheads and would never agree? So firmly convinced did he grow of the obstacle he had thought up that he even regretted he could not marry the girl. To avoid tormenting himself and Gashitsa, he stopped visiting her despite all pleading and tears.

Harvesting time had begun and the fields were dotted with ricks which seemed to be pleading for the threshing-floor. The corn stalks on the hill stood as proudly as oaks, exhibiting their fat cobs; and the grapes in the vineyards grew yellow and swollen.

Mosh Kostaki's red-pepper face burned even ruddier as he looked over all this wealth. "I must see Ion married by autumn!" he decided. As he did not at all keep his intention to himself Ion soon learned of it and not only agreed, but left the choice entirely to his father's taste.

With the blessings of his father, therefore, he was soon spending his leisure peering into the dark eyes of thick-set Domnika, and came to wear her little copper ring—the first link forged for him by Hymen.

And Gashitsa?

She lay by her mother's side on the family's outdoor bed. Her father was pacing the yard, murmuring a prayer to the starlit sky. She could hear his sighs and snatches of prayer accompanied by the nocturnal croaking of the frogs at the pond in the valley and the clicking of the long beak of the stork nested on the neighbouring roof. Gashitsa was annoyed with her father for praying so long. If he would only go to sleep! She was awaiting her lover tonight and was anxious to get away to the vineyard. But would Ion really come?... Of course he would! It was urgent that he should, because she wanted to talk to him very earnestly. Ah, that Ion! How her heart did ache for him! And her head was so tormented with thoughts of him! She was too weary to think any more. Only shreds of thought and images flickered in her mind, rankling in the heart and vanishing.... She could see him with the broom on his shoulder when flushed and handsome he had strutted to and fro in the cellar. Then, there was the time in the vineyard when they had sat amid the leaves and he had caressed her, talking of their wedding and future life together. The traitor! What was that people were saying about Domnika? Had he really deserted her for another? It could not be! Never, never! He was probably stealing up the path to the vineyard right now to put his arms about her and tell her when he would send his father to urge the suit.

"And who is it that nests in the vineyard by night? Just let me catch him and I'll break every bone in his body!"

She heard the angry voice of her father and began to tremble. She was terribly afraid, afraid terribly for Ion! She would have to hurry to warn him. She sat up on the bed and grew wide awake. It was a dark moist night and the frogs were croaking. Her father kept turning from side to side, moaning at the other end of the bed. It was time to run. Ion would be waiting. But she could not get away now; her father was still awake and might notice. . . .

Gashitsa lay back pretending to sleep. A sweet fatigue gradually overcame her and sleep pressed her eyelids gently together. She struggled against this however, listening eagerly to her father's breathing which grew more and more even.

He was asleep at last, and she could get away.

Gashitsa slipped from under the blanket, put her bare feet down cautiously, and finally vanished round the wall.

The vineyard was quiet. Wave after wave of the vines descended to the valley. Gashitsa plunged into that sea and found the familiar corner. Ion was not to be seen. She sat down beneath the bushes, hugging her knees and determined to wait. The warm air carried the odour of the black earth to her from under the dense shrubbery.

The fragrance and the vine-rods and the fading grass all reminded her of the happy moments in her life. She thought of Ion embracing her, promising that he would love her for ever. . . . And now? . . . She would have to tell him today. . . . Oh! There was someone approaching! . . . Probably he! . . . But no; it was someone passing down the path to the village. . . . She would tell him that he had been deceiving her long enough. . . . Wasn't that Ion coming?... She could hear something stirring far away.

Gashitsa peered over the bushes, her body tense. It wasn't he, but only a horse grazing on the hillside; the stillness of the night had caught up its heavy tread.

"Merciful God! When would he come?... It was late.... And it was so necessary, so awfully necessary that he should come and learn that soon.... Oh, how shameful! How would she ever tell it to him? ... But it had to be done, because he would then give up Domnika and send the match-makers to her father.... But why wasn't he coming?... Could it be that he would not come?... Wasn't that the crowing of a cock?

Gashitsa strained to listen.

Somewhere near by a cock crowed hoarsely and was echoed clearly and melodically by another whose call was at last caught up by a ragged chorus of crowers breaking the stillness of the slumbering village.

The girl sat rooted to the spot.

"No, he was not coming.... But he must.... He must.... He must.... He must ..." she repeated, stubbornly clinging to the thought, concentrating upon her one desire with all her might. No.... He had deserted her!... But wait, she would make him sorry!... But then, what could she really do to him? He would marry! And she? She would be deserted, dishonoured and with child. Disgraced! For ever disgraced! Laughter would rise about her like straw in the winds! And father! Dear God!

And Gashitsa wept, the large tears streaming not unpleasantly over her cheeks and falling on her childish pouting lips.

Gripped by the chill in that late hour, she shivered and wept, though somewhere in her heart a small soothing voice kept saying:

"Perhaps he'll come? Perhaps!"

It was only by morning that she returned to the house, weary, frozen and disconsolate, but determined to meet with Ion and thresh things out frankly and to the end.

Though Ion guiltily avoided Gashitsa, she managed to intercept him. He was driving an empty cart to the fields for a fresh load of wheat when she hoisted herself on to the back and hid until they were well out of the village and concealed from everyone by great clouds of dust. Only then did she touch his hand, and Ion turned frightened and surprised.

"How did you get here? What for?"

"What for? Because I waited long enough for you to come to me. When are you going to send the match-makers?" Her voice was sharp and accusing, but Ion could not hear over the rattling of the cart.

"What did you say?"

"When are you going to send the match-makers?" she shouted irritably at his very ear.

Ion slightly reined the horses.

"I'm not going to," he said firmly.

"Is that so? And what about my shame? How are you going to make good for that?"

"My father won't have it!" the young man dodged, his eyes wandering.

"So it's your father you've thought of now? And before? But what's this?" she cried suddenly and clutched his finger resplendent with the cherished ring he had got from Domnika. "But he doesn't mind if you pay court to fat-nosed Domnika? Does he?"

Ion was hurt.

"What's that to you? You've climbed on to someone else's cart and have the gall to scold! Here, off with you!"

"I won't get off until you say when we marry."

"That'll be when I've hair growing over here!" he re-torted angrily, tapping his palm. "Get off!"

Gashitsa clung to the side of the cart, but was wrenched loose. The cart rumbled on.

"U-u-h!" She shook her fist at him as she arose and shook the dust from her clothing.

Choking with tears and anger, she ran towards the village wailing, but soon took hold of herself, dried her cheeks with her apron and turned homewards.

There was nothing for it but to tell her mother and plead for help.

So horrified was her mother that she forgot even to scold. "We're disgraced! Shamed! We've got to think of something."

Aunty Prokhira was sent for at once. She was a re-nowned authority on all such matters. The messenger found her in the street winding yarn on to a spindle and muttering.

When they heard the drag of torn shoes beyond the door and caught sight of the spindle, Gashitsa and her mother anticipated the ponderous figure in a padded jacket; she would be wearing a black shawl over her head and another around her neck, and between the two they would see the great nose, which at first glance looked less like a nose than a whole face.

Gloating, Aunty Prokhira questioned Gashitsa long and well on the saucy details and authoritatively de-clared:

"You've got to go 'pe-koptor'.... That means—on to the stove with you, my girl!"

On to the stove! The girl vividly pictured this humil-iating custom, the inevitable heart-rending altercation with Ion's parents, the enemies of her father, and the wild scenes that sometimes accompanied the practice. The shame of it all!

The things that awaited her in the next few days were so bitter, so tormenting that she would rather have sunk through the earth. But what could she do? The earth would not swallow her and she had to go on.

It was arranged that Aunty Prokhira would take Gashitsa to Ion's cottage in the evening when all were home, and then come back to tell her mother the outcome.

Prokhira turned up after dark and took Gashitsa away almost by force. The girl was as in a fever. Her feet seemed to cling to the ground; her heart throbbed and her head could hold only one wish: that the path would go on for ever.

"Don't grieve!" Prokhira soothed. "You're not the first to go *'pe-koptor'*! That's how Katinka Sandina married Nikhalaki last year, though his mother tried to drag her off the stove by the braids. She got an awful thrashing from the father and another from Nikhalaki. Her poor body was black and blue for a month or even two. And yet...."

Gashitsa was not listening. They had already turned the familiar corner and could see the reddish lights of Ion's windows. She hung back from the gates, but Prokhira pushed her through unceremoniously.

"You go on! I'll wait here."

Quickly she ran across the yard, seized the latch and pushed the door.

Mother Anika had just opened a huge chest, while father Kostaki was extracting an ember from the stove to light his pipe.

"Good evening."

Gashitsa first kissed the hand of father Kostaki and then of mother Anika. Without another word she ran precipitously to the stove, scrambled to the bedding on top and hid behind the chimney.

The old folk stared at each other and had the same thought at once.

Dropping the lid of the chest with a bang, Anika darted to the stove and mounted, while Gashitsa curled up in a corner, a trembling little animal.

"Why did you come here?" Anika demanded severely.

"Why did your son come to me?" snapped Gashitsa.

"My son? And how about all the others who called on you? We know what you girls are like today! Get off that stove!"

"Not if you kill me! Everyone knows that no one came to me but Ion.... It was he who led me to sin, saying he would marry me.... And now...." Gashitsa sobbed.

"*Nunte shi Bukovina!*" thundered Kostaki who had been listening. "What's all this? Where's Ion?"

He flung open the door and emitted a roar that set the windows rattling:

"Ion! Ei!"

Ion had barely put his foot across the threshold when his father seized him by the shoulder and dragged him to the stove.

"What does this mean?" he snarled into his son's ear, pointing.

Ion froze when he saw Gashitsa.

"Yes.... That is, I ... and she," he faltered.

That was all he could say before he was whisked away to the outer passage. Kostaki slammed the door behind them.

Terrified Gashitsa heard a great to-do in the passage, the sounds of blows and Kostaki's hoarse exclamations:

"With my enemy's daughter! So you'd ruin that girl! I'll knock all the others out of your head! *Nunte shi Bukovina!* You'll send the match-makers to father Shtefanaki tomorrow!"

Kostaki re-entered the room, breathing hard, approached the stove and shouted:

"Get out of here at once, you hussy! Go to your father and tell him that tomorrow I, Kostaki, will send the match-makers on behalf of Ion! Do you hear? That's what you're to tell him!" Gasping for breath, father Kostaki sat heavily down on a bench.

"Good God, good God!" moaned Anika, overcome by the unexpected calamity. She urged Gashitsa to go home, but the sobbing girl declared she would not leave until the match-makers had been sent.

Anika had to arrange a pallet for her on the stove and after a whispered talk with her husband before the icons turned out the light and lay down beside the girl.

Ion spent the night in the yard. He could not fall asleep for a long time, thinking of the events of the day, of his crushed hopes of marrying Domnika. Fingering his forelock, he sighed with loneliness in the dark.

When he went to the threshing-floor with Gashitsa at his side the next morning, he said not a word, pretending not to notice her.

But before very long, while shouting at the tethered horses straining for the sheaves of wheat on all sides, he stole a glance at her now and then, saw her muscular arms skilfully shaking the sieve, winnowing the grain, scattering it over the threshing-floor like snow, and felt the harshness melt within him into resignation.

April 15, 1896

THE WITCH

Aunty Prokhira bustled into the cottage of Ion Bro-ska, her neighbour, with a vivacity hardly in keeping with so staid a figure as hers. Her pallor, her heaving bosom under the flimsy peasant's blouse, the black kerchief awry and especially her bare chunky legs told Ion that something extraordinary must have happened. Before he could exchange so much as a glance with his Maritsa bent over the evening meal by the oven—something which he never failed to do in emergencies—Aunty Prokhira let out a scream: "Witchcraft!" and collapsed on a bench.

"Whatever is the matter with you?" cried man and wife.

"Witchcraft!" she blurted again.

"Whatever could have happened to you, Aunty Prokhira?" Maritsa rushed to her, leaving her pots to destiny.

"I've seen a witch!" came Aunty's bomb-shell. Ion's longish face grew even longer, while Maritsa's dark eyes blazed.

"How? Where? When?"

Aunty Prokhira regained some breath.

Her story began with catches and gasps and a world of sighs. She went to the beginning of things. In minutest detail she reiterated all that they knew so well: she described her cow which was black but for some white patches on the back and the mouth and had clean udders, each as big as a small barrel. She recalled with great accuracy how the cow was fed, how much milk she had given and of what quality. Encouraged by the attention of her listeners, Prokhira went on to tell of the family relations of the gentry to whom she sold her milk. And lo and behold: the cow began to lose weight, gave no more milk and let no one near her. Neither sacred water nor incense had helped in the least. And when the old medicastress was summoned she had pronounced but one word: "Witch!" To think of it! Aunty Prokhira, of course, had felt it all along. Hadn't she noticed something white near the barn, something that flitted through the barn door only the day before? And then.... Prokhira pursed her lips, letting her eyes roam the cottage before they fixed on her hosts.

The two were burning with impatience.

Ion's long face and Maritsa's glittering eyes deeply gratified Aunty Prokhira.

"I finished my housework and just had enough time to do the milking. The sun was about to set and there was I only now getting the pails. I didn't want that witch to get the evening's milk, and so pushed the door in with a pail—when out jumps a white dog, whisking between my legs! That's witchcraft, I tell you! Holy saints! That was the witch! My blood boiled. You know how it is with me! I'll kill her! I'll kill her if it's the last thing I do! I grabbed the buckets and went after her. She flew across the yard—with me after her, ran along the fence—with me after her, jumped a ditch right into Mitrokha's kitchen garden—and me after her. I could've swallowed my heart. I'd lost my shoes and thought I'd drop dead. We reached your vineyard and shot straight for it. Her tail went down as she crouched, and then over the fence she sailed! I threw my pails across and,

Lord have mercy on us! I looked around and what do you think, dear neighbours? There was not a trace of her anywhere! Only my pail hanging on a bush and your Paraska staring at me near by."

"Our Paraska?" gasped man and wife.

"Yes, your Paraska! With her hair streaming and vine leaves sticking in it. My flesh crept, the way she ogled me! Witchcraft, I tell you! I can't get over it even now."

Aunty Prokhira was still fighting for breath.

Ion and Maritsa said nothing. Ill at ease, they had a disturbing thought, something that could not be expressed in words.

Ion was tongue-tied, and a vague smile hovered on Maritsa's lips.

Then all three broke into talk at once. All the hallmarks of witchcraft were reconsidered in detail as well as the prescribed methods of breaking its spell: their own and other people's stories about witches and other evil spirits. Ion and Maritsa heaped advice upon Aunty Prokhira. Maritsa was especially vehement. She shook her fist and swore that had she been in Aunty Prokhira's place, she would have run down that witch even at the price of her head.

Apparently reassured, Aunty Prokhira talked louder and more confidently, though some lurking thought seemed to trouble her at times, coming nearly to the tip of her tongue. It had grown late, and she looked down at her bare feet with some show of haste: she meant to stop at Mitrokha's where she had lost her shoes in the kitchen-garden. She would ask Mitrokha to find them for her as early as he could tomorrow, because she intended to go to market in Kishinev before dawn. She had heard that the Broskas were going too; and at last she went away.

As soon as she had gone, Maritsa turned to Ion, facing him hard. Ion withered under that stare.

"What are you looking at me like that for?"

"Why shouldn't I? You'd better go and see what your daughter is up to in the vineyard. I'm fed up with the bitch. The moment you're out, she's out too! Trapesing about the kitchen-garden, in the weeds or in the vineyard. All the work about the house is left to me. But as soon as I say as much as a word, she turns those saucer eyes on me so that my flesh creeps. She'll poison me one day, I swear. You'll have your bit of joy then! She never says anything when there are people around, but lets her tongue wag about me to you. I'm this and I'm that; I'm drinking wine and carousing in the night!"

"But she's never said anything of the kind."

"Don't tell me that! Blood runs thicker than water. If she were really a decent girl, she would behave like one. Where's she off to when all good people go to church? Wandering in the weeds or in the vineyard with the dogs. Have you ever seen her in church even once? Have you or have you not? And what is she doing in the vineyard night after night? What's she up to now?"

Ion merely blinked, because he did not know what Paraska could be up to in the vineyard by night. His inability to lash back with a suitable answer infuriated him. He shouted, his hazel eyes blazing: *"La draku!"** It's not me, but you who ought to know what the girl has been doing at night. You're not her mother, but ought to keep an eye on her just the same, *o sout-draku!"***

The usually complacent Ion so surprised Maritsa with this outburst that she could only stare with her dark eyes.

"Keep harking for the devil and there'll be some more of him in our cottage!"

---

* To the devil with it!
** A hundred devils!

The forgotten supper spoke with its fumes. Maritsa hurried to the oven, and Ion suddenly realized what a hot stove could really be like. Which was the hotter of the two, he thought, Maritsa or the oven? The whole hearth was aflame, acrackle and aboil as though a mess of fiery dragons were fighting to the death. He flung himself from the cottage. On the steps outside, he filled his pipe, sat down and took a deep breath of the crisp night air.

The moon was just peeping over the old black barn. The pea-creepers, the acacia- and apricot-trees threw sharp shadows across the yard, black lace stitched with silver. There were windows glowing here and there and on one side there lay the heavy braid of vineyard dwindling into the shadows of the rugged hills. There was a shout and a laugh in the street near by.

Ion was disgruntled and puffed hard at his pipe thinking how unjust his wife had been. Well, what else could one expect from a stepmother? He thought about his kitchen-garden and vineyard which Paraska had put to rights with her own hands. Neither Maritsa nor he had so much as touched anything there. The poor girl had done all the work herself. She was a quiet hard-working girl. Why was she always gadding about—and so shy of people? He visualized the scene described by Aunty Prokhira: the white dog leaping over the fence into his vineyard with a pail sailing behind it and landing on the bush where Paraska had stood with vine leaves in her hair, looking at Prokhira with surprise.

He stirred uneasily. What could she have been doing in the vineyard? Why should she be frightening people? He got up impatiently and went to the corner of the house from which he could see the vineyard.

"Paraska! Where are you?" he shouted, cupping his lips to keep his voice from spreading. His "where are you?" rang loud and sonorously. Never reaching the vineyard, it bounced from the wall of nut-trees and returned to Ion. He stood for yet a while and, hearing no answer, shrugged and went into the house where Maritsa had served the supper.

He could not fall asleep for a long time, lying next to his wife on their bed in the passageway. In spite of himself, he was still listening, waiting for something, irritated by Maritsa's luscious wheezing. The quiet patter and then scraping of bare feet reached his ear at midnight. That must be Paraska cleaning her feet of the clay in the vineyard. Ion yawned, blessed his mouth with the sign of the cross and fell asleep.

Daybreak found the Broskas preparing for market. Paraska had got up long before and was busy over a folding-ladder. She was obviously avoiding her stepmother. Coming face to face with her at last, Paraska felt such a wave of hatred in the elder woman's look that she shied away and slipped from the house. Ion had meant to speak to the girl several times, but could not somehow. Only when they were at the point of leaving did he say, assuming a gruff manner:

"You stay in the house, and don't go trapesing about, because ... because...." Perhaps he finished the sentence when he was out of the house, for the girl did not hear it.

Paraska was alone now.

Her tasks about the house were quickly done and everything was spick and span. She made a breakfast of yesterday's corn gruel and then kept indoors remembering her father's bidding. Passing a little mirror fitted in the wall, she could not help stealing a glance, though she knew that this would give her only pain.

Paraska was a plain-looking girl and, therefore, as she thought, unhappy. Her short stocky figure, toil-worn hands and especially her face drove her to despair. How many times had she looked at herself in this mirror and

40

how many times had her heart filled with resentment over such ugliness! She could not help trying to smooth the lines of her face, but it was useless to try. Her skin grew no smoother and the spots she had rubbed merely grew blotched, while the mirror reflected the selfsame face with the biggish nose, the drooping lips and the red spots she had just made. Bitterness surged in her and overflowed in hot tears from her grey eyes lacklustre like the tin spoons in the cupboard. Rebellion! The quiet shy Paraska was ready to rebel against destiny. She gritted her teeth, knitted her brows, clutched at her hair which flowed down over her convulsively shaking shoulders. What good was there in those sable brows resting over her eyes like an eagle's outspread wings? They only gave her an owlish look. What good was there in all that long hair, a girl's pride and beauty, washed and cherished with the secret hope that they would ever flow about a young fair face and never about one like a dried apple?

Often, when overcome with this despair, she sank into reverie with wet cheeks on the bench in the corner. Sweet and soothing dreams stole upon her unawares, stilling her grief. Like the Tsarevna Frog of the fairy-tale, she shed her ugly shell to be revealed in all her luxurious beauty—tall and slender, with snow-white face, star-like eyes, in short, the direct opposite of what she was. The waves of love surged in her heart like the floods of spring.... The handsomest young fellow in the village.... Merry-making on the green.... The envious glances of her friends.... The holding of hands.... The quiet dark nights filled with ecstasy, a kiss and infinite happiness....

Paraska could sit about that way for a long time, feasting on her dreams. But one glance at her little mirror and it was all gone. An ugly face peered out of it. She was sure that it lay hidden under that smooth glass surface especially to remind her of her loneliness and bad luck.

She had had two joys, but was deprived of both. The first had been her mother, gentle and loving. The mere memory of her vague image made her tears flow. She had died and Maritsa had come instead. The other joy had been.... No, that was something she dared not think about, for it made her heart ache until she could barely breathe. It is all too easy to scatter a dream cherished by a lonely heart!

Why should she, an ugly duckling, have dared to raise her eyes to the proudest eagle in the village, one as handsome as the new moon! A lizard in love with the sun! But a lizard would surely be happier, because it could bask in its rays at least, while the eyes of her own sun, Todoraka, would never come to rest upon her. Their warmth belonged to stepmother Maritsa. The moment she saw them together her blood froze. Her heart had turned to a stone so cold that it burned. Its aching gave her no rest.

Her loneliness grew ever drearier in this world harbouring such vipers as her stepmother. She had drawn away then from the company of the girls and the young men without regret. She had always been the last among them anyway because of her ugliness. She gave up all the walks, songs and parties and even her own home to avoid the dagger glances of her stepmother. There was so much malice, scorn and undisguised hatred in those eyes that Paraska flinched with a feeling of unknown guilt and wished she could dwindle to a speck.

Her only refuge was her father's vineyard, the dumb witness of her dreams and anguish. She loved that sea of woolly green with its coolness, seclusion and tranquillity under the blue vault of the sky. She had put so much work into this plot of land, rearing with her own hands those verdant vines with delicate tendrils and clusters under the broad leaves. Those were true and undemanding friends and their company was comforting.

She stayed in the vineyard every day until late at night.

And now her father, whom she loved for his kindness and pitied for the injustice he suffered at the hands of Maritsa, had forbidden her even to go to the vineyard. Why? She could not understand. She sat about tormented by her idleness. It was past midday. The hot sunshine poured through the windows. Only the flies buzzing under the ceiling broke the stillness of the room. She went out into the yard and heard snatches of songs: there were gaily dressed girls walking down the street. Paraska clambered into the barn much resembling a wicker basket, where cabbage was stowed instead of corn. Perched on a heap of cabbages, she thrust her head through a wide crevice.

A few girls whom she knew walked past the barn. But instead of greeting her, they darted timidly aside and cried: "That's her!" They all pointed and fled away with skirts rustling. Paraska wondered. She looked around for the cause of their fear. There was nobody. She thrust out her head, looking after the girls. Granny Anika was approaching with her grandchildren. Paraska was glad to see them. The old lady had always seemed so sympathetic. But now, to her surprise, Anika looked up at her wildly, gathered the children into her fold and hurried past without greetings.

Paraska was puzzled. What had happened to them all?

Sensitive as always, she was deeply hurt and lay still on the cabbages until evening.

The sun was setting when she remembered that it was time to cook supper, because father and stepmother would soon be back.

The Broskas returned earlier than usual. Word had spread rapidly between Ion's friends that Aunty Prokhira had caught a witch who turned out to be none other than his daughter Paraska. Several versions were afoot, and the girl figured as a witch of long standing in each of them. When one of the tales came back to Ion he flew into such a rage that he almost came to blows with his neighbour who had told him about it as friend to friend. Finally, the two of them drank a glass at the nearest pub, but while they were doing so, Ion heard such weird things about his daughter that his superstitious head was at once filled with strange and unaccountable recollections of his daughter's behaviour, things that both disturbed him and made him angry.

Trouble may visit anyone, who knows? Never had he doubted the existence of witches and he felt a cold chill at the thought that his own daughter could be one.

Maritsa fanned his fears with her enigmatic smile and dubious shake of the head, which was to imply that she had known it all along, but had preferred to say nothing. In the grip of superstitious fear, his imagination was whetted by darkness and begot many pictures truly terrible. He decided to see if Paraska was still wearing her cross. Witches were afraid of such a thing, as everyone knew. Maritsa agreed with him.

As soon as the Broskas came home, Paraska began to think anxiously of a pretext to leave the house. Ion, however, was so eager to reassure himself that he bade her to stay. Paraska thought this strange, for she was not used to attention from her father. She was even more surprised when her stepmother approached the oven and ostensibly on the sly, but actually for all to see, made the sign of the cross over the vessel of mamaliga. Ion ordered Paraska to unfasten her blouse at the throat. At which, the girl clutched her throat and stood stock-still, staring at her father.

Ion lost his temper. There she was, the witch, knowing very well that something was wrong.

"Undo your blouse, do you hear?" he bellowed.

Paraska shuddered and began unfastening her blouse. She could not manage it, however, because her fingers were trembling and the button would not come out of its loop. But the blouse was undone at last, revealing her dusky breasts and the little silver cross between them on its black ribbon.

Ion took the cross, felt it in his fingers and showed it to Maritsa. Without moving from the oven, the woman looked at it, shook her head, but said nothing.

Ion felt greatly relieved, though ashamed of himself in the presence of his daughter, who stood quite still, timid and confused as before, without refastening her blouse.

"Cover your breasts, for God's sake! And better stay home, instead of running about at night."

Paraska flushed with shame, covered her breasts with her arms and rushed from the room.

Ion exchanged glances with his wife. Maritsa shrugged with the mysterious air so typical of her of late. Then, in an unusually high-pitched voice she began to complain about people's malicious tongues. Perhaps the girl was not at all to blame? True, she was strange and kept to herself, but there could be nothing to those rumours, of course. Deaf Mariora had sworn that she had seen Paraska perched on the well, had seen her clearly in the moonlight as she had sprinkled something down. And Iordokhy Karabush had complained that the folds of his gates had been fastened together with bast, after which his horses had grown feeble, and that such a thing could have been done only by Paraska. They had heard all sorts of things at the market. What a shame! But of course it was only a pack of lies.

Ion was somewhat surprised to hear Maritsa defending her stepdaughter, but no less depressed by the reiteration of the facts. Yet he had seen the cross with his own eyes—and no witch could wear a cross. But then again, perhaps it had not been a cross, but only some satanic charm. He did not know what to do and was deeply troubled.

A difficult, inexplicable time came for Paraska. Everything had changed and grew stranger and stranger.

Father must have been watching her. No matter which way she turned, she always felt his intent gaze. Maritsa's attitude too had changed. She had become quite sugary, especially in the presence of her husband. Yet she never failed to make the sign of the cross over everything that her stepdaughter had touched, doing it in a way that she was sure to notice. She made the sign of the cross over a pitcher of water from which the girl had drunk, over the oven which she had approached and over the hens which she had fed. It was all so depressing that Paraska preferred to spend her days in the vineyard again.

The vineyard, however, was no longer as secluded as it used to be. Often, as she sat under a bush, pensive or wringing her hands, a whisper would reach her. She would look around and see a pair of eyes burning at her through the foliage. She was being watched, and they were whispering about her. But why? Sometimes, too, she noticed that people shrank away from her, replied to her greetings gruffly, pointing at her with malicious looks. What was the meaning of this? What did they want of her? What harm had she done them? Did she interfere with anyone by being ugly, poor and unhappy?

Filled with sadness, she wetted the broad caressing leaves of the vines with her tears.

The inevitable happened at last. Neither Ion nor Maritsa were at home that day. Paraska hanged two pails on the shoulder pole and went to the well for water. No sooner had the children playing on the square by the well noticed her than they scattered in all directions and hid behind the trees, peeping at her through pert eyes. Only the sparrows kept hopping about, pecking the ground at the base of the well. So touched was she because they had not flown away that she took out a bit of bread and scattered some crumbs. It was such fun to see them snatch the bits from each other. While the birds were still feeding, Paraska drew her water and put the pails back on the pole ends. Suddenly, something struck her sharply between the shoulders. She screamed and turned. Lumps of earth, pebbles and stones showered down upon her.

"*Shedz bineshar!*"* Paraska shouted, shaking her fist.

The children seemed to have been waiting just for this. They scurried out of their ambushes with shouts, whistling and hallooing. She thought of defending herself at first, but when the stones and lumps of earth turned to a hail she hurried away, feeling that she could not cope with them. She ran steadying her pails, followed by the children as by hounds in hot pursuit; they kept pelting her with lumps of earth as they ran.

"Halloo!" shrilled long-legged, twelve-year-old Iokash, Aunty Prokhira's son and evidently the ringleader. "Hit her! She's a witch who steals the milk from the cows."

"Witch, witch! She steals the milk from the cows! Witch!"

Paraska suddenly halted The word ran through her

---

* An oath.—*Tr.*

like fire. Recent scenes flashed across her mind, illuminated by the one word: "Witch!"

An uncontrollable fury seized her, and with an ani-
mal-like howl she turned upon the children. The one
pail fell at her feet, while the other splashed water
upon her. She did not notice. Seizing the pole, she attacked the boys who ran away frightened by her outburst, but still shouting: "Witch, witch!"

Paraska flew after them like a tempest, her eyes burning, her breast heaving, her hair dishevelled. The boys
were so terrified that they grew even more shrill and
ran for their lives. Coming into full tilt with a fence,
Paraska grew aware that none of her attackers were
any longer in sight. She cursed them again and ran
home sobbing. As she ran, people looked at her, wet,
dusty and with dishevelled hair. She sank to the
ground in the kitchen-garden, sobbing. Now she knew
why Father had wanted to see the cross, and why her
stepmother was for ever making the sign of the cross
over the pots and pans, and what those malicious
glances meant. The injustice of it was unbearable. This
terrible grief had come to her for no fault of her own.
She was a witch. But that was a filthy, stupid lie! She
was ready to get up and shout to all the world: "It's a
lie!" But meanwhile, it seared her heart no matter how
she beat her head against the ground, weeping.

The fresh news spread over the village like wildfire.
The story ran that Paraska had been casting her spell
over the well by broad daylight, that she had been spilling something into the well and towards the four ends
of the earth. The villagers would not draw water from
that well any more and demanded that the Broskas have
sacred water sprinkled over it at their own expense.
Ion was constantly beset. No one was afraid of him
any more and bluntly told him all that was said about
his daughter. It turned out that not only Prokhira's

cow had stopped giving milk, but about a dozen more had fallen victim to Paraska's witchcraft, to the unspeakable grief of their owners. It was up to Ion to make amends. But then what could he do? He was constantly on tenterhooks.

He was overjoyed when Aunty Prokhira came to give him advice and brought her husband, Ioch Galchan, with her. The latter had come with a bottle of white wine. Maritsa served some biscuits and the council began. The first to speak was Aunty Prokhira, an earnest and experienced woman. She was not satisfied with Ion's declaration that he had seen the cross. That might have been only a satanic charm of course. This is what should be done: Paraska must be taken to church on Sunday. When the choir would begin to sing "Ye Cherubim!" she must be watched closely. If she was really a witch she would never be able to endure this and would bark and whine like a dog, a true sign which had exposed more than one witch!

Ioch, a stout, ruddy-cheeked Moldavian with shining eyes and a clipped bristling moustache, laughed with a wave of his hand.

"That's all nonsense! Old wives' talk! What you ought to do is to see if she has that thing."

"What thing?" His wife stared.

"Well, the thing that every witch must have—a tail."

Neither Ion nor Maritsa could claim to have looked for one.

"There you are! And that's the first thing you should have done. A witch cannot do without a tail. Who's ever seen a witch without a tail? She ought to be examined carefully." He was willing to help. He would make no mistake.

But Prokhira protested. She looked ominously at his ruddy fat face and oily smile. She knew that man inside out, could see through all his thoughts and wishes. He would do better to sit still and keep out of things which women knew better.

But Ioch stood his ground. Inspection was the thing. If there was a tail, she was a witch; if not, she wasn't.

Their opinions differed. Ion and Prokhira supported the first method, relying on the church. Maritsa was inclined to agree with Ioch. But it was Prokhira who finally got the upper hand. It was decided that next Sunday Paraska should be taken to church, and they would see what they would see!

Paraska learned of their decision by chance. The village talked of nothing but the Sunday service and how she would whine like a dog to show her witchy nature.

Strangely enough, Paraska received the news indifferently as if it were no concern of hers. She had grown so weary and apathetic of late. It was as if she and the world were two runners who would run on for ever and never overtake each other.

What did it matter? There was no happiness for her. and death seemed dearer than life.

Sunday came in three days. The rumour that a witch was to be taken to church had attracted so large a congregation that many were left jostling on the steps. The girls in their Sunday dresses did what they could to protect their starched folds in the crush. The young women kept whispering to one another, burning with impatience. All heads turned to the door whenever anyone entered. Some of the men had climbed to the choir gallery for a better view. Aunty Prokhira exulted as if at her own name-day party. She strode about as importantly as the sacristan who was lighting the candles. She exchanged whispers with some, nodded to others, waving to still others. Ioch wore his usual oily smile even here, casting glances at the young women and whispering to his neighbours. But there was no sign of Paraska. The priest appeared at the holy gates and began the service, and yet there was no Paraska. The impatience of the people mounted. At last there was a commotion near the door, and a wave of excitement swept from the rear to the front rows. Paraska came into the church, her eyes lowered, a figure timid and shamed. In her neat but not festive dress, she walked down the aisle that had been cleared for her, an avenue perhaps too wide for someone so insignificant. Maritsa followed with the air of an innocent victim; Ion walked behind. Hundreds of eyes turned on Paraska as if seeing her for the first time. Those in the rear pressed forward, craning. When Paraska approached to take her place near several girls they shrank away from her as from something unclean. The circle around Paraska was so big that any dignitary could have envied her. To her it was only depressing. To evade those malicious looks, she kneeled and addressed herself to God, kind and merciful, to Him who could see all injustice and who knew who was innocent. She prayed with the troubled crowd surging about her. The melting tenor of the dark young priest who put so much feeling into his chants was lost upon the congregation, for everyone was tensely expectant, watching the service carefully not to miss the "Ye Cherubim!" That was when the witch would be sure to reveal herself by whining and barking like a dog. The overcrowded church grew stuffy. The congregation was a single breathing, coughing and sweating mass. The warm vapours mingling with the incense and the smoke of the candles hung in the air like a great stifling cloud. It seemed that a bolt of thunder must leap from this charged atmosphere and shatter the walls. As the "Ye Cherubim" hymn drew near, everyone's eyes grew wider. All necks ached from the strain of watching and quaking. The tension grew unbearable. Then came a lull like the quiet before the storm and the choir broke forth and mounted in volume: "Ye cherubim!" There was a ripple of animation as though a chill wind had swept by. Faces grew longer and paler and all eyes bored into Paraska who continued to pray, on her knees as before. While praying to God, protesting about the injustice, she too had been waiting for the moment subconsciously. And no sooner had the solemn choir begun its gentle strains than something within her clamoured wildly for expression. Cold beads of perspiration stood on her brow. She barely managed to suppress a scream. She crossed herself convulsively, bowing again and again, crushing her fingers in a frantic clasp. Could it be true? The people around her were waiting, holding their breaths, their lowering eyes upon the prostrate witch. But the Cherubim passed by as peacefully as a summer's night. The mist cleared and it was obvious that nothing extraordinary would happen. The crowd was visibly annoyed. For a minute or more they stood quietly as if puzzled and waiting for something more. Still nothing happened. Paraska kept crossing herself and bowing, and sickly smiles appeared on the lips of some women. The crowd stirred as if awakened, cheated and disgruntled. Paraska had made them feel silly.

There were some who left at once. Ioch was excited and muttered something to his neighbour. He looked at his crest-fallen wife whose eyeballs had turned heavenwards, demanding explanation.

The service was over and the crowd poured from the church. There were voices of pity for Paraska, claiming that she had been unjustly slandered. Aunty Prokhira felt ill at ease. She had advised this method herself, had in fact proclaimed it from the house-tops and now it had ended in smoke. Ioch Galchan, on the other hand, was full of glee. He had known it all along, but they had not listened. He continued to insist that the girl be examined. She was a witch if she had a tail, and not if she had none. That was all there was to it. There was no other method.

There were not a few who agreed, and even Prokhira finally lent a sympathetic ear. Anything to distract attention from her predicament. Her plea now was that this witch was cunning, malicious and experienced.

Walking hand in hand with Maritsa, Ion was much comforted. He was sure that the whole story was nonsense and was glad that it was over and done with, that all minds were at rest and he need not go to the expense of having the well sprinkled with holy water. He expressed his satisfaction to Maritsa who responded rather coldly. She looked at Paraska with distaste. Pale and obviously disturbed, the girl was hurrying homeward with her eyes lowered.

The stars were shining over Paraska. The night was dark and still. The thickly woven vines were trailing over the soft earth; their entangled tops forming canopies of dense foliage heavy with grapes nearly ripe. The mysterious transformation had gone on within the grapes under the hot sun all day. Reddish or yellowing, the half-transparent berries seemed to be dozing in the veil of vapours amid the leaves. They were protected from the evil eye and all afflictions by goat, cow and horse skulls mounted on the posts set up haphazardly throughout the vineyard.

Paraska sat in her favourite spot under a spreading bush. Open-eyed, she saw nothing but the overcrowded church. They were singing "Ye Cherubim" and there was something rising in her throat so that she could barely suppress a wild outcry. What could it have been? Why that queer impulse? The question had given her no rest for several days. She felt that something strange was happening to her since that memorable Sunday. She would begin to pray, but find that she could not. There was some power stifling her from within, clamouring for expression in a wild scream. Or she would feel that she had become as light as a wisp of down and was nearly ready to float into the air. More and more often her thoughts turned to things sordid and mean. She thought, for instance, of flying to Prokhira's cottage, settling on her cow's back from the air and kicking at the animal's sides with bare feet. She would gallop on it with streaming hair until the creature fell dead. Or perhaps there was something she could do to Maritsa? She could turn her into a dog, a lean mangy dog with tail between its legs. The dog would be slinking to the table, cold and starving, but they would only say: "Away with you!" The dog would then run to Todoraka and he too would kick her away. Yes, she could do such things. She felt almost capable of them. Good God!˙What was she thinking of? So the people were right after all! Perhaps she was really a witch? But no! Paraska shuddered and rubbed her eyes, trying to disperse these queer pictures and thoughts. She must pull herself together. The Evil One was plaguing her because she did not pray and had forgotten God. She crossed herself, therefore, collected her thoughts and raised her eyes to the glowing sky. She began her prayer loudly.

The tip of the moon was rising over the hill. It was slipping from the grip of the black clouds lining the horizon. Its silver stole gradually over the vineyard, fingering the leaves and lighting up the grape clusters. The skulls on the posts gleamed more whitely, casting long-horned shadows. One leaf stood out alone vibrating with its tendrils.

Paraska had not yet finished her prayer when it seemed to her that a sheep's skull as white as snow had winked its hollow eye at her. She stared hard. No, she had only imagined it. Once more she raised her eyes and continued her prayer when someone seemed to have winked on the right. She looked to see who it was and found a cow's skull grinning at her on a tall post. Her blood froze. The skull kept grinning, holding her with the hollows of its eyes.

Something stirred. She looked, and saw nothing but a moonbeam reaching from behind a bush like a gigantic white arm. She trembled, afraid to turn her face to see the skulls again, yet drawn to peep once more at that of the horse. She did not dare. Suddenly, she was sure that there was someone standing behind her. She stiffened, sprang to her feet, wheeled and saw only the horse's skull she had been afraid to look at. The object hung brilliantly white in the moonlight and there was no mirth in it. In the grip of a foreboding, she was sure that something might happen at any moment.

The skulls so horrifyingly white and the black bushes with their curling vines and the moonbeam seizing upon the bush like a great white hand filled her with icy, paralyzing fear. She wanted to run away, but could not. Her feet seemed rooted to the ground. Her dilated eyes seemed fixed on some far-away object as upon something terrible. But recovering from her spell, she wandered quickly away with short uncertain steps as though intoxicated. She blundered through the thickets, shuddered when the wet leaves touched her face or neck.

Paraska walked about distracted for several days. Her mind kept turning on the same thoughts. She recollected everything she had heard about witches since childhood and compared all the omens with the strange moods that had disturbed her of late. The conviction grew upon her that she was a witch and the horror of it mounted within her. She did not go to the vineyard any more, for she felt that the skulls would laugh at her and taunt her with the word "Witch!" At night, she lay awake for a long time on the porch, tormented with the thoughts which she could not shut out.

One day, at dawn, she felt that something unaccountable had happened to her. She could not say whether she had slept or not. But again, she felt as light as a wisp of straw. She was chilled to the marrow and felt something as solid and clammy as a snake brushing over her legs. She found that it was a tail, a long solid tail with a tuft at the end such as cows have. Horns had sprouted from her head, raising her hair. She could not see, but felt them. A wild rage shone in her eyes and seared her heart. In a twinkling she was swept high in a vortex carrying her over the earth. On she flew with the howling wind fanning the evil flames of her witch's heart.

In the morning she was found lying unconscious before Galchan's house. She was revived and carried home. After this, she sat on the porch, pale and hunched, surrounded by curious onlookers. She answered no questions and was afraid to stir for fear of feeling the long snake-like tail tickle her legs.

The event caused great excitement. Though reassured by the trial in church, the villagers were now aroused again. Ioch Galchan's method which he had taken good care to explain to everyone had become very popular. Everybody agreed that only a tail was the doubtless stigma of the witch, and that only its presence or absence could put an end to all conjecture. Ion was beset on all sides. He ought to agree to have his daughter examined. If he did not, they would find a way themselves. The village would tolerate no evil.

Tormented by superstitious fear, Ion agreed to everything. He was sick unto death of the whole story and would heartily have liked to see an end to it.

The inspection was fixed for next Sunday. When it came, Aunty Prokhira was in the Broskas' cottage all morning. She had come when the people were still in church. She helped Maritsa clean the cottage with the air of a priest at a consecration. Paraska was waylaid in the yard and summoned to the house. Prokhira saw to it that she would not get away. The grim woman was sure that the witch would slip out if only given the chance. It would be useless to look for her then. So cautious was Prokhira that she fetched water herself when the girl was thirsty. She bolted the outer door and kept whispering with Maritsa, explaining the details of the plan and making signs to Ion who stood anxiously looking out of the window.

Paraska grew suspicious. It was easy to see that something extraordinary was afoot, and she carefully watched the glances of all who were present. After some whispering with Prokhira, Maritsa went out and returned with deaf Mariora, a huge woman with bulging eyes and rough muscular hands. Crossing the threshold she sniffed at everything, until she caught the fragrance of the white wine which Ion had hidden behind the oven. Observing that it was sinful to drink while the others were at church, she nonetheless poured a glass and downed it with great relish.

The nearer the end of the church service, the more often did Ion look out of the window. At last he saw a group approaching the house. Soon, there were people converging upon the cottage from all sides. There were young women among them in holiday dress. Still influenced by the solemnity of the church they had just left, they crowded about the door. Behind them were the men, young and old. Only Ioch Galchan stood among the women, talking animatedly.

The girls and youths kept somewhat aside, but the children clung to the windows like flies to a carcass.

The sight of the crowd filled Paraska with mortal fear. They had come to kill her, to drown or to burn her at the stake as had been done to witches in olden times.

Like an animal at bay she rushed about the cottage, her eyes wild with fear. At the same time Prokhira and Mariora seized her hands. Ion stood by the door determined to die rather than let the girl escape. With her hands clasped beneath her apron, Maritsa regarded the scene with her usual smile.

Paraska screamed, struggling in their hands: "Let me go! You'll kill me, you will!"

"There, there!" the two women soothed, pulling her to the bed.

Before she could realize what was happening, Paraska found her dress over her head as strong arms flung her on the bed. She was gasping for breath like a trapped animal under the heavy bulk of deaf Mariora. The muffled shrieks that escaped her were like the cries of a stuck pig.

Prokhira gave the sign and Ion opened the door upon which the crowd outside had been impatiently banging. The people surged into the passage, but Ion barred their way, intending to let them in singly or in pairs.

They were impatient and noisy. Everyone wanted to be the first to see the tail. The most persistent were those whose cows had perished. Galchan wanted to be the first, but the young women would not let him, claiming that a man should not cast eyes on the girl's shame. This made Ioch furious, insulting him as the author of the entire affair. Scolding and jostling, he made his way to the door.

Ion let the women pass in twos and threes. They filed by the bed inspecting the visible part of Paraska as intently as they would the cows at the fair. Disappointed, they would make way for the following group. Paraska struggled no more. She realized that she was neither to be drowned nor burned, and so lay submissively. The people walked by with an air of passing some exhibited relic, touching her from time to time. Paraska could not see them, but could guess by the feel of the hands or by the voices just who it was that was visiting them. Now she could feel the hands of Aunty Anita who lived near the church, now the hands of Granny Domnika, the mother of Iordok, the best young man in the village. Paraska was suffocating in her clothes wrapped about her head, but resistance was impossible, for the strong hands of the women over her kept her firmly down. And so, bent nearly double, she lay accepting the guests as they came, one after the other, as if to celebrate her name day.

Meanwhile, a heated argument began in the yard. Ioch Galchan insisted on his rights of authorship and fought hard to reach the cottage. Yielding to his insistence finally, Ion decided to take council with the most venerable women who, after brief consideration, decided that Ioch should be the only man to be admitted out of respect for his share in the event.

He approached the bed, excited and flushed, his oily eyes shifting from Paraska's skirts to her rather pleasing stockings. He stood for some minutes, obviously disappointed, then slapped Paraska nonchalantly and weightily pronounced:

"No, she is not a witch."

At this point, Prokhira and Mariora let go of the girl who at once thrust her head out of her clothes. Though her cheeks were flushed with shame, her heart raced joyously. Sweet tranquillity flooded her body. She was sure now, as were the rest, that she was not a witch.

June 30, 1898
Chernigov

CHRYSALIS

Triste comme un beau jour pour un
coeur sans espoir

F. Copée

The plain cart drawn by one horse bumped mercilessly over the road whenever the wheels plunged
out of the ruts. The constant shaking brought an ache
to the chest of Raisa Levitskaya, the local schoolmistress, a circumstance of which she was glad, for it took
her mind from ugly scenes of the recent past. These
thoughts were still as hot within her as the fragments
of a freshly exploded shell. Try as she would to dismiss them, she still saw the haggard, Jesuitic and irate
features of the priest as she drove him publicly out
of the school. She could not have done otherwise, for it
had been impossible to bear his eternal denunciations,
his campaign against the local school, his instigation
of the peasants and interference with her work. Her
nerves had snapped and she had finally made a scene
in front of her pupils and the peasants. The priest had
gone to complain to the inspector again, as well as to
his superiors, while his wife had burst into the school
with her servant, broken all the flowerpots, and, her
green eyes flashing like those of a cat, had pounced on
the "impertinent schoolmistress," incoherent with rage.

She would have laid hands on the mistress if the latter had not escaped. Then came the inspector, a member of the district board, and the ensuing inquiry ended with her transfer to another school where she was now going. As soon as the exams were over, she collected her poor belongings and, unwilling to stay in that village with the priest another day, set off at once. Though she had come far from the scene of her troubles, the disgraceful matter still haunted her like a nightmare, filling her heart with anger. This was the second time in the thirteen years of her service that she had been compelled to change her post because of trouble with the local priest. Who could tell what lay in store for her. She would no doubt find another priest there and his wife.

Fortunately, the shaking made her chest ache so badly that she could not brood too long.

The white sand extending from the edges of the road threw up its dust veiling the distant strips of forest. The ornate birch-trees floated by with streaming braids, like those of the mermaids. The knotty shaggy willows on both sides of the road clutched at the ground with bared roots, like predatory birds clawing their prey. It was May, but the sultriness was that of summer. Webbed clouds drifted high in the hot sky, while something ominous was brewing in the west, rumbling fearfully in the distance. Raisa kept looking in that direction, wondering if the storm would overtake them. The mere thought of it gave her a chill of fear. In response to her pleading, the driver clicked his tongue over the beast and then lashed its dry ribbed hide, but with little results.

The cart trundled into the forest. It was very still and there was a pungent fragrance of resin. The needles of the pines were sharply etched against the fresh green of the young birches. Wherever the birches had ousted the pines, all seemed flooded with green fire-works. Now and then they would pass a wild pear-tree in bloom or a bird-cherry tree whose clusters of white blossoms filled the air with honey.

When they came out of the forest, the fields tipped downward and the cart continued to roll over the narrow rough road, zigzagging amid the winter rye.

At last they saw the village. It stood in the marshes, concealing its shabby cottages under the branches of spreading willows. From a distance, it seemed that these were not cottages at all, but ricks of rotting straw.

The cart clattered down the street and Raisa looked about with curiosity. Most of the houses were black with age and had dark mossy cornices. The mud'dy yards were dotted with greenish puddles. Deep pools pitted the street as well. The stamp of poverty lay on everything. The cottages and their tenants, the eternal diggers of the earth, had acquired, as it seemed to Raisa, the colour of earth and had themselves turned into objects of nature.

A peasant walking down the street looked much like the stray root of an oak. His face was as dark as tree-bark, his hands were hard and chapped, the crevices saturated with earth. His legs, too, were as ponderous as tree-stumps. A young woman hurried from a cottage and looked up at the newcomer shielding her eyes. The sun shone on her bronze calves giving them the hue of a near-by willow bent over a wicker fence. A group of old men sat drooping on a pile of logs, hardly distinguishable themselves from the dark seasoned wood. Dirty urchins were playing by the fence surrounded with pigs and dogs. Meagre piglets wandered about on spindles of legs, their bellies coated with mud. The odour of manure hung everywhere. By the pond in the valley there were several young women pounding the linen they had washed, their tucked-up skirts showing their legs which were as red as those of a stork. At the edge of this village there was yet another village, one peopled with the grey crosses under which the tillers of the soil had found their last repose. Farther on there was a field—level, greyish-green and bare but for the red skirt of a peasant woman which stood out like a lone wild poppy. At the turning of the road, a white church gleamed behind some spreading maple on a hill. Raisa's heart fell, and she gritted her teeth. Well, it would not be the first time: she would fight if need be.

A new school stood facing the church. It was a tall, metal-roofed building perched on the hill like a magpie on a fence. The cart turned and rolled into a large yard overgrown with tall grass.

The school proved to be locked, but Raisa walked round the building, looked into the windows, which breathed an untenanted atmosphere, and tugged at the padlock of the back door. There was no one around, only an unknown man who stood beyond a fence leaning on his elbows and watching her.

"Could you tell me where the key to the school is kept? I'm the new teacher," she said to him.

"Tatyana must have it; she's the care-taker.... You there! Run along and fetch Tatyana. She's weeding her stepmother's witchen-garden."

These words were followed by a patter of bare feet as something white flashed beyond the fence.

Raisa seated herself on the bench to wait for the care-taker. There was no sign of life. The white church nestling amid the massive trees was pleasing to look at. The driver had unharnessed the horse and put it to graze in the yard, while he lay down beneath the cart.

Half an hour passed before the gate slammed and Tatyana appeared on the path. A dry, spare little old maid, she came clutching the key in earthen fingers, eyeing Raisa with distrust.

"A good day to you!"

"Good day. Please open the door. I'm the new teacher."

Tatyana bolted to the door like a skirted soldier, admitted Raisa and hurried to the cart to get her things.

Raisa's steps echoed through the empty rooms. She could hardly breathe in that musty air pungent with the odour of pine wood. She flung open the windows and the green-stained light filtered into the room. She caught sight of a blue patch of sky.

Meanwhile, Tatyana had carried her things from the cart, brought some water for washing and lifted a samovar out of a sack by its ears so violently that it tinkled.

"Shall I prepare the samovar?"

"Please do."

While the care-taker busied herself with the samovar, Raisa inspected the building.

It was a large building, spacious and newly built. The sun flooding the big windows had scorched the high walls of pine board until the resin sweated from the cornices. The yellow desks stood piled in the corner, covered with dust. A blowfly kept buzzing plaintively at the window, while a spider wove its web between a bookcase and the blackboard. She passed from room to room and found them all quiet and empty. The school reminded her of a beehive upset in the sunshine.

She was to occupy two small rooms; the bedroom was nothing more than a cubbyhole. There was room only for a bed, a small table and her suitcase. When she lay down, she felt as though she were at the bottom of a deep well with bare pine boards sweeping to the mouth above. The other room was a trifle larger and the windows faced the white church and the trees.

While the teacher was having her tea, the care-taker stood by the door studying her and her belongings. Finally, she made so bold as to sit down at an edge of the red sofa and began a conversation with the intention of both learning and telling all she could.

Raisa, for her part, learned that the school had been empty since Fast, when the former teacher fell ill and soon passed away. She had suffered terribly, the poor lonely creature, and had lain in the room which was now Raisa's. If not for the reverend's old lady, there would have been no one with her in her last moments.

"So the priest must be an old man?"

"Oh no, he's not. He's a widower and has a daughter in her teens. It's his mother I was talking about. He's a rich man and owns a big farm near by. There are no other gentry about, and so the people work on his land to earn some money or make amends for their sins. He's been quarrelling with the deacon over the collections."

Raisa heard of the latest quarrel in all its detail, just what the priest had said to the deacon, and he to him, and what had happened after that, and what effect the quarrel had had on one-eyed Semenikha whose husband was a cousin of the deacon's godmother. The care-taker's story went on and on, spreading like a ripple from a stone cast into water, involving more and more people, confusing all odds and ends until Raisa could understand nothing and stopped listening to the garrulous little woman.

She put her two rooms somewhat in order and arranged her bed, to which she retired very early. She could not sleep. The candle kept flickering on her table at the head of the bed and she lay on her back between the fresh sheets, staring at the pine walls for a long time. In the dim light they seemed even narrower and even more reminiscent of the bottom of a well. Yes, she was lying at the bottom of a well, and real life began only way up there, where there was a patch of light.

Life! She lay thinking about it. She had turned thirty and what had she got out of life? There had been something like real life only in her final years at the clerical school when the seminarists used to call on her in the guise of relatives, bringing the forbidden books, talking of love for people, of politics, and even saying that there was no God. It was both terrifying and exciting. She had hidden the books jealously and read them until her head ached. The new thoughts had set her trembling, and she had felt such affection for the "poor" people that she had wanted to die for them at first, but then changed her mind. She felt superior to the girls she knew and to all who surrounded her for that matter. She was filled with a sense of new power and yearned to be rid of the school's walls in order to serve the "poor" people. She finished the school at last and her father, a poor psalm singer, took her home to the village. But there were none of those beloved long-suffering "poor" folk there, for such could never be near, but far away. There were only the peasants whom Raisa knew very well and did not like overmuch.

Life was none too happy in that poor home of hers where there was never an extra morsel. True, father did his utmost to have Raisa dressed no worse than a priest's daughter, and give her every opportunity to attend all weddings and other festivals where she was likely to find a groom among the clergy. No suitor was to be found, however, for the girl was neither rich nor handsome; and so life went its dreary way until two years afterwards, when all hope was gone, Raisa had to accept a post as a school-teacher. She had been teaching for thirteen years! Drying like an apple in an empty box for thirteen years! At first she had soothed herself with the thought that she was not unnecessary to the world at least and was serving a lofty cause, but this idea palled from day to day, losing its colour until it was lost itself. Her humdrum existence flowed through a narrow rut, bringing no joy. Her interests grew so narrowly professional that outside of them she was as out of place as a fly in autumn. That, indeed, was what she called herself: a fly in autumn. She had even wondered more than once whether or not she was really fond of her school. She was of course. She was fond of her work which had cost her her voice and brought that pain in her chest, the work in which she fought a constant battle against the schoolboys, their parents, the priests and the authorities. She was as fond of it as a peasant of his ploughing, reaping or the hard bench on which he could rest his aching body.

Still, there was a hungering in her heart.

True, it had more than once burst into blossom under the fickle rays of happiness. It had flowered on the quiet, but, losing all hope of casting a seed upon fertile soil, it withered like her face, hands and chest and became like a field flower in a glass case.

And so, even more lonely in this alien village, she lay tossing at the bottom of her well, thinking with something like fear that the time was near when she would have to come to the surface and face a reality centred about such trifles as her relations with the local priest.

The day was breaking when she fell asleep.

She was awakened by a voice outside the window.

"I saw someone come to the school yesterday and said to the priest: 'I wonder if it could be the new teacher.' The reverend sent me to Tatyana to learn if it was true or not."

As though something had stung her, Raisa sprang from her bed and knocked on the window-pane. What concern was it of his? This was no clerical school, but one belonging to the local authorities. She did not want to have anything to do with him. As far as she was concerned, he was merely a teacher of catechism and nothing more. And even that not now, not on school holidays. "This is outrageous!" she thought indignantly.

When Sunday came she did not go to church. Just out of spite. She kept wandering through the empty rooms, read the old books, sat in the orchard or talked to the school children who had brought her strawberries to make her acquaintance.

During the holidays, she did not go anywhere, for her father was dead and she did not want to disturb her relatives.

The priest showed no sign of himself and she grew calm.

She liked best of all to sit by the window in her "parlour" from which she could see the white church amid its massive trees. At sunset sometimes, the church assumed a rosy hue and the tree-tops were tipped with gold.

One evening, when she sat admiring this play of light, a figure rose before the window. Startled, Raisa jumped up and ran to the door, when she remembered that both doors opened into the yard where she would meet the priest anyway.

Instead, therefore, she ran across the class-room, opened the window and lept out. The priest tried the door-knob several times, paused for a while, then went round the building and found Raisa standing back against the wall.

Both seemed embarrassed.

He doffed his hat, showing that the flush of his uneasiness had spread even to his bald head.

Tense and pale, she watched him with frightened eyes.

He had meant to call on her. He knew that she had come and had expected to find her among the congregation on Sunday. But there had been no sign of her in the house of God. She was a stranger and he begged her, therefore, to come to him in case of need, for he was her nearest neighbour. Though hers was a secular school, he thought that the church and school should go hand in hand.

He failed to notice the spark in her eyes at his last words.

"My mother and I would be so happy if you would call on us sometimes. My daughter Tasya will be home during the holidays. It may be more cheerful for both of you."

Raisa was tormented by the question as to whether she should invite him in or not. She, too, had sprung from the clergy, and could not help respecting the cloth, but her extreme dislike for this guest won out.

"He had better go," she decided and just stood listening.

The guest seemed to grow tired of standing. He glanced about for a place to sit down, and then carried his rather feminine figure in its surplice to the garden bench.

Raisa sat down gingerly.

In the half-hour that Reverend Vasily sat on that bench he complained of the drunken, lazy congregation who cared so little for the church, asked her who she was and where she had come from and even mildly reproached her predecessor for her inability to instill the spirit of humility in the young generation.

Raisa answered in monosyllables, but Father Vasily overlooked this good-naturedly. As he took his leave, he invited her once again to visit him.

Raisa now rushed into the house, her cheeks aflame, and with an unpleasant feeling of having left something undone. "I ought to have invited him in. This was his first visit. But who cared? But what if he had taken offence? No, dear reverend, I do not need your precious acquaintance."

Their acquaintance, however, was not interrupted. The reverend's mother once sent her a plate of raspberries, and one day, too, when Raisa had a fever and the priest heard of it through Tatyana, he sent her some powders of quinine, and afterwards made inquiries about her health.

Nevertheless, Raisa appeared neither in church nor at his home, though she was certain that his family was hurt. "Well, let them be!" she would say stubbornly and turn her head from the window facing the white church in the embrace of the green giants.

May was gone and the heat of June began. On one especially sultry day Raisa was disturbed with an inexplicable anxiety from early morning. "There's going to be a thunderstorm," she thought with fear. And indeed, the dusk fell rapidly after the sultry calm until the darkness was almost complete. The black effaced the sky and earth, and there was a blacker strip on the horizon. There was a flash way out at the edge, as though a giant match had been struck. Fire then whipped at another spot and then at the former. The sky seemed to be winking. Feeble at first, the ragged flares grew more intense. It seemed that a wave of flame was rolling through the strip of black to break out at its ends.

Then came a flash in a new spot. The lightning lost some of its lustre, but the thunder mounted. The black kept winking uninterruptedly and seemed to be smirking wryly. Raisa's anxiety grew. The cloud might pass harmlessly enough leaving nothing more menacing than distant flickers, but then it might not. As ill luck would have it, she had dismissed Tatyana and was in the empty school alone. She lit the icon lamp and curled up in a corner as far from the window as possible, quivering whenever the windows came ablaze and the furniture, caught in the hellish light, seemed to scatter and run apart from their stealthy conclave.

The night was descending rapidly.

New and darker blots crawled from the horizon over an earth equally as sinister. The yard was as black as the interior of a chimney, but the lightning grew brighter, redder and, finally, dazzling white. When the blinding avalanche tore apart the pall of the night, the silhouettes of the poplars, windmills and cottages were etched in a frame of fire and vanished like a vision. The stillness was fraught with uneasiness and fear; even the warm air seemed breathless like a frightened child. It was as if a dragon were stealing over the hushed soil, baring its black fangs in a fiery maw. The trees trembled in its breath and all things hid away. The monster drew nearer with widening jaws and quickened gasps of fire swelling to a roar. An extraordinary thing happened then. The inert air was set whirling, chasing madly about as though crazed with fear. Helter-skelter it ran whistling and wheezing, lacerating its face on fences and walls, catching up the sand and leaves and all that it found in its way. The black monster pursued hotly, trodding hugely over the ground and breathing fire.

A roar shook the earth, set the window-panes rattling and made Raisa's heart leap.

She could not repress a scream. Even before, every peal of thunder had wrested a groan from her, shaking her from head to foot. Her dilated eyes and pale face, suddenly haggard, shone in the dark. She felt as if her hair had turned to wire and something unspeakably cold were clasping it. Her limbs were icy and alarm welled over within her. When the cannonade began and its heavy charges swept the sky, Raisa wedged herself into the corner, facing the holocaust with horror. The icon lamp went out and she could not muster the strength to get up and light it afresh. The heavenly salvos grew more frequent and vehement, vomiting arrows of fire, glowing kites and spouts of flame. A barrage on one side was at once echoed by one on the opposite until the earth heaved underfoot, the walls creaked and the desks in the adjacent room seemed to be dashing about like a maddened herd.

The cannonade was long and persistent.

Then there was a pause as though before a new vast effort, and suddenly the whole of the sky split apart along a blazing crevice and came thundering down. The church seemed to rock and the walls to crumble until all was blotted out in dead quiet.

. . . .

"You're still alive, I hope, *Panna* Raisa?" she heard a strange voice say.

In the flare of a match that he lit, she saw the stocky figure of Father Vasily in his white surplice. His huge canvas umbrella seamed with copper clasps was streaming and his high boots were covered with mud. He brought the moist freshness of summer rain into the stuffy room, and Raisa felt relieved.

"My goodness, what's happened to you?" he cried as he saw her at the point of swooning, her pale yellowish features and dilated eyes.

"What's happened to you?" he repeated anxiously, lighting a candle hurriedly and holding it to her face.

Raisa stared at him wide-eyed, though she seemed to recognize her guest.

Father Vasily closed three fingers of his puffy, almost feminine hand and made the broad sign of the

72

cross over her, sweeping her face with the moisture of his sleeve.

"In the name of the Father, the Son and the Holy Ghost...."

"Is the storm over?" Raisa asked as she got to her feet, looking fearfully about.

Of course it was over. It was a splendid shower and how clear the sky now was. It was a real tempest. When the last bolt came, he had thought that it struck the church and rushed out to see. But no, all was well, though the lightning must have struck somewhere near the church and school. Then it had occurred to him that Raisa was alone, because she had dismissed Tatyana. He wondered if she was frightened, especially when he noticed that the school doors were opened. It was worse than he thought. How was she feeling now? Better, thank God! Why was her room so stuffy? She would have done better to open the window. She had been afraid, but now the sky was clear and starry and the air still and pure. Didn't she think so too? She would feel much better now. Could he be helpful? Should he send someone to fetch Tatyana? She had not completely recovered as yet. Well, he would not send anyone if she didn't want him to, but it would really be the best thing. He would send her some beverage brewed of grass. Half a glass of this would return the colour to her cheeks and soothe her heart. He wished her a good night and hoped that she would rise refreshed in the morning.

As he took leave, his puffy hand, white surplice enveloping his almost feminine figure, his pale face, grey eyes and bald crown spread such tranquillity that Raisa was loth to let him go. Besides, she was grateful.

"Won't you stay for a while?" she asked timidly, clinging to his hand. "Are you in a hurry? My samovar must be ready by now. I got it going before the storm. Won't you have some tea?"

Before he could answer, she vanished into the dark of the adjacent room.

The samovar was puffing cheerfully. The oil-lamp under its white shade gilded the fresh pine boards. The aroma of brewing tea mingled with the freshness after the storm and the stars shone through the windows. The glasses tinkled in Raisa's hand. Her thin figure in a white smock seemed to toss about the room like a feather in a breeze. Her dark eyes shone, her cheeks were slightly flushed and there was a ring in her voice, as though the electric storm that had passed had dropped a spark into her frail body.

His legs crossed, Father Vasily sat puffing at his cigarette, surprised at the sudden change in the teacher's mood and not displeased with it. Nor was he displeased with the golden cleanliness of the samovar, the milky lamp-shade, the pine boaɪ ls, his hostess's frock and the sky of stars.

Raisa had not quite recovered from the storm, as was evident by the slight tremor of her fingers as she set the glass before her guest, her nervous movements much too rapid, her shining eyes and elation. It was easy to talk to Father Vasily now: it was as if he were an old friend.

It turned out that she had been acquainted with his deceased wife. Fanya had been two forms her senior at school and she remembered her very well. So she had died eight years ago? Raisa had never heard of it.

"My only consolation is my daughter Tasya. She'll be here tomorrow or the day after."

Whenever Father Vasily mentioned his daughter, his face would soften and his eyes glow. He was glad of the opportunity to speak of his pet, while Raisa was truly interested in the girl.

They recollected many common acquaintances. There were many surprises in store for Raisa. She would have never imagined, for instance, that that pock-marked lanky seminary student as red as a Dutch cow, the one who had lisped the ideas of Feuerbach to her, now wore a *Kamilavka*, a diamond cross and had worked his way up to Eminence.

"Is that possible?" She could hardly believe her ears.

"Honestly! But didn't you read about it in the *Eparchial Gazette*?"

No, she had never read that newspaper at all. And he promised to bring it to her.

And thus a host of memories and tidings of deaths and promotions, of the sad or happy destinies of mutual acquaintances hovered over them and the singing samovar, bringing back long-forgotten events and faces, cherished hopes and feelings of long ago.

When Father Vasily had left, Raisa threw herself into her bed at the bottom of the well.

The receding perspective of the rising pine boards over which the darkness fluttered did not disturb her now.

She still saw the bulky figure, the calm face, the shining eyes and the three plump fingers pressed together over her forehead.

Two days later, a twelve-year-old girl with pixy ears and a round head between angular shoulders came skipping to the school. Her quick dark eyes were those of the late Fanya, and Raisa knew at once that this was Tasya. Her poorly cut calico frock did not conceal her little figure. The white stockings clung tightly to her plump legs and the loose ends of her red slippers flapped like the ears of a sucking-pig. She skipped by oblivious of Raisa and clattered through all the classrooms, peering into all the corners as if inspecting her own home. At last she came upon Raisa and stood stock-still, embarrassed. But not for long. In a moment she showered the teacher with questions. Did she have a sister? Were the cherries ripe in her orchard? Did she have the same head mistress at her school? What sort of jam did she like best? As for herself, she liked any kind, and so on.

Tasya grew attached to Raisa at once, would not let her go, begging her to come home with her at once. Raisa agreed.

They found no one in the rooms of the priest, but Father Vasily soon came and was very happy to see them.

"Quick, Mother!" he called to the next room, wiping his perspiring crown. "We have a guest!"

There was a tripping of taps, much like those of a goat crossing a wooden bridge. This was followed by the appearance of a small old woman in black in the doorway. She carried a cane, which explained the tapping.

"Quick, Mother!" she mimicked her son. "A fine guest indeed! The teacher! She ought to have come here long ago!"

She crossed the floor with a series of taps, giving no heed to Raisa, and seated herself, muttering: "Quick, Mother! The teacher, the teacher!"

Despite this far from friendly welcome, Raisa felt a surge of sympathy for the quaint old figure in black. Her hair was caught up in a black kerchief as in bygone days and her face peeped from under it like a baked apple.

"She's for ever grumbling," Father Vasily said apologetically.

"She's for ever grumbling!" the old woman reiterated, rising. She tapped across the room, took another seat and continued her muttering.

It was evident that nobody minded her.

Meanwhile, Raisa saw Tasya sink to her heels before a little oven, reach into it and, after some fumbling, draw out a jar of jam. Carefully removing the wrapper, she put her sooty finger into it and then to her mouth, sucking ecstatically, her button eyes twinkling like those of a little animal and her pixy ears flushing as though someone had pulled them.

Father Vasily spoke proudly of his farm. He led Raisa to the apple-trees he had planted himself, acquainted her with the odour of the stables and the mud of the cowsheds and convened his whole quacking, gobbling and clucking kingdom of domestic fowl. But of all the animals gathered in the yard of the priest's farm, the liveliest and most curious seemed Tasya whose tiny figure darted between the calves or encroached upon the flocks of geese raising a great honking.

Then they drank tea on the veranda in the quiet sunset. There was something very restful about the bulky and kindly figure of Father Vasily, the incessant muttering of the old woman, a sound much like the endless ripple of a brook, the kittenish springiness of Tasya, their simple conversation and the surroundings. Through the open doors, Raisa could see the portraits of the bishops over the old mahogany furniture, a solemn gallery which quite belonged to this little company in which she did not feel at all alone.

The ice was broken, and Raisa was glad when Tasya would come to her in the early morning, pleading with her to come to the woods and fields. Sometimes, they would take Father Vasily with them He too would pick mushrooms with them, unbending with difficulty in his white cloth. When his strands of hair were wet with perspiration, they would let him rest, but soon come running to watch him lying on the grass, puffing at a cigarette, and bring the mushrooms they had picked.

Raisa soon won over the old woman: she made the

jam preserves, helped in the kitchen and looked after the maids. The old woman was very pleased and expressed her appreciation by grumbling at her as well. They grew to be a family of four.

The Sunday dinners were especially delicious. Immediately after the service, Tasya would beg Raisa to come to their house, and the teacher would go to the kitchen to prepare some delicacy or other for the little sweet tooth. Flushed after standing by the oven, she would rush into the dining-room with her sleeves rolled, clatter the plates and help the servants set the table. She would then drive Father Vasily from the sofa where he lay reading the newspaper.

"Please go to your room. You're such a nuisance here," she would cry cheerfully.

Dinner inevitably brought an old argument as to how many glasses of vodka Father Vasily had drunk.

"You've had five!" she exclaimed indignantly. "It does you so much harm, but you keep on."

"What sort of a teacher can you be, if you can't count to five? I had only four."

"No, five! I forbid you to have any more, do you hear?"

"What next?"

"That's what's next!" Raisa would retort, snatching the bottle away.

But determined to defend his rights, Father Vasily went to war with Raisa, turning into a servant of Mars instead of one of God. There was a great fuss and bother. Little Tasya would shrill like a stuck suckling and the old lady grumble, shifting from place to place, tapping the floor until the plates rattled.

Victory usually went to the weaker side and everybody was pleased, though Tasya's appetite always seemed to grow so sharp after the tussle that great inroads were made into the dessert.

They went to see the haymaking, the beehives or just walked in the fields.

Father Vasily grew used to the teacher. He would sometimes ask her to see to the farm-hands weeding the sugar-beet or bring dinner to the haymakers, which she did with great zest Time passed at these pleasant occupations all the more imperceptibly, because she felt quite at home in the family of Father Vasily. As summer drew to an end, Tasya had to return to school and all were saddened. though Father Vasily now had more reason to pay frequent visits to the school and talk to Raisa about his darling. Besides, he brought her the *Eparchial Gazette* which he was far too lazy to read by himself. The announcements in small type attracted their attention first. Familiar names occurred now and then, and the various events in the lives of the local clergy were described in some detail. Raisa at first showed interest merely to be polite and avoid hurting Father Vasily's feelings, but then grew absorbed herself in the accounts of former acquaintances at the seminary. Sometimes the post arrived when Father Vasily was not at home, and Raisa then would be the first to read the announcements and wait impatiently for Father Vasily to share the news with him.

"Have you heard that Father Arkady has been transferred to another parish? And Father Theognost has received promotion," she would say as he arrived.

"Really? How do you know?"

"Here, you can read it for yourself."

And they would bend over the newspaper so that the black shock of Raisa's hair would tickle his bald crown.

Father Vasily soon found something for himself to do at the school. When the parents brought their children for acceptance, Raisa tried to get acquainted with them, and Father Vasily was very useful on such occasions. He knew every peasant in the neighbourhood, his life, character and thoughts. He knew his wife and children and his riches, earthly and spiritual.

"This one may be accepted," he would pronounce, rocking importantly in his chair. "His mother is a pious woman and never misses a service."

"Oh, it's you, Ivan! So you've brought your youngster to school too? You want him to be as sharp as you, no doubt? No, don't accept that one. I know him too well."

"Have a heart, Father! Don't be angry with us! I'm not to blame for the cattle roaming into other fields."

And so an argument would begin about some cattle or some rye that had been stolen. Father Vasily would grow angry and flushed, insisting that the boy should not be admitted. Though annoyed, Raisa thought it rude to remind the priest about her rights in front of the others. But when she learned that the peasants had fallen into the habit of coming to the priest to beg admittance for their children before they came to her, she grew indignant and spoke her mind. Father Vasily, however, not only managed to reassure her, but somehow gave the matters such a turn that she indeed felt obliged to him. How could she help thanking him and listening to him. He knew everything and could do anything. If the roof had to be mended at the school it was he who found the men to do it. If dry fuel was to be stowed away for the winter, it was he who saw to it that dry wood was duly brought. If she had to call on the local board or go to town, it was he who furnished the horses and so on.

Raisa was really grateful to him for numerous kindnesses and advices without which she would have been in a more difficult position.

Besides, she truly liked him and found him handsome. His high forehead seemed so calm and noble.

His grey candid eyes gave his face a soft light. He was unhappy too, for had he not lost his wife so long ago? There were times when she felt a tenderness and mother's solicitude over his broken life. It was easier for her, therefore, to overlook Father Vasily's weaknesses than anyone else's.

After Tasya's departure, Raisa decided to board with the priest's mother. The three of them thus shared their meals every day, and this could not help but bring them closer together. Raisa even found that she could exert some influence upon him. Gradually, she was able to curtail the number of vodka glasses he drank over his dinner until he gave up drinking altogether. When he told her how much he could drink and how much he had drunk at times, her heart was filled with pride at the thought that she had been able to eradicate a habit so deep-seated and pernicious.

They spent the long autumn evenings together at the round table in his dining-room in the dim light of an oil-lamp. They talked endlessly, accompanied by the grumbling of the old lady, remembering Tasya, her babyhood, her pranks and the things she had said. They made plans for her upbringing and future. The atmosphere in the dining-room grew warmer and even more family-like.

The bleak autumn surrounding the house and drizzling over the windows isolated them from the whole of the world. They were a trio marooned on a deserted island and felt especially near to one another for that reason.

Sometimes they read long and dreary books the last pages of which were missing, books which they had rummaged out of the dusty heaps in the lumber-room. It was Raisa who did the reading, while Father Vasily ponderously paced the room, his hands thrust deeply into the pockets of his surplice, his head pensively bent, his figure throwing the shadow of a shaggy bear upon the walls.

The old lady who sat dozing would suddenly awake to find fault with some word or other, fall to grumbling and tapping the floor with her cane in such a rage that Raisa would have to stop reading for a time. She was easily appeased, however, and Raisa's quiet voice would go on as before, with the rain drubbing the house and the shadow of a bear sliding along the walls.

Most festive were the evenings on which Father Vasily read his sermons prepared for the coming Sunday. He would draw the smoking lamp nearer, push a few unruly strands behind his ears and turn into a despot. The slightest noise or even an approving remark of the old lady drove him furious. As he read his manuscript, his grey eyes would ignite as he ejaculated vigorous words in his vibrant, somewhat nasal voice. His cheeks flushed and his brow carved by a deep furrow, he flagellated his congregation like a prophet of the Bible. Thieving, disobedience, inebriety, sloth, the annihilation of the spirit and the body hung over their heads like clouds menaced by even darker clouds of retribution charged with sulphur and the fires of Hell. Amid these lowering clouds the stout figure of the inspired prelate stood out like the dove of innocence, fastening the eyes of the two women.

"I'll grind them to dust, the sinners!" Father Vasily threatened his imaginary congregation.

Though it all seemed powerful and beautiful enough, there were some passages which could not satisfy Raisa. She felt that some of his ideas needed clarification and development, and others ought to be struck off altogether. Besides, his allegories were not always consistent. But Father Vasily could not bear criticism. That which he had written must stand!

"I won't change a word!" he would cry in a passion.

Yet Raisa insisted and argued, which led to heated altercation until she was sometimes hurt by a careless word dropped by the prelate. The matter usually ended with Raisa reaching for a pencil and making some corrections and additions with which Father Vasily finally agreed.

On Sunday Raisa would go to church as early as she could, anticipating the sermon with impatience. She carefully observed its effect on the congregation—especially in those passages which she had altered. She was sure that the women sniffed with greater feeling at these spots and that the men looked more intelligent then.

The sermon came out very impressively, thought Raisa, and Father Vasily seemed so worthy of its success. The rays of his glory were shed also upon her, poor schoolmistress, for it was a part of her self too that had influenced the masses, and this raised her in her own estimation.

Imperceptibly she grew attached to him.

She felt this especially on the days when Father Vasily visited the bishop or attended an ecclesiastic congress, so that she was left alone in the evenings. On such occasions she would roam listlessly about her immaculate rooms, unable to occupy herself with anything. The school then seemed like nothing more than a coffin of pine boards.

Hardly knowing what to do with herself, she would take refuge with the prelate's mother. They would spend the entire evening talking about the lofty spiritual qualities of Father Vasily and how unfortunate he must have been to be widowed when he was so young.

She would come home in a strange mood and unable to fall asleep for a long time. She would lie on her nunnish bed in the dim light of a candle, a strange warmth surging in her breast. It reminded her of the thrill of taking communion when she was a girl, of the warm prayers that then came from her languishing heart. It was a long time ago.

She would have liked to recapture those minutes and enjoy them again, but could that be done?

She lay hoping that it would come back, that pure childhood experience, that it would renew her parched heart like a spring shower. She both hoped and was afraid to hope for it to come.

But come it did.

Blissfulness descended to her lonely heart from the dark heights into which she stared, and her heart burst into blossoms luxurious yet frail as the legendary fern's flower.

She fell asleep warm and refreshed, ashamed and comforted like a child after a long cry.

After such a night sometimes she would rise feeling as though there were cold steel in her heart; it pierced, lacerated her heart, driving her to despair.

"I should not indulge in such illusions," she would say angrily. "Enough of playing at hide-and-seek with reality. I'm not a child. If my life has been a failure, I shall not be able to sugar it with a sweetmeat in a bright wrapper. I must not deceive myself and live on vain hopes. I do not want anything or anybody. No, nothing and nobody!"

At such moments she did not want to see anyone, did not go to dinner and turned thin and yellowish overnight, her feverish eyes growing as piercing as a knife.

Troubled because she had failed to turn up at dinner, Father Vasily would come to the school himself. She would call to him from her bedroom then, claiming that she had a headache and wanted to see no one. But he would finally enter her room, sit down beside her, soothe and amuse her until she was calmed.

That was another reason to be grateful to him.

She missed no opportunities to make amends, taking Father Vasily's health under her special supervision. If he went into the cold ante-room or yard hatless as of old, Raisa would come running after him with his hat and scarf in her hands. He accepted these attentions absently at first, but was finally annoyed, especially when she made scenes about it, complaining of his carelessness.

She could not understand how one could neglect the health of a man not only responsible for a family, but also for the fulfilment of social duties. High-minded and endowed with a powerful gift of speech, he must bring his influence to bear upon people. He must live for loftier aims, for the benefit of his congregation. He was the bearer of a mission.

She talked to the peasants about his mission. They nodded agreement, but sometimes expressed surprise over the discrepancies between Father Vasily's sermons and actions. This made her very angry and she withdrew into herself, disgusted with such ingratitude.

Except for these moments of dissatisfaction, Raisa found great joy. She had never imagined before that such a simple and obvious matter as fasting, something to which she had given hardly any attention, could be a source of consolation.

As she had her meals with the old lady, she too began to observe the fasts. She grew thinner, therefore, and paler, feeling great weakness from the fasting and the work at the school. This continence which so raised the spirit in her weak body gave her great pleasure.

Another source of pleasure was the matin service. Afraid to oversleep, she would spring from her bed in the dark room grown chilly overnight and look anxiously at the clock. It was too early. There was a wintry night beyond the windows, stars trembling in the frosty air, the lights of distant houses twinkling like the eyes of wolves. She would wander then through the rooms dimly lit by the candle, shivering at the touch of the chilly air, her steps ringing through the emptiness. In her black dress (she never wore any other colour now) and black kerchief, she would run to church with the peal of the bell, as eager as a young nun. The caretaker would still be sweeping the floor under two yellow streaks of light falling from above. The dust of human steps rose to dim the crude icons and relieve the poverty of their gilding. The night still hovered beneath the ceiling, quivering plaintively in the last shattered peals from the belfry.

Still smoothing the strands of his hair wet after his morning wash, Father Vasily would stride through the church to the altar, hurriedly shaking hands with Raisa as he went. Archangel Gabriel's gates gave way to him and he passed on, vanishing behind the altar.

The lights were gradually lit here and there like stars in the twilight. The dark emaciated faces of the saints stood out from the icons. There was a shuffling of feet at the entrance and vapour streamed from the mouths and nostrils of the cold waiting crowd.

There was a sanctity in the atmosphere ready for prayer. Raisa would stand behind the chair on the right side before a medieval icon. The old psalm singer stood behind her venturing a few tentative notes. Then the service began. Raisa recollected the prayers she knew; some of them were poetic, she thought. She poured out her heart now as she stood on her knees, looking up to Father Vasily as if expecting him to take her prayer to God. Whispering the humble words of supplication, she observed the movement of his red lips under the dark moustache, his shining grey eyes, and was sure that his high sweeping brow shed a soft light.

When he raised his plump hands through the smoke

of the incense to the first rays of the morning sun, appealing to God in his gentle, somewhat nasal baritone, Raisa's heart too floated to the heights, dissolving there like the smoke of the incense in the gold of the sunbeams.

She was the first to kiss the cross. With awe and trepidation, she pressed her lips not only to the cold metal, but also to the soft hand of Father Vasily as though the blessing of God himself would penetrate her through this kiss.

She would come home at peace with the world, her body weightless as though she had grown even thinner, her back aching but her breathing easier. She sat down then in her modest room, laying the table with a fresh cloth and eating a sacred wafer, this divine flesh of God, in a mood that brought back the festive days of her childhood.

Her work at school exhausted her, giving little satisfaction. She was interested more in her altered views, feelings and trend of thought. It was all so new and unexpected. She was not surprised, however, by these changes, and could not, indeed, understand how she could have ever lived otherwise, how she could have ever refrained from drinking from the sources that lay in her own heart. She had been robbing herself. And now, thanks to the divine will and Father Vasily, new ways had opened before her and her heart found fresh nourishment. She felt as if she were a chrysalis growing bright wings within itself against the day of flight. Humbly, she thought of herself as of the disciple of Father Vasily. She felt the necessity to see and hear him constantly and spent all her leisure time in his house. She felt that her day had begun only when she saw him at last and was quite willing to strike out the rest.

When on Christmas Eve Father Vasily felt slightly

unwell, Raisa gave all her time to his recovery, acting the nurse with such zeal that she annoyed him.

One night she awoke with a distinct and dreadful thought: Father Vasily was dying! She could have sworn that someone had whispered to her that he was dying. She was afraid to think of it, and yet could visualize his pale face, eyes closed, resting against the arm of the old lady and his breast heaving with agony.

She put on some clothes and ran from the school as if in a trance. There was a bluish glitter to the snow and all objects seemed sharply cut in the crystal air. It was so still and desolate around her. The snow crunched under her shoes (she had forgotten to put on her galoshes), and nearly running, she could visualize the lights in the windows, the swinging doors, the groans and sobs, the deathly pale face supported in the hands of the old lady, while his numbing lips pronounced her name.

"I'm coming!" she whispered, hurrying on.

She moved as fast as she could, though her legs trembled and nearly gave way. Terrified that she would not come on time, she sent her soul ahead as messenger. She was sure that if she could only reach him before it was too late, there would be a miracle and he would recover. The blood seemed to pulsate in her heart alone, for it alone seemed ready for struggle. She felt that she might fall at any moment, but mustered her last strength, trying to get every part of her to move as fast as she could. At last she saw the lights and found herself leaning against the gate. It was locked, and she peered through one of the crevices in it, catching a glimpse of the white house which stood like a block of ice with black sleepy windows. Even the dogs did not stir.

She closed her eyes, her shoulder against the gate. It was not joy but utter exhaustion that she felt. It was as though the blood that had coursed through her heart had turned to vapour in the cold clear air, leaving emptiness behind.

When she opened her eyes she saw only the white snow tinged with blue, the hard glittering road, the squalid cottages propped on black stems like mushrooms. She could even see her footprints quite distinctly. So there had been no nightmare.

She was ashamed.

She slowly returned with hanging head.

"What if someone had seen me?" she thought, looking fearfully around. She was afraid to meet a witness of her nocturnal escapade.

The stillness was complete, except for the watchman's rattle which sounded so suddenly that Raisa almost fainted.

On the next day she learned that Father Vasily had had a restful night and was almost well.

Father Vasily was annoyed with her incessant solicitude. On his way out of the house, he was always thoroughly inspected with the result that he was swathed with so many kerchiefs that one might have thought he was on his way to the other end of the earth. As for the sweater she had knitted for him, he was not permitted to take it off all winter. Every cough, be it ever so slight, brought on a torrent of reproaches for his carelessness. Absence of appetite prompted anxious inquiry, while a good appetite brought admonitions not to overeat. Father Vasily was highly irritated. It was a conspiracy against him. What did she want of him, this old maiden?

"You watch my every morsel, but take nothing yourself. You'll soon look like a sacred relic."

Raisa was hurt by his rude tone, but obediently bore his despotism and said nothing even when he dismissed Tatyana and hired another care-taker who did nothing at all at the school, loafing constantly about the priest's kitchen. Nor did she protest when he dismissed her two best pupils out of hand to settle some score or other with their parents. Still, his scorn for her feelings was painful.

Father Vasily himself perceived nothing, but Raisa very well saw that he was avoiding those long debates and talks which she liked so much.

They spent the evenings together, but not as of old.

After tea the old lady would settle down by the stove with a sieve filled with feathers before her, half dozing as she plucked at them for down.

"Shall we read?" Raisa would ask, timidly reaching for a book.

"No. I'm tired of it. What is there to those novels anyway? I can't imagine for whom they were written. Perhaps for old maids to warm their blood on."

With these words, Father Vasily would look askance at Raisa and yawn. He would shuffle about the room still yawning, or fall back on the sofa and yawn again with such gusto that his jaws cracked.

"You'd better go to sleep or you'll get your jaws out of joint!" the old lady would remark, plucking her feathers.

"Perhaps I should. I'm sleepy for some reason." Father Vasily would yawn again and retire, though Raisa still sat in the dining-room.

At times, he would sit down over the records of his church books, oblivious of Raisa.

At other times he would grow capricious and be unbearable, jibing at her expense, mocking her exultation, her superficiality and contradicting the things he had previously stood for. The old lady felt that she had to intercede on behalf of the embarrassed and saddened Raisa, scolding her son and tapping her cane to interrupt the unpleasant conversation.

When Tasya came home for Christmas their relations improved. Father Vasily grew pleasant and cheerful and Raisa was happy as if everything unpleasant had been wiped from her memory.

But this spirit of accord was short-lived, for Tasya soon went away and Father Vasily sulked again. He would wander about the room with lowered head, wondering what to do with himself. One evening finally, he went to the cupboard, extracted a bottle of vodka and poured himself a glass. Raisa stared with frightened eyes. After some pacing, he poured himself another. She looked on horrified. But when he poured himself a third, she arose, bowed wordlessly and went away.

Without troubling to remove her things or light a candle, she collapsed on the sofa in her room. She lay there inert, oppressed, defeated. Her only thought was that she was lonely, a lonely bleeding heart in a dark pine coffin. A dog howled in the yard in a melancholy long-drawn note. She could have howled like that too if she had had the strength. But what for? She would do better to keep lying there without stirring, without hope until this darkness turned into eternity. She would be like a flower between the pages of an old book. She did not want to hear the ticking of the clock, the howling of the dog or any other sound reminding her of life. Let there be only stillness and the unrelieved pain of a lonely frustrated heart. Let it bleed to death.

How long she had been lying that way she did not know. She remembered only that suddenly she felt someone's soft warm hand on her heart. She opened her eyes and saw Christ bent over her, his soft white hand lying on her heart. Terrified and ashamed, she sprang up with a scream. The vision vanished and she lit a candle with a trembling hand and then wiped the perspiration from her forehead. She was not sure whether this had been a dream or a vision, but still felt the touch of the warm hand on her heart.

Raisa grew resigned after that, humbly accepting Father Vasily's rudeness, his jibes and indifference, while he, for his part, seemed to enjoy wielding power over the old maid and expressed his scorn more and more often. Humility was her only defence, and the more rudely he spurned her, the more sacrificing her efforts became. She would have willingly given him the last drop of her heart's blood. If he were to kick her like a stray dog, she would cling to his leg with love and humbleness. Humility shone from her large eyes and in every line of her yellow emaciated face. She drew her strength from this humility, finding bitter delight in it and subtle poetry. She accepted his rude antics as expressions of energy and indomitable will and explained his changing, inattentive and often downright scornful attitude by the fact that he lived by loftier ideals and could not be expected to pay heed to trifles. In her humility, she was ready to sacrifice her heart to this extraordinary man, as she had been taught by Him who had left the warm touch of His hand on her heart, by Christ—she was sure it was He. Never had she felt more affection for Him. She prayed to Him and conversed with Him in her solitude, and He understood.

Meanwhile, she was wasting away.

Her strength was ebbing with the thaw waters.

"You had better consult a doctor!" Father Vasily would say, fixing his eye on her waxen features.

She did not answer, but regarded him with lucid melancholy eyes.

She was glad of the spring: she could now place fresh flowers on the altar before every service. That was a token of her sacrifice. She would rise at dawn and ramble through the green dew-drenched meadows, adding flower to flower.

"Perhaps you are in love and having your trysts at daybreak round the village!" Father Vasily joked when he learned of her strolls at dawn.

After the service, Raisa took one of the bouquets home. She felt that it had changed somehow: the aroma and colour had grown more intense and fresh, as though God's blessing had descended upon the flowers during the service and compelled them to open their cups. Raisa pressed the flowers to her lips and heart and put them in a glass on her night table.

She set up a kind of altar woven with fragrant grass and flowers, fresh and dry. Her room came to look like the cell of a nun, for its walls were hung with black clothes and the bed was white as snow. Father Vasily's photograph stood conspicuously beside the bookcase.

The services were not enough for her, and she kneeled before her altar, looking at Father Vasily, thinking of Christ. She would utter her prayers, numbed by the fragrance of the flowers, her head swimming from the ailments of her heart. To Him alone she opened her heart and complained of her life so drab, colourless and meaningless. She stood in a wilderness, joyless and cold. She did not want such a life. What was the good of it? Why had He breathed fire into her soul if it was meant only to turn her heart to ashes? He witnessed her suffering. Let Him, therefore, take her unto himself and give her the happiness which she had never known on earth and which she desired more than drink in fever. At His feet nailed to the cross she laid her lonely heart and the power of her love. He was kind and merciful and she would serve Him eternally, be His slave for ever. Let Him soothe her sorrow! Let Him quench her parched lips.

Let Him put a hand on her heart and calm its rebellious beat as He had done once before. O Lord!

Numbed by the fragrance of the flowers and her head swimming with the ailments of her heart, she raised her hands, immobile in her plea for a miracle and consolation, and consolation would come at last.

The meak figure of Christ would descend to her, His grey eyes shining gently, full of a caress. He lifted her who was so frail in His hands, and she felt that she was floating from earth. The touch filled her with inexplicable happiness. Her head spun deliciously and the blood coursed once again through her parched heart afire with divine joy. Irrepressible tears streamed down her cheeks.

". . . Don't you see?" Raisa went on with the story she was telling her former schoolmate who had paid her an unexpected visit. "Can't you see that he's an extraordinary man, not just a simple village priest? If you only knew his lofty thoughts and noble heart, his high-mindedness, his spiritual purity, you would be charmed with him, I'm sure. He's handsome too. His grey eyes shine so softly, and there is such nobility and calmness in his pale face and high brow! His hair is somewhat reddish, but does not spoil his looks at all. On the contrary, his lips seem fresher because of that—and his voice is so musical. I want you to see him. It is not everyone who likes him, but that's because he is very energetic and has an indomitable will. The village is no place for such a man. He's frittering away his energy here. Now imagine my grief! He's going to stay with Father Ivan during the church holidays."

"But why grieve? Let him go."

"You don't understand. You don't want to understand... He must not go. It's no place for him. There'll be only drinking, cards and orgies. He must be strong and stand above them all. He gave up drinking. I begged him so much not to go. Can it be that I.... Can it be that he...."

Raisa sobbed. She could not go on for the spasms in her throat.

She sat very still, the large tears rolling down her face which was so wretched and full of anguished inquiry. Wringing her hands until the joints cracked she stared dim-eyed into the distance.

"You don't see," she began again, turning her wet face to her friend.

"On the contrary, I see it very well: you're in love with him."

"What did you say?"

"I say that you are...." She did not finish, because Raisa shrank back with a scream, like a wounded bird.

There was a blinding flash and a chasm gaped before her, a black bottomless pit. She was sinking into it, and the church, rosy in the sunset and framed amid the green maples, faded from her vision.

September 20, 1901
Chernigov

ON THE ROCK

A Water-Colour

Both the sea and the grey shore could be seen from the coffee-house, the only one in this Tatar village. The clear blue of the sea fading into infinity seemed to pervade even the enclosed colonnaded porch through its open doors and windows. Even the sultry air was stained with blue, dissolving the contours of the distant mountains descending to the sea.

It was a sea wind that was blowing. Its salty chill attracted the guests who, ordering coffee, nestled down near the windows or other parts of the porch. Even the proprietor, the lame Mehmet, who anticipated the wishes of his guests by calling to his younger brother: "*Jepar ... bir kavee.... Eki kavee!*"* put his head out of the door and removed his Tatar skull-cap to bathe it in air.

While Jepar, flushed with heat, fanned the oven and rapped the coffee urn to make a good *kaimak*,** Mehmet kept gazing at the sea.

"There's a storm brewing," he remarked without

---

* One cup of coffee. Two cups.
** Foam on the coffee.

turning his head. "The wind is freshening. The boats are taking in their sails."

The Tatar visitors turned their heads to the sea.

True enough, they were trimming their sails out there on a black skiff heaving shoreward. Fat with the wind the sails strained in the hands of the boatmen like huge white birds. The black vessel listed and lay about on a blue wave.

"She's turning this way," Jepar rejoined. "I know her. She belongs to the Greek who brings the salt."

Mehmet too recognized the boat. This was not unimportant to him, for besides his coffee-house, he also kept a shop in the village, likewise the only one in the vicinity. In addition, he was the local butcher. One could not do without salt.

When the boat was near, Mehmet went down to the beach. The guests swallowed their coffee and hurried to follow. They crossed the narrow street in a group, rounded the mosque and descended a rocky path to the water's edge.

The blue was foaming near the shore. The skiff danced hither and thither, plopping like a fish, but was unable to make the shore. The great moustached Greek and his mate, the *dangalak*, a trim, long-legged young man, fought hard at the oars, but could make no progress. The Greek then dropped the anchor, while the *dangalak* quickly threw off his coat and rolled his yellow trousers well above his knees. The Tatars ashore exchanged some remarks with the Greek, while the surf rolled boiling to their feet and hissed back.

"Are you ready, Ali?" the Greek called to his *dangalak*.

By way of reply, Ali flung a bare leg over the gunwale and slipped into the water. Adroitly accepting a bag of salt from the Greek, he threw it over his shoulder and waded ashore.

His spare figure in a blue shirt and yellow trousers, his bronze skin, wind-burnt face and the red cloth about his head contrasted sharply with the blue. Dropping the bag on the sand, he waded into the sea again, thrusting his reddened calves into the creamy foam and wandering farther into the lavender waves. Approaching the boat he watched warily for the instant when the gunwale would come level with his shoulder so that he could receive another of the heavy sacks. The boat strained against its anchor like a chained dog. Ali lept to and fro, oblivious of the surf slapping at his legs. Whenever he missed the opportune moment to catch a sack, he was compelled to cling to the gunwale rising and falling with the sea, like a barnacle fastened to the side.

The Tatars stood in a group on the beach. There were flowery clusters of women on the flat roof-tops in spite of the heat.

The sea grew more and more impatient. Sea-gulls plunged from the lonely rocks and scudded over the waves with mournful cries. The water grew livid. The smaller waves were fused into masses of undulating glass stealing shorewards to collapse and explode in foam. There were flashes of white under the keel and the craft seemed to be riding on white-maned horses. The Greek cast anxious looks at the sea. Ali increased his stride to and from the beach, bespattered with the foam. The edge of the sea grew yellow and turbid. The inrushing water brought not only sand but pebbles, and, receding, dragged back what it had brought with a rumble like that of a monster gnashing its teeth. Within half an hour, the tide had lapped over the pebbles, flooded the adjacent road and was creeping towards the bags of salt. The Tatars on the beach had to step back to avoid wetting their shoes.

"Mehmet! Nurla! Give me a hand! The salt may get wet! Ali! Come here!" the Greek lamented.

The Tatars came into motion and, while the Greek was still bouncing about in the boat on the waves, casting angry glances at the sea, the salt bags were carried to safety.

Meanwhile, the sea continued to encroach. Its monotonous rumble swelled to a roar. It had been as dull at first as the rattle of death, but then it thundered forth like a cannon in the distance. A grey web of clouds slid over the sky. The turbulent sea grew dark and dirty, dashed up the shore and burst over the rocks into streams of sullied white.

"Oh-ho! There's going to be a storm!" Mehmet shouted to the Greek. "Pull in closer! Beach her here!"

"What's that you're saying?" the Greek shouted hoarsely, trying to make himself heard through the din.

"Beach her here!" cried Nurla with all his might.

The Greek got busy over his chains and ropes amid the rising chaos. Ali rushed to help him. The Tatars threw off their shoes, rolled up their trousers and waded in to help. The Greek recovered his anchor at last and the black boat riding the muddy brine with which the Tatars were splashed from head to foot moved to the shore. The crowd of wet men striding through the wind-swept sea hauled their burden on to the land as if it were a marine monster or a huge dead dolphin. It was grounded at last and tied firmly to a post. The Tatars shook the flakes from their clothes and helped to weigh the salt. Ali helped too, though glancing stealthily at the village when his master was engrossed with the customers. The sun hung low over the mountains. The Tatar houses lay straggled over a rocky spur of the heights. They had been hewn from stone and had flat earthen roofs one beneath the other like a structure of cards. There were no fences, gates or streets. The paths wound up the rocky slopes, vanished under the roofs, but appeared here and there by the stone steps. All was bleak and barren, except for a solitary vine that had reached one of the roof-tops by some miracle. From below even this seemed only like a dark wreath against the deep blue sky.

But a wondrous world unfolded far beyond the village. Groups of boulders, ruddy with the evening sun or blue with overhanging woods, rose in the valleys green with vineyards now veiled in grey. There were bald round mountains casting long evening shadows like huge tents. The grim peaks in the distance were like petrified clouds. Meanwhile, the sun had flung a golden net over the valley, which enmeshed the rosy rocks, the blue forest, the black tents and set the peaks ablaze.

In this fairy panorama the Tatar village was a small disorderly heap. It was only a garland of slender girls returning from a *chishme** with tall pitchers on their shoulders that enlivened the stony wastes.

A brook flowed through the deep valley near the village, winding amid the nut groves. Forced to turn upon itself by the surf of the sea, the brook burst its banks and enveloped the tree-trunks, reflecting their leafage, the motley frocks of the Tatars and the naked bodies of the children on the shore.

"Ali!" the Greek shouted. "Help me to pour the salt!"

Ali could hardly hear his master over the voice of the sea. A salty mist of spray hung over the beach. The wrath of the sea was mounting.

These were waves no longer, but water spouts, tall and ominous, with white crests scattering torn shrouds. They rolled on interminably, gathering fresh waves,

---

* Fountain.

tumbling over them and hurling fresh sand on the shore where all was drenched until every hollow was filled with water.

The Tatars were startled by a sharp crackling, and the onsweeping waters enveloped their shoes. It was an unusually tall wave that had dashed up lifting the boat and hurling it against the stake to which it had been tied. The Greek ran to the boat with a great cry: there was a hole in the side. He screamed his rage and cursed and wept, but in a silence imposed by the roar of the elements. The boat had to be dragged still farther and tied down again. So disconsolate was the Greek that when night fell and Mehmet invited him to come to the coffee-house, he would not go. He and Ali continued to haunt the flying mists of the roaring sea in the wind which cut them both to the bone. The moon had risen and was strolling from cloud to cloud. In its light the bursting surf was like drifts of snow. Tempted by the lights of the village, Ali at last convinced the Greek that they ought to go to the coffee-house.

The salt was brought to these Crimean villages once a year, and was usually left with his customers on credit. Wasting no time the next day, the Greek ordered Ali to mend the boat, while he went to collect the debts owing to him in the villages. He had to go by the mountain paths because the lower roads had been under water since the day before.

When the water began to subside in the afternoon, Ali took to his work. The wind fingered his red headcloth as he hammered away, singing a song as monotonous as the unchanging beat of the waves. Good Moslem that he was, he spread his kerchief on the sand and began fervently to pray when the proper hour came. In the evening he kindled a fire and cooked a pilau of wet rice he had found in the boat. He even thought of spending the night here, but was invited to come to the house by Mehmet. There was enough room at the house now, because it was crowded only once a year when the grape buyers came.

The interior was quiet. Jepar sat dozing by the oven ornate with shining pots. The fire within seemed to be dozing too. Whenever Mehmet woke him with the shout "*Kavee!*" Jepar would start up and rush to the bellows to wake the fire. The blaze bared its fangs in a shroud of sparks, setting the copper pots aglow, while the fragrance of fresh coffee filled the room. There were flies buzzing under the ceiling. The visitors sat about the broad tables covered with red cloth. Some were playing dice and some cards. The tiny cups of coffee stood everywhere. The coffee-house was the heart of the village. All interests of the people who lived on the rock were centered here. It was the favourite place of the most revered guests, among them the severe old Moollah Asan in his turban and long robe which hung loosely on his bony frame. Black and stubborn as an ass, he was much respected for it. Another who came here was Nurla Effendi, a giant of a man who owned a red cow, a wicker-work arba and a pair of oxen. Still another frequent visitor was a well-to-do *yuzbashi* (the head of a hundred), the owner of the only horse in the village. They were kinsmen all, like all the inhabitants of this forgotten place. But this did not prevent them from being divided into two hostile camps. The bone of contention was a spring which forced its way out of the rocks and streamed through the kitchen-gardens in the heart of the village. It was this water alone that gave life to everything that grew on these rocks. When one half of the village, therefore, had turned the stream to flow through their own kitchen-gardens, the other half were grieved over their perishing onions. The two most wealthy and influential men had vegetable gardens on opposite sides of the rivulet. Nurla was on the right and the *yuzbashi* on the left. When the latter turned the water to his land, Nurla stemmed the water a little higher and turned it back to his own. Those of the left bank flew into a rage therefore, and, forgetting their kinship, sought to save their onions by breaking the heads of their opponents. Nurla and the *yuzbashi* were the leaders of the opposite camps. The *yuzbashi*'s party was the stronger, because Moollah Asan supported it. Their enmity made itself felt in the coffee-house as well. Whenever Nurla's followers played dice, the *yuzbashi*'s party would look at them with loathing and sit down to cards. There was only one thing the two parties had in common: both drank coffee. Mehmet, who had no vegetable garden and as a businessman stood above such party strife, kept hobbling from Nurla to the *yuzbashi*, trying to soothe and reconcile them. His fat face and shaven head shone like a skinned ram. An anxious spark always lurked in his cunning red eyes. He seemed to be perpetually worried over something, always engrossed in one calculation or another. He would run about the shop, his cellar and the visitors. Sometimes, too, he would hurry out of the coffee-shop, throw back his head and shout: "Fatma!" A female shade then separated itself from the wall of the house above and came in a great veil to the edge of the roof.

Mehmet would toss up an empty bag or two and order her to do something in his strident voice as abruptly as if she were a servant. The shadow would then withdraw as unobtrusively as it had appeared.

Ali saw her once. He stood near the coffee-house, watching her yellow slippers descend the stone steps which linked Mehmet's house with a lower tier. A bright-green *ferejeh** hung handsomely about her slender figure from her head to the red trousers. She descended unhurriedly, carrying an empty pitcher in one hand and holding a fold of her *ferejeh* with the other in such a way that a stranger could see only her almond gazelle's eyes. She turned them upon Ali, dropped her lashes and moved on as unperturbed as an Egyptian priestess.

Ali knew that those eyes had penetrated his heart and he would carry them for ever.

Her eyes never left him. He saw them while mending the boat on the seashore and singing his sleepy songs. He saw them everywhere: in the waves as transparent and brittle as glass, in the huge shining rocks. They looked at him even from the cups of coffee.

Often, too, he looked at the village and saw the vague figure of the woman on the roof over the coffee-house under a lonely tree. She seemed to be facing the sea as though demanding that he return her eyes.

Ali soon became a familiar figure. The girls returning from the *chishme* showed their faces as though unwittingly when they met the handsome young Turk. They blushed and quickened their steps, whispering with one another. The young men liked him for his cheerfulness.

On summer evenings, so quiet and fresh, when the stars hung over the earth and the moon over the sea, Ali brought forth his *zurna* which he had obtained in Smyrna, sat down by the coffee-house or near by and talked with his native land in melancholy but thrilling sounds. The strains of the *zurna* drew the young men to the spot. They well understood that eastern song and soon an old game began in the shadows of the stone houses interwoven with moonbeams: the instru-

*A woman's cape.

ment would reiterate one tune, simple, monotonous and as endless as the song of the cricket. It would go on until one's heart burned and mind wandered; and the Tatars caught up the refrain:

"O-la-la! O-na-na!"

On the one side lay the great mountains and their mysterious streaks of light. On the other lay the tranquil sea, breathing in its sleep like a child and quivering under the silver beams.

"O-la-la! O-na-na!"

Those who watched from above, perched on their stony nests, could perhaps catch a glimpse of an outstretched hand in the moonlight, or shoulders twitching in a dance, and could hear again and again the endless:

"O-la-la! O-na-na!"

Fatma was listening too.

She had come from the mountains, from an outlying village where other people lived with their own customs, where she had left her friends and where there was no sea. The meat vendor had arrived, paid her father more than the local suitors and taken her away. He was an unkind strange man, like all the people here. She had no family, no friends, no well-wishers. This was the edge of the world and there was no returning.

"O-la-la! O-na-na!"

There were even no roads, because when the sea was especially angry it flooded whatever paths there were. There was only sea everywhere. Its blue hurt her eyes in the morning, its green waves continued to undulate by day, and at night it breathed as heavily as a sick man. In good weather its calmness was irritating. When there was a storm it spat and howled like a beast, keeping one awake. Its sickening odours even penetrated the house. There was no getting away from it. Sometimes it even teased, wrapping itself in mists as white as the snow in the mountains. One might think that it was gone, if it were not sighing and moaning beneath the pall just as it was now:

"Boom, boom, boom!"

"O-la-la, o-na-na!"

It would struggle beneath the mists like a swaddled child, but then it would toss itself free. The long shreds of mist would then crawl upwards, clutching at the mosque, lingering over the village and penetrating the houses and huts. There were days when the sun could not be seen, just as it was now.

"O-la-la, o-na-na!"

She would come out on to the roof of the coffee-house very often now to lean against the tree and look at the sea. But no, she was not watching the sea, but only the red kerchief on the stranger's head, as though hoping to see his eyes, large and black, the eyes she had been dreaming of. Her favourite flower, the saffron, had blossomed on the sand by the sea.

"O-la-la, o-na-na!"

The stars hung over the earth and the moon over the sea.

"Did you come from afar?"

Ali was startled. The voice came from above, from the roof. He looked up and saw Fatma under the tree whose shadow concealed him.

"From Smyrna," he stammered, blushing. "It's far away."

"I'm from the hills."

A pause.

His blood stirred like a surge of the sea. He could not take his eyes from the lovely Tatar.

"What could have brought you here? Are you not sad here?"

"I'm a poor man and homeless—without a star or a stalk of my own. I live by the work of my hands."

"I have heard you play."

Another pause.

"It was cheerful, as cheerful as our high hills. We had music and cheerful girls. There was no sea about us there. Is there a sea where you came from?"

"No, not near."

"Not so near that you can hear its breathing?"

"No, we have sands instead. The wind gathers up the hot sand and makes it grow like the humps of a camel."

"Shush!"

As if by chance, she revealed her white, well-kept face and put a painted finger-nail to her fulsome lips.

There was no one in sight. The sea lay before them like another sky, and the lone figure of a woman flitted over the square of the mosque.

"Are you not afraid to talk to me, *hanim*? What would Mehmet do if he saw us?"

"Let him do as he likes!"

"He'd kill us if he did."

"What care I?"

The sun had not yet risen, though the peaks were tinged with rose.

The boulders stood out darkly and the sea still slumbered under a haze. Nurla was descending from the Yaila, almost compelled to run to keep pace with his oxen. He was in such a hurry that he failed to notice that a sheave of grass had slid on to the backs of the oxen and was spilled over the road whenever one of the tall wheels caught on a stone and jolted the wicker-work *arba*. The sturdy black animals swung towards the village, tossing their large shaggy heads, but Nurla managed to turn them and soon drew up near the coffee-house. He knew that he would find Mehmet at his establishment and tore open the door.

"Mehmet, Mehmet, come here!"

Mehmet sprang up and rubbed his eyes.

"Mehmet, where is Ali?"

"Ali? Somewhere about." He turned and saw the empty benches.

"Where is Fatma?"

"Fatma? At home, asleep."

"They're up in the hills."

Mehmet stared at Nurla, then crossed the room and looked through the window. He saw the oxen still bestrewn with grass. The first ray of the sun was fingering the sea.

Mehmet returned to Nurla.

"What do you want?"

"You've lost your mind. I've told you, haven't I, that your wife has gone with the *dangalak*. I saw them when I was coming back from the Yaila."

Mehmet's eyes started from their orbits. Pushing Nurla aside, he rushed out, waddling on his crooked legs, and climbed the steps to the roof of the coffee-house, looking indeed like a man who had lost his mind.

"Osman!" he shouted hoarsely, his hands about his mouth.

"Sali! Jepar! Bekir! Come here, all of you!" He bobbed in all directions as though crying "fire!" "Usein! Mustafa!"

The Tatars appeared sleepily on their flat roofs, while Nurla echoed Mehmet down below.

"Asan! Mahmut! Zekeria!" he bellowed.

The alarm swept over the village, bounding upwards from roof to roof and rolling back, everywhere bringing forth more and more people. Red fezzes popped from everywhere and sped down the steep paths to the coffee-house.

Nurla told what had happened.

Mehmet, livid and half mad, devoured the crowd with his eyes. Finally, he ran to the edge of his roof and sprang down as lightly as a cat.

The turmoil rose. The kinsmen who but yesterday had broken one another's heads over the supply of water now stood united as one man. It was not Mehmet's honour alone that was at stake, but the honour of the tribe! A mangy *dangalak*, an alien.... It was outrageous! And when Mehmet reappeared with his sheep knife flashing in the sun and thrust into his belt, the tribe was ready.

"Lead on!"

Nurla started the procession with the lame butcher at his side, leading the long line of their angry kinsmen.

The sun had risen high enough to bake the rocks, and the Tatars continued to climb upward over these paths so familiar to them, a straggling line of ants. Those up ahead kept their silence, and only a few words were spoken in the rear. Nurla was like a hound on the scent. Flushed and angry, Mehmet limped badly. It was still early, but the boulders were as hot as ovens. The fleshy, poisonous leaves of the spurge clung to the ponderous sides of the huge rocks cupola'd like great tents or jagged like a frozen toss of waves. Vitriolic green crawled down to the edge of the sea through the wilderness of boulders.

The barely perceptible track, almost like the prints left by a beast, was lost in the rubble as it swung somewhere about a jutting rock. At this moment there was a refreshing chill and the Tatars took off their fezzes to cool their shaven heads. But then they had to enter the cruelly heated ovens once more, the grey airless sun-scorched spaces. Doggedly, they climbed higher and higher, with bodies bent forward and swaying on their bent Tatar legs. They walked on along the ridges of dark narrow chasms, brushing the rocky walls with their shoulders and plodding on as sturdily as mountain oxen. The farther they came, the harder was the walking, the hotter the sun, the harder the stubbornness of their red shining faces and the fiercer their eyes.

The spirit of the towering barren rocks, which had died in the night, but had grown as warm as human bodies by day, added its heat to theirs, goading them on to vengeance as relentlessly as the grim Yaila. They were determined to intercept the fugitives before they could reach the neighbouring village of Suaku and put to sea.

True, Ali and Fatma were aliens and could easily lose their way. That was the fondest hope of the pursuers, but the fugitives were nowhere in sight, though Suaku was already near. The heat grew unbearable, for the relieving moisture of the sea to which they were so accustomed could not reach to these heights. Descending and mounting the steep inclines, their feet loosened avalanches of pebbles, a source of irritation to the angry, though weary procession. There was no sign of their quarry, while in the village each man had left one task or another. Those in the rear were falling behind, but Mehmet kept driving on with unseeing eyes, his head tossing like that of an infuriated goat and his whole body bouncing with his limp. Hope began to dwindle. It was clear that Nurla had brought the news too late, but still, they kept on. The tortuous bed of grey-sanded Suaku was caught sight of several times.

Suddenly Zekeria, one who walked in the forefront, whistled shrilly and halted. All eyes turned to him as he pointed silently to the high rocky bar jutting into the sea.

A red kerchief had flashed there for an instant and vanished. Mehmet emitted a muffled roar and all hearts were set racing. The same thought occurred to everyone at once: if they could trap Ali on the bar he could be taken easily. Nurla quickly thought of a plan. He put his finger to his lips and, assuring himself that all were listening, divided the procession into three groups which were to advance upon the bar from three sides. On the fourth side the rock fell abruptly to the sea.

Every man grew as alert as at a hunt, and Mehmet alone seethed with fury as before, piercing the rock with ferocious eyes. Finally, they caught sight of a green *ferejeh* among the rocks, and behind it the slender figure of the *dangalak* arose as though he had just grown out of a boulder. Fatma was climbing somewhat ahead, as green in her garb as a bush in spring, while Ali in his tight yellow trousers, blue vest and red kerchief was as tall as a supple cedar. He seemed a giant against the background of the sky. When the pair reached the summit, a flock of seagulls took flight from the neighbouring boulders, specking the blue of the sea with their wings.

Ali must have lost his way and was probably talking of this to Fatma. They looked anxiously over the precipice, trying to find the path. The calm bay of Suaku lay before them in the distance.

Fatma suddenly screamed. Her *ferejeh* fell and she found herself gazing into the bloodshot eyes of her husband whose head came into view over one of the rocks. Ali wheeled and saw Zekeria, Jepar, Mustafa and all the others who had listened to his music and drunk coffee with him swarming up the jagged rocks on all sides, hand over fist. This was no longer a silent horde, but an onrushing roar of guttural voices. There was no escape. Ali stood very straight, his feet firmly on the stones, and waited with his hand on his dirk. The challenging grimness of a young eagle was written on his features.

Fatma hovered behind him like a sea-gull. There was the hateful sea on one side, and the even more hateful butcher on the other. She saw his ox-like eyes, the blue gash of his mouth, his shortened leg and the sharp knife he used for slaughtering sheep. Her soul took wing and flew back to her native village in the mountains: there was music and her eyes were covered; the butcher was leading her away to the sea to be slaughtered like a sheep. She threw her hands to her face and lost her balance. Her blue cape spangled with yellow half-moons flashed but once over the brow of the rock and vanished amid the cries of the sea-gulls.

Petrified, the Tatars for an instant forgot Ali over this simple, unexpected death. Ali was not aware of what had happened behind him. His eyes shifted from one to the other, like those of a wolf at bay. What were they waiting for? Surely they were not afraid? He saw their flashing eyes, fierce red faces, distended nostrils and bared teeth—and then the wave of hatred broke upon him like the thundering surf. Ali defended himself. His knife plunged into Nurla's arm and wounded Osman, but then he was torn from his feet, and, dropping, saw Mehmet's knife descending to his ribs. Mehmet hacked away with all the fury of a betrayed man and the callousness of a butcher, though Ali's breast no longer moved and his handsome face had sunk into eternal repose.

It was all over and the honour of the tribe was saved. The body of the *dangalak* lay bleeding on the rock near the trampled torn *ferejeh*.

112

Mehmet seemed drunk. He was stumbling about on his crooked legs, waving his arms. His movements were absurd and purposeless. Pushing aside the curious who were bending over the corpse, he seized Ali by a leg and dragged him away. The others followed, and as they returned by the same path, over the same hills, the Ganymede head of Ali bumped over the stones, sprinkling blood. The bobbing head seemed in permanent agreement, saying: "Yes, it is so." The Tatars followed quarrelling.

When the procession entered the village, the flat roofs alive with women and children seemed as flowery as the hanging gardens of Semiramis.

A host of curious eyes followed the procession to the edge of the sea. On the dazzling sand stood the listing black skiff like a dolphin tossed ashore. A blue wave as fulsome, pure and warm as the breast of a maiden rolled shoreward and broke in delicate lace of foam. The sea melted with the sun in a shining smirk which spread far over the Tatar villages, the gardens, black woods and reached even to the grey sun-baked boulders of the Yaila.

There was mockery in all things.

Wordlessly, the Tatars raised Ali's body, put it in the boat, pushed her out to sea accompanied by the anxious cries of the women on the flat roofs, cries much like the plaintive calls of the sea-gulls.

The boat hissed over the pebbles, plashed through an oncoming wave and halted rocking. There she stood with the playing waves lapping her sides, spraying her with foam and imperceptibly bearing her seawards.

Ali was drifting away to meet Fatma.

January 10, 1902
Chernigov

THE DUEL

They had just finished the evening meal—*Pani* Antonina and her daughter's tutor Ivan Poddubny. He arose from his seat on the couch, lightly jostling back the round table with the remains of their supper as she offered him her hand to kiss. This he at once proceeded to do and not on the side usually kissed by acquaintances, but on the palm and higher.

Far from resisting, *Pani* Antonina tossed back her head, eyes tearfully green and eyelids red as they always were after the brandy, and gazed fondly upon the curly head of the young man. With her free hand, she raised her sleeve, fingering her arm.

"Here. . . . And now here."

His lips pursued a blue vein up to the soft rounded forearm shining in the pale light of the dining-room.

When suddenly—crash! And crash again!

The window-frame rattled.

Both jumped, turning frightened eyes upon the black window-panes where the snow-caked boughs of a tree seemed to beg entry.

"Who's that? Who?"

"My husband! And he's seen everything!"

Rooted to the floor before the juggernaut of catastrophe, they heard the doors shatter as someone thudded up the stairs. It was the master of the house who bounded into the room, in coat and hat and snow-covered overshoes, puny, but with quivering beard and angry eyes.

He had raised his left hand long before he reached the dining-room and now flung it towards the door, shrieking:

"Get out!... Out of my home!"

Ivan Poddubny changed colour. His objection died in his throat. He swayed for some reason, and raised his hand to steady himself. With hanging head he shambled uncertainly through the dining-room, passed the master of the house and crossed the next room to the vestibule. Behind him, he could hear *Pani* Antonina pleading tensely with her husband:

"What have you done!... Nikolai!... You're mad!"

"Get out!... Out of my home!" screeched *Pan* Nikolai in a voice not at all his own as he stamped his rubber overshoes.

While the tutor donned his cloak, his ten-year-old pupil Lyuda ran into the vestibule, frightened by the noise. She was half clothed: her short white skirt supported by white straps could not reach her stockings, leaving her knees bare. She turned imploring blue eyes on her father, her small hands folded over her chest.

"Papa!... Papa!... Please don't drive *Pan* Van away!"

That was the name she gave her favourite teacher. Her father hardly noticed her. He ran into the vestibule with waving arms, shouting:

"Took him into my home as I would a son, a respectable human being, wined and dined and payed him.... Ha-a-a!"

Pani Antonina was still talking and Lyuda piping, but Ivan was no longer listening; he found his hat, mechanically plucked *Pan* Nikolai's umbrella from the corner and sped into the street.

There was a sharp current of frosty air... lighted windows here and there ... voices ... the warning cries of the coachmen!... And he found himself in a deserted back street. It was as if *Pan* Nikolai's banishing left hand still hovered before his eyes and the blood rushed to his cheeks. His ears were still ringing with the cries: "Get out!... Out of my home!..." It's scandalous!... A disgrace! His head swam and he plunged on, choking, hardly conscious of anything, his cloak unbuttoned and someone else's umbrella firmly under his arm.

The moon was setting, and the snow sparkled as though the stars had fallen from the heavens. The contours of trees, houses and fences were painfully sharp—and so firm, as though hewn of marble. Yes, they were strangely calm, curiously strong. The blue light seemed barbed, as though frozen to crystals.

The tutor was hardly aware of all this, lunging on down the street with only one want: to get home and hide from mankind, from shame.

"Get out!"

The words haunted, pursued him, drove him on pell-mell.

There were coaches and he should have liked to engage one of them, but remembered that he had five kopeks too little.

Poddubny flung into his room and fell on his bed without turning on the light or shedding his overcoat.

The events came back to him agonizingly. Besides his awareness of disgrace, of the insult that now made his blood run hot, he realized that he had been absurd. He had been driven out like a cur, and had left like a puppy, obedient, inarticulate and cowardly. She would never forgive his disgrace, his philistinism. He should have said something, done something.... But what? He did not know. This was the first time he had ever had an affair with so important a lady. Poor teachei of lower middle-class parentage, he had been driven from school and had never dared to let his sinful thoughts run higher than to a servant or poor young lady who could afford to dress up only on holidays and whose hands were always reddened with work. And then, this forty-two-year-old lady of noble birth and owner of a rich estate had hurled herself into his arms so unexpectedly and imperiously that he had not dared to spurn her. She had taken full possession and needed him every hour and every minute, every day and every night. She insisted that he had good taste and knew how to strike a bargain and therefore compelled him to buy buttons for her, thread, material and furniture. She dragged him endlessly about the shops. Then, she decided that Lyuda should study more, and instead of giving her an hour of his time he had had to give three. When dinner-time found him still at lessons with the little girl, he was invited to join the family at the table.

She had taken him to concerts and theatres when her husband was busy, and had also assured her husband that the tutor was the best fishing companion he could find. He had to listen to her music, to a lot of music, though he understood nothing of it. Often, he had been kept so late that it was not she but her husband who begged him to stay for the night. They had put him up in the small room which once belonged to the governess. Before descending for a cup of coffee in the morning, he had carefully removed the grey female hairs from his clothing.

When he arrived to give his lessons he found the house empty, nearly lifeless. Her husband was at his office. Lyuda would be playing somewhere at the end of the garden or with friends. The servants would not dare to show themselves anywhere in the rooms and the mistress would be sure to be busy over her toilet, peering out with straying hair and bare arms to call to him. She would kiss his eyes, cheeks, lips passionately, endlessly tickling him with strands of hair smelling of some bitter-sweet pomade; she would fling her bare arms round his neck until his head spun.

"Ivas!... Ivashechko!... Ivanko!... My own, my little darling!..." she would moan between kisses. "You are my Lord and Master, blood of my heart, poem of my life! You're my Romeo!"

Then she would demand to be kissed, offering her neck and shoulders, her high, as yet well-preserved breasts, raising her arms so that his lips could reach her arm-pits and laughing nervously because of the tickle of his moustache. She turned in all directions, ogling him with greenish eyes under reddish lids, and the crow's-feet and creases of her face would smoothen under his caresses. Then, she would draw a sheet of paper folded several times from under a pillow and press it into his hand hastily, stealthily.

"That's for you!"

The tiny feminine handwriting and blue ink told him that it was another letter from herself.

While tutoring Lyuda, he would furtively open and read it. His little pupil could do whatever she pleased.

The letter, first of all, was very, very long, covering some five or six pages. It was written in the old flowery style fraught with allegories and long tortuous exclamations. The whole of it gave off the specific familiar bitter-sweet smell of pomade and carried the moist traces of kisses, not allegorical but real, distinctly stamped upon the paper to join the words as illustrations. "If only you could peer into the well of my passion and, radiant with the divine luminescence of love...." "How I should love to dwell for ever upon your breast, to live there in happiness beyond description, in mad ecstasy to drink the dew of your kisses, kiss your footsteps and embrace even the air you breathe." "You are my Lord and Master, my life and my death...."

She wrote such letters at least twice a day, slipping them into his hands, delivering them to him through Lyuda, hiding them in the pockets of his coat or sending them by post. The drawers of his desk were overflowing with these letters of even blue lines saturating his room with the specific bitter-sweet. To each letter she stubbornly demanded an answer, long, passionate, filled with unearthly emotion and knightliness. She was determined. He was duty-bound to bare his soul to her. And so he sat painting word scenery to her theatrical ebullience, tormenting himself, sweating, but finding nothing suitable. If he brought a reply that was pale and brief she went into tantrums, stabbingly accused him of mediocrity, philistinism, but then collapsed on his bosom, entwining him, stuffing even fatter and longer letters into his pockets —and all this in some light dress leaving her body as accessible as possible. In fits of intensified tenderness she would drool over the cigarettes she was for ever smoking, pop her own between his lips or snatch away his, her greenish twinkles under the rose lids crinkling with pleasure at the corners. He was tortured by such love, tickle his pride though it did. There was nothing he feared more than to appear comical in her eyes. And now: "Get out!" And he had got out like a cringing dog.

Poddubny moaned like a wounded man. It was his own fault! He should have done something—anything! But what? Hit him? No! Fling a glove into his face?

But where find a glove? Challenge him? The devil knows!

His eyes chanced upon the window and he groaned. The window depressed him terribly. He rose from the bed and drew the curtains; then returned and buried his head in the pillow. His soul rankled with inexpressible, formless displeasure. His head seemed swollen and empty but for some flitting recollections, chaotic and incongruous.

She had come to him in the room of the governess. "Kiss me!" But when he had grown too determined she was stricken with panic.

"I'm afraid ... afraid, my darling, I'm afraid..." she would whisper, her eyes filled with terror, and the folds at the corners of her mouth deepening painfully; she would push him away, looking anxiously about.

He had nothing to fear and would not listen, but she would squeak and thresh about like a fly in a web. These schoolgirlish mannerisms in a woman far from young were highly irritating.

"Oh, ah!... My darling, my only one ... I'm afraid.... There's someone coming.... Oi!"

She would run away, leaving him filled with craving.

There were times when she was simply cruel. For evenings on end she compelled him to listen to music, particularly classical music—Bach, Haydn, Beethoven—and after some fugue or symphony, played with understanding and expression, would rotate sharply on her piano stool, triumphantly demanding:

"Like it?"

"Why yes ... that is, no ... you see..." he would mumble.

She would measure him with angry eyes.

"Ass! You don't understand anything...." She would trundle about turning her back on him and he would sit depressed, guiltily aware that she had spoken the truth. She was capricious, passionate, sentimental and old. Her behaviour reminded him of the stale French novels.

"Papa'chka! Don't chase *Pan* Van away!"

He could still see the clear pleading eyes of the child, her thin arms, long legs and wavy white skirt.

Why had they aired their family filth before this innocent soul?

How he hated this official with his splotched face, quivering beard and shrill voice; he hated him for being the husband of his mistress, for the shame brought on himself, for his own cowardice. With what delight he would have thrashed him now, crushed him with his weight, clutched his throat!

But what would she have said?

"Philistine! Scandal-monger!"

What she needed was the stage properties ... a duel!

The last word escaped from his lips and made him sit up sharply, staring wide-eyed into the dark.

The stodgy scene came to his mind's eye from some old novel: a green patch of turf and the seconds in high hats. He was pressing the trigger.... There was a puff of blue smoke and *Pan* Nikolai was slumping forward, a red splash widening on his white shirt-front.

Poddubny squinted, trembled and pushed his head back into the pillow.

No, that was something he could not do. Never!

He lay shuddering, trying to forget about blood. He was finally soothed by the thought that *Pan* Nikolai would never agree to fight a duel. He was an official and highly respectable. He would be sure to report the matter to the police at once. Yes, that was probably what would happen. And then things would be still worse. There would be an investigation, the police, a trial—and he would find himself in a most absurd position. But what was to be done?

Poddubny lay pondering in the dark, hearing the rattle of the watchman's night-stick.

"Very well then!" he said to himself, sitting up again. "You've done a nasty thing; you've crawled into someone's home and taken someone else's wife.... Be bold enough then to take the consequences. Take her away. Take her to your nest even if there are only ten kopeks left in your pocket, take her even with your meager means. But what about the child?"

A lump rose in his throat, breaking into fitful laughter. "But she's a hag! Something that's been left over! Never!"

The duel seemed better and better. He would wash his dishonour away in blood.

And he could see the scene again.

There was an exchange of shots and something sharp and hot pierced the very spot where his humiliation hurt him most; he felt even relieved for an instant—and then he was both a corpse and a hero!

There would be talk about him then, and sympathy for him and tears and long, long tender letters in blue lines on expensive paper, letters he would never read.

But there were two sides to his perception and while visualizing the effects of the duel, he very well knew that it was all an idle fancy, sheer stupidity and that he would never, no, not for anything in the world, put his head in front of anyone's pistol.

"Philistine!" he heard someone's voice close at his ears.

Wrestling with his reason, he continued to watch the duel.

What would happen to him when he died? The first

thing was that he would most certainly stop breathing. And so he had stopped breathing and lay perfectly still. The blood in his veins grew cold, turning into jelly; his limbs grew drawn out, absolutely inflexible, as though made of cardboard. His head was empty and his bosom too. It was impossible to close his mouth or get the slightest sound out of his throat.

A fierce impulse wrung a croak from his throat; he felt for his body and bent a hand.

It was perfectly revolting! He protested with all his being!

Suddenly he sprang from the bed, burning with an idea. It was still hazy, more illusive than a zephyr, undulating gaseously; and from the core of him there rose the essence of his nonentity, all that was false and compromising, hydra-headed monsters ogling him green-eyed and filling the air with a stench that turned his stomach.

But he had it at last, the idea, it was his to grasp!

He would challenge him to a duel, but by letter; and the letter would have to pass through the hands of Antonina—and she would never tolerate excesses one way or the other.

Nearly cheerful now, he jumped to his feet.

The window was greying through six patches in the curtain; the pale winter's light fingered the room. Daylight grew over the snow fallen in the night.

Poddubny lit a candle.

In what spirit was his letter to be written? He did not know exactly. Where were those old novels he had had about? They would give him the trend. He began to rummage among his books. Where the devil had they got to? Well, never mind! He knew only that he would sign: "Contemptuously yours...." That was a brilliant idea; it would show his full contempt.

"Dear Sir!"

Stop! The thoughts rushed to his head now, but were crowded out by the phrases; it was not easy. Crossing and recrossing his lines, he copied them again and again and at last concocted something of a letter:

"Dear Sir. You allowed yourself to abuse me unpardonably yesterday. Only blood shall wash out such an insult. I beg you to name the time and place and my seconds shall be at your service. Most contemptuously yours, Ivan Poddubny."

But then he put a line through "Most contemptuously yours," changing it to "Respectfully yours," copied the whole and addressed it: "To Madame Antonina Tsyupa personally for Nikolai Tsyupa."

That was that.

It was still early: half past seven. The Tsyupas usually rose at about nine. Poddubny paced the room, his eyes on the clock. Time stood still. At last he tossed his cape about his shoulders and went out.

There was much snow; it was warm and sunny. The fluff had poured over the earth and the buildings, softened the lines of the fences, caked the trees, branches and twigs enlacing a clear sky and stealing gold from the sunbeams shimmering in patterns between blue shadows on the ground. The sun and air caressed his cheeks and the pines shone so freshly green beneath their coating of white that he felt this was not winter but spring attired in dazzling flakes.

A crow flew down to perch on a fance.

How to make sure that the letter come into the hands of Antonina? And how to avoid running into *Pan* Nikolai who sometimes walked out earlier than the others?

The cattle was being herded to the slaughter-house, a forest of horns and hoofs and rusty hides.

How good it was to breathe; one could almost drink the air like sweet warm milk.

The sun lit a crystal starlet on a frozen bough.

The letter seemed to burn in his pocket. He would have to send it into the house with someone. She would come out to receive it. A letter? From whom? Let me have it! Aha! The colour would rush to her face, and she would turn to take it to her husband.

The street was deserted. There were two rows of white houses under white roofs, and between them only snow. Wisps of smoke straggled skyward. A soldier ran by with a basket. "Hey! Soldier! Hey!" The man stopped and approached with bulging eyes.

"Deliver this letter.... It's that house over there. See those two windows? Hand it to the lady of the house. Do you hear? You'll get ten kopeks." He felt for his pocket.

He paced the pavement, waiting.

The soldier came back, bowing humbly.

"Did you give it to the lady?"

·"She took it from my hands."

"Well then, here!"

Poddubny returned to his room. What would happen next? What was the end to be?

The day was long, endlessly long and anxious. The sky smiled at noon, setting the roofs adrip and filling the room with gold.

Poddubny paced the floor, thinking.

He could hardly get his dinner down; his mouth was dry and his temples heavy.

Finished with his food, he fell back on his bed, cold, apathetic, insensible and expecting nothing.

Something would happen, no doubt.

Grey shadows roamed the room; the window faded and the deeper gloaming enveloped his heart. There was no one about, no one and nothing.

Knock.... Knock....

On whose door?

"May I?"

"Please come in."

It was he ... *Pan* Nikolai, hoarse and shifty-eyed. He made no move to take off his coat and did not offer his hand. He sat down instead.

Poddubny felt for the matches with shaking hands, but could not light the candle.

"Don't trouble."

But Poddubny kept striking match after match.

"You ... you see ..." croaked *Pan* Nikolai. "Please don't be angry! I was drunk yesterday. Just drunk, nothing more ... not a thing more! ... Well, then if I was drunk, you see...."

Aha-a-a! Why of course! He was drunk—drunk as a coachman!... Nothing more!... Not a thing more!... How could it have possibly escaped him—that *Pan* Nikolai had been drunk? He had been filled to the gills —as full as a tun of vodka, as a whole pot-house full of harpies!... Ha-ha! How could it possibly have escaped him?

"Lyuda is lonely without you.... Please come to your lessons tomorrow and forget about the things that happened between us...."

Ha-ha! The old drunkard; he had been drunk as a ... and nothing more. Of course he, Poddubny, would come to lessons tomorrow.... Ha-ha.... Everything in him was giggling, bubbling, laughing; he would have gladly seized this gentleman by his hoarse throat, though anxious to show neither his exultation nor his craving.

Very well, he would come... and nothing more.... Ha-ha-ha!

And about the letter not a word! The swine!

. . . .

Poddubny had a good sleep—slept through all the night like a dead man. At about noon, he slipped *Pan* Nikolai's umbrella under his arm and hurried off to his lessons. The familiar feeling of a teacher hurrying to his lessons soothed him. It was only when he entered the vestibule and saw the stairs down which he had slunk the day before yesterday, and especially when he set the umbrella in the corner, that the recollections poured over him like a bucket of icy water, laming him for a moment.

Lyuda already stood on the threshold of the room, hopping about on her long legs and extending her pipe-stem arms to *Pan* Van.

"*Pan* Van ... *Pan* Van!" she shrilled, ogling him with loving eyes just like Mama.

They got down to their lessons at once.

Everything went as of old; they were interrupted even at the usual hour and called to luncheon.

And so he passed through the same rooms from which he had so recently departed, saw the dining-room and *Pan* Nikolai and *Pani* Antonina seated at the table.

Pan Nikolai shook hands dryly. There was a worn look about *Pani* Antonina, but she was shining nonetheless and, choosing a suitable moment, thrust such a ream of papers into his hands that he did not know what to do with them.

They ate in silence, though trying to make conversation. *Pan* Nikolai was polite, attentive—perhaps a trifle too much so. He kept moving the plates towards Poddubny and pleading, though turning his face away:

"Why don't you have something?... Try some of this...."

His "s's" in "something" and "this" were so sharp that it seemed his mouth was a nest of wasps.

Ivan Poddubny had not yet quite recovered and kept eating with lowered eyes, eating endlessly, to insensibility, with a doggedness and all the eagerness with which he was being pleaded.

Pani Antonina kept dropping her napkin, bending to pick it up and pinching Ivan in the leg.

Sometimes she would reach over and put his hand on her knee.

Lyuda sighed and raised her eyes to the icon.

"I thank you, good merciful Christ!... Everybody is happy now!..."

February 8, 1902
Chernigov

APPLE-TREES IN BLOOM

I tightly shut the door of my study, unable any longer to bear the suppressed wheezing that filled the house. There was my child dying in the bedroom. I had been pacing the study for three sleepless nights, my nerves as taut as the strings of a harp responding even to the slightest stirring of the air. My lamp under its broad cardboard shade divided the room in two—the upper half in darkness and the lower in light laced with shadows. My untouched bed made on the sofa was a source of especial irritation. The snow lay clinging outside to the black windows and my room seemed to me much like the cabin of a ship drifting on a dark ocean with my loneliness and horror. Curiously enough, I was aware of every detail, though entirely in the grip of sorrow. Passing the table, I even readjusted a photograph. That's the way it ought to stand, I thought. But there was no end to the wheezing. I could hear it though the door was closed. I would not go to the bedroom. What for? I could visualize my daughter, her little bare hands on the blanket. I could see her chest heaving under her little shirt and her parched lips struggling for air. Though usually so shy, she now gladly threw her arms around the doctor's neck. My poor little kitten! She was so obedient now. It wrung my heart. If only it were over!

I listened, my heart sinking at the slightest noise. I felt as though something extraordinary was going to happen. A strange being with huge black wings would penetrate through the window, glide across the room, cry out and a life would snap. I listened. The house was not asleep. There was something great, though invisible, alive within it. I heard its breathing and sighing, its heart beating, its pulse throbbing. I knew that its name was alarm, that it crushed the air in its embrace. How I wished to be rid of its oppression, to leave this house and walk away!

I kept pacing the room in measured steps from corner to corner. I could not feel my feet under me, did not guide them, but let myself be carried by them. I was like a wound-up mechanism and only my mind kept weaving its own web of thoughts, like a spider. The infinite spaces of the night stared through the window. A watchman was striking his rattle somewhere in the distance. For how many centuries had it disturbed the night with its wooden cry! How many generations had it survived! It had always brought a sensation of communion with our distant ancestors. There was something simple and pleasing in this clatter, promising to guard our tranquillity and sleep in the desolate night. Why not use this scene of night for the novel I had begun? It would do for the part in which Christina found herself in a forgotten hamlet after leaving the vast city where she had left her husband. She could not sleep and opened the window to watch the trees in bloom, an ocean of soft black waves. The village was asleep and stood about like a congregation of rocks. There was not a sound, not a patch of light under the overcast sky. There was only the fragrance of the blossoms and the rattling in the distance like the heartbeat of an invisible giant. It was all so new to Christina, so unexpected. She felt. . . .

I shuddered. Good God! What was I doing! Had I forgotten? My daughter was dying! I put my ear to the door. She was wheezing. It was so hard for her to breathe, she was in such agony, poor little bird! Her wheeze made me catch at my own breath, and I breathed deeply as though this would make it easier for her.

I was feverish. A cold chill spread through my body and my jaws were trembling. I had not slept for three nights. Grief had been devouring my heart. She was my favourite. I pitied myself, felt so wretched and lonely. I shrank into myself, with grimacing face, a tear rolling from my eye.

What was that? The door banged and there was a pattering of bare feet. Had the end come?

I stood very still, my heart barely beating. I heard the pouring of water and the clang of metal against a pail. It was Katerina. She had brought something into the room. In my mind's eye I could see the sleepy distraught woman. She had been rushing to and fro all night. She was also fond of our Lenochka, a kind soul.

And then all was quiet again, but for the wheezing, the mark of encroaching death.

Where could I escape the sound? I could not bear it any more, and yet I was sure that I would not leave the room. How could I? That wheezing held me to the spot, for as long as it lasted I would know that the child was alive. And so I walked on and on, aching all over because of this wheezing.

It was late. The lamp was smoking and flickering. I saw the flame rise and fall like the breast of my child. Horrified I watched the struggle between darkness and light, and it seemed to me that the moment the light would be out, the soul must depart from the child too.

How superstitious I had become! I lit a candle and then mustered the courage to extinguish the lamp. The room grew darker. The contrast of light and shadow was gone. There was only a great sad chiaroscuro. My room grew so sad! I dragged my weary legs past the ashy furniture, my bent shadow dragging behind. My mind was still infested with thoughts. What were they? Trivial and desultory matters, but the grief was still there. Someone within me kept asking: "Do you want a bit of herring?" "Herring? What do you mean?" It had been merely the question of an outsider and was easily brushed aside. "Hydroquinone, hydroquinone, hydroquinone...." Why did I like that word, repeating it at every step, afraid to miss a syllable? It was somehow soothing to my swollen eyes: it gave them a rest, a sweet rest, and conjured up infinite green meadows. I could hear neither the wheezing nor the rattling.

The clock in the dining-room struck two sharply and loudly. The two strokes fell on me like thunderbolts, like the blade of a guillotine; they almost killed me.

When there is grief and foreboding and the soul is as taut as a tightly drawn cord, it is best to stop the clock. To watch the hands at such a time is to prolong one's agony interminably. Should one forget about it for an instant, the reminder will come like a brick fallen on one's head. It will surely tick away the limits of all patience as its long fingers crawl to the minute of catastrophe.

The green meadows faded from my inner eye and again I heard the rattling.

The window was greying and everything reappeared in the room as it had been: the yellow flame of the candle flickered as before; the shadows swayed and the blacknesses hung in their places. And yet there was something new—probably the grey window. So sensitive had I become that my eyes could now grasp things they had not seen before. I could even see myself pacing the room amid the cumbersome and alien furniture. I could even see my heart without a grain of sorrow in it. Well then, let it be death or let it be life!

The door creaked and the doctor entered my study. He was a dear old friend and had come straight from the bedside of my child. He pressed my hand and looked into my eyes, and I understood. There was no hope, his honest eyes told me. There was nothing more he could do and he was going away. My wife stood on the threshold watching the doctor go. Her eyes, full of hope and supplication, followed him across the room as though he were carrying the life of our Lenochka with him.

She turned to me then, her swollen eyes, dark from sleepless nights and anxieties, shining with tears— and beautiful. Her dark hair collected on her neck seemed so soft and warm! I saw it all to the minutest detail. I saw her dear tear-stained face, her bare throat, the low forward cut of her collar fragrant with the warmth of her young body. As she rested sobbing on my breast, I was conscious that she was not only a friend, but an attractive woman. Though as in a dream, I realized that my mind retained the thought: "Don't cry! Not everything is lost. We'll still have...." What viciousness! How could this consolation occur to me when that little throat was in the clutches of death. Lenochka was dying. No, it could not be. It was wild nonsense. Who would take her from us? Who needed her life? Who would dare to take her while I still lived, flesh of flesh, my Lenochka, my joy, my only child? It could not be! This was absurd!

Starting at the groan that came from the bedroom, my wife rushed to the bedside, while I lunged about the room like a wounded animal, scattering the furniture in a fury, as though bent on destroying everything. "That's vicious, absurd!" something shouted within me, and I gritted my teeth to shut out the pain in my heart. "That's outrageous violence!" I protested with all my being. "It's the law of nature!" insisted a voice behind me, but I would not listen and kept rushing about the room. The grossest words came to my lips and I pronounced them, fearful of my own voice. My jaws were cramped and cold sweat stood on my forehead. I subsided into a chair, shutting my eyes with a palm. "Ah!"

I sat there for a long time.

Had the wheezing ceased or had I imagined it? Was it the end? My wife did not answer. Nor was she sobbing. But perhaps the child was better? Better, my little girl? Perhaps it would all end happily: she would fall asleep and her eyes would smile to her papa tomorrow? Was that really impossible? Was I not near death as a child, abandoned by all doctors. And yet.... Good Lord, was there any power one could supplicate?

Was she still wheezing? No, she seemed to be breathing easier. If she could only fall asleep! If she could only fall asleep! Perhaps I was mistaken when the doctor left. He could not have looked me so boldly in the eye if....

A wild cry, the cry of a mother, made me jump up. My legs refused to obey me, but still I ran, seeing nothing and overthrowing everything in my way. I could not find the door at first and finally ran into my wife who was wringing her hands. I understood. The end had come.

The child was beyond help, and it was she who needed me now. I embraced her, soothing, and saying things that I did not myself believe, and kissing her cold tear-stained hands. With the help of Katerina, a sedative, kisses and cold water, I managed at last to calm her and draw her from the bedroom. She did not scream any more, but wept bitterly. It was the best thing for her, poor dear!

I rushed to the bedroom. What for? I did not know. Something drew me there. I paused at the threshold and looked, feeling that my face had sunken and my eyes, dry and unblinking, were covered with horn. But it was all there, as in a nightmare.

My little darling, already drained of colour, lay on the large white double bed in the middle of the room. A faint wheezing still escaped her parched lips and tiny bared teeth. I saw the glassy stare through the half-closed lids, and my brain caught at the details, registering everything: the large white bed, the tiny body, the faint light of dawn fingering the room, the burning candle forgotten on the table, casting its deathly hue on the face of the child through its green shade, a splash of water on the floor and the reflected glitter of the candlelight on the bottles of medicine. I must not forget anything, neither the small ribbed person heaving under the sheets, the golden, no longer glossy curls scattered over the pillow, nor the warm odour of the already chilling body.

All this, I felt, would be necessary to me some day ... necessary as material. I felt this plainly, and yet knew that it was someone else who was saying this, someone else—within me. I knew that he had usurped my eyes and avid artist's memory to record the picture of the end of life at the dawn of life in spite of myself. But how horrible I felt. My own callousness wrung my heart. I had to leave the house at once.

The apple-trees were in bloom. The sun had risen and was gilding the air. How warm and sparkling it all was! The birds sang high in the blue. Absently I plucked an apple blossom and pressed it, dew-drenched, to my cheek. The rosy petals were scattered by my rough touch. Had not the same thing happened to my child?

But nature sparkled for all that.

What the scene of grief had failed to do, the scene of joy accomplished: I began to weep. Tears of relief dropped like the petals and I looked with regret at the green empty cup in my hand.

I was loth to return to the house and stayed in the orchard for a while. It was all over. Perhaps she was better now? How could I know?

It was all over! But it was so hard to believe, to agree with it. Only six, no, five days ago she was scampering about this garden in which I heard the pattering of her bare feet. Who has not noticed how joyful is the sound of the pattering feet of a little child! It seemed like yesterday that we had stood under our favourite cherry-tree ablossom in a gay bouquet. We had stood hand in hand with upturned faces listening to the bees above. Through the lace of blossoms we could see the blue sky, and below the spring sunshine frolicked on grass.

And now....

She had been such a joy to us. We had so often laughed at the things she said.

When I brushed my hair she would say: "Father is sweeping his head." She called my collars "rings." She could not pronounce the letter "r."

Would I ever forget how she would come to kiss me good night in her little night-gown, all warm and rosy with chubby legs and arms. She would hold her gown with one hand, embracing me with the other and offering me her hot cheek to kiss.

Would I ever forget how happy I had been, toying with her silky hair and looking into her blue eyes, the eyes of my own soul, except that it was a soul that was better, purer and innocent.

But what was she like now, my tiny daughter? No, I must not think of that. She was no more. Where had they put her? What was she like? I suddenly wanted to know. I broke off the best of the twigs of the blossoming apple-tree, heaps of them, and carried them into the house. I did not know in which room she would be now, but entering the first, saw the table and on the table....

So that's where they laid you, my little darling. How big you seem to have grown! As though you were not three years old, but fully six.

I lay the blossoming twigs about her, flowers as tender and pure as she.

Then I looked at her.

She lay so straight, her arms stiffly at her sides, as unnatural as a doll in a box. She wore a short white frock and the little yellow tasselled shoes I had bought for her recently. She had liked them so much.

A candle burned at her head, shedding a warm artificial lustreless light in the broad day. It quivered on her dead cheeks like kisses.

I looked at the waxen body and was seized with a strange feeling: it seemed to me that this was an alien object to me, that it had nothing to do with the living body in which the warm blood had flowed, that it was not this that I had loved and was sorry for, but something quite different, still living in its gold aura in my memory.

And my memory, that inseparable secretary of mine, had already recorded the picture of this limp body amid the apple blossoms, the play of light on the bluish cheeks and my strange feelings.

And I know why you have recorded all this, my tormentor. It will be of use to you some day ... as material.

My little daughter, are you not angry with me?

September 10, 1902

LAUGHTER

P*ani* Natalya, pallid and sleepy, pushed the door to the dining-room ajar and saw Varvara already busy with the dusting. Fastening her morning frock as she went, she asked with a softness probably of fear:

"Have you opened the shutters?"

Varvara stopped dusting, eager to comply.

"In a minute."

"No, no, on the contrary. Let them be shut all day!" said *Pani* Natalya hastily.

Stocky Varvara raised her broad sallow face.

"The town may be unquiet again today. There may be bad people about. I'm afraid someone may break in. Don't go to market. Have we enough food?"

"We have no meat."

"Never mind. Prepare whatever there is. Don't go out and let no one in. We're not at home to anyone. Say that everybody is away. Unless it is one of our friends."

Pani Natalya spoke in low tones, almost whispering into Varvara's ear, her short-sighted grey eyes wandering uneasily.

No sooner had Varvara left the room than *Pani* Natalya looked cautiously around. The room was dark, but for yellow rays penetrating the shutters and diffusing in hazy streaks. *Pani* Natalya bent and white as an apparition tried the bolts of the shutters, and then went on to inspect the adjoining room. From time to time, she put her ear to a window on the street side and listened intently. The vague sounds seemed unusual and alarming.

How would the day end? It was bad enough that the Cossack horsemen had trampled and mauled the people and that so many had fallen to their bayonets! And now, they had turned the mob against the intelligentsia! How often had she pleaded with her husband: "Let us go away and take the children with us." But no, he did not want to. And now it was too late. Dear God! What was it all for?

She thought of the sordid, stupid leaflets that had been snowing the town for days, calling for the massacre of all enemies of the government. And their name too had been listed. Yes, indeed, the attorney Valerian Chubinsky was a man hateful to the police, and so they too had been put on the roll.

The children were laughing and shouting in the next room, and *Pani* Chubinskaya descended on them at once. "Shush, for God's sake! Will you stop that noise!" Her long white sleeves flapped like the wings of a startled bird. Lines of agony marred the corners of her mouth. She kept looking at the window as if afraid that these carefree voices might be heard outside.

Varvara was very helpful. The composure with which she moved to and fro, collecting the clothing and helping the children to put on their stockings, the reassuring heavy padding of her bare feet and her concentrated air were somehow soothing to *Pani* Natalya. It seemed safer with such a loyal and sensible companion about.

"Varvara, have you been out?" asked *Pani* Natalya.

"No, but I have stood by the gates for a while."

"Well.... Are the streets quiet?"

"There were some people who came and asked to see the *pan*."

"Oh, they did? Who were they?"

"I don't know. Just some people."

"Were they carrying anything?"

"Some sticks."

"Oh!"

"I told them that the *pan* was not at home, that everybody was away."

"That's good, Varvara. Very good. Remember, dear, to say that there is no one at home. Dear God!"

"Varvara!" called the irritated voice of *Pan* Chubinsky. "Why are the shutters closed?"

Pani Natalya stopped Varvara and went to the dining-room herself. Her husband, half dressed, stood narrowing his weak eyes. Without his spectacles his face framed with fair hair seemed shapeless somehow and confused.

"Let the shutters be closed, darling. It's I who ordered it so. You know how things are today. I won't let you go anywhere."

"Nonsense, let them be opened at once."

"Oh, dear! But I beg of you! For my sake, and for the sake of the children!" *Pani* Natalya's high cheekbones reddened.

Pan Valerian was angry.

"What nonsense! We can't escape!" But at the back of his mind he felt that his wife had done the right thing.

Varvara soon brought the samovar and the family sat down to breakfast.

There was something odd about the half-darkened room. Yellow patches of light quivered on the walls and the cupboard, and the shutters rattled in the gusts of wind. Awed by the extraordinary atmosphere the little boy and girl spoke in whispers, while *Pan* Valerian drummed the table absently. The tea before him grew cold, but he still sat biting at strands of his blond beard, gazing vacantly over his spectacles. He had noticed that some suspicious figures had been trailing him for some time. At night, it often happened that someone would loom behind the window and shrink away when seen. Only the day before, a string of oaths had followed him down the street. "One of those damned orators!" a swarthy chunk of a man hissed with flaming eyes as *Pan* Valerian turned with surprise. He had said nothing about it to his wife. Then again, he recalled an ocean of heads. Endless numbers of them, heads everywhere, sweating, flushed faces and thousands of eyes turned upon him through the rising mists. Hot waves of this ocean seemed to flow over him as he spoke. The words had lept from him like birds of prey. His speech was a success, it seemed. Simply and vividly he had described the contrast of interests between those who gave work and those who took it; he had done it so clearly in fact that he at once understood it better himself. When they applauded he knew that their conscience had been awakened. That was all very well, but what was to be expected today? What would happen?

Chubinsky looked at his wife who sat very upright, tensely listening. There was an expression of bird-like fright on her face.

It was maddening to have to keep those shutters closed. What could be happening behind them in those mysterious river-beds that were streets carrying strange ominous currents ready to burst their banks and sweep far and wide.

A knock on the shutter made *Pani* Natalya jump. Everyone stiffened.

"What are you afraid of?" *Pan* Valerian asked angrily. "It's probably some urchin or other and you imagine God knows what!"

Varvara rushed from the kitchen.

"What's happened, Varvara?" *Pani* Natalya gasped.

"*Panich* Gorbachevsky is here. He came through the kitchen door."

"Ah, of course, let him come in."

The student Gorbachevsky already stood behind Varvara, thrusting his head over her shoulders.

"What's happening? Tell us about it?" said the host in lieu of greeting.

"Things are rather bad. The Black Hundreds have been sitting about all night at Nikita's. They've been drinking and talking about their first victim. They've decided to deal first of all with the 'orators' and 'democrats.' "

"Good God!"

"Don't be afraid, *Pani!* Perhaps nothing will happen. Though there really seems to be some suspicious commotion in the streets," he added as an afterthought. "They wander about in groups of three or four. Their faces are pretty fierce, and the sight of an intellectual just makes their eyes burn. May I have some tea?"

Pani Natalya poured him a glass with trembling hands, splashing some of the liquid as she offered it to him.

"What else have you heard?" asked *Pan* Valerian pacing the room.

"Thank you. When I passed the market I saw a great crowd. Vodka was being handed out to them free. There were some mysterious confabs going on. What about, I cannot say. I only heard some names: Machinsky, Zalkin, yours...."

"Good God!"

"But there's no need to be worried. That's the usual thing on Sundays—crowds of men drinking vodka.

142

May I have some bread? Thank you. Still, I'm rather surprised at you. Couldn't you have left town for a time? I saw the shutters down as I passed and thought you were away. I knocked only to find out when you were expected back. And here you are, sitting about.... You're running a great risk."

"There you are! How many times have I pleaded with him: 'Let's take the children away.'" *Pani* Natalya was almost in tears, pressing her hands to her heart with anxious eyes on her guest.

"Well, it's too late now," shouted *Pan* Valerian still pacing the room. He was smoking furiously, cigarette after cigarette, dashing the blue wreaths apart with his head, leaving them to trail like mists in the mountains.

"The things that are happening, oh, dear, oh, dear!" These words came in a high-pitched feminine voice.

Everybody turned to the kitchen door and saw a plump little woman dart in, a shaft of light behind her. Her hat was awry and her dishevelled red hair ablaze like a bit of fire she had carried in from the street.

"How dark it is! Is anybody in?"

Greeting no one, she hurried to the table and collapsed on a chair.

"My dears, how glad I am to find you all well! I even thought.... It has begun.... The crowd is moving through the street with the tsar's picture aloft. I just saw them beating Sikach."

"Which Sikach?"

"The young one, the student. He did not bare his head before the picture. I saw him hatless and all bloody. His vest was torn. They were tossing him from hand to hand and beating him. His eyes were red and wild. I could not look on. It was too awful! And do you know whom I saw in the crowd? Just plain people: peasants in grey Sunday jackets and high boots, just plain respectable toilers in the fields. They were the people from our village: so quiet usually, so sensible and industrious."

"They're the worst of the lot, Tatyana Stepanovna!" Gorbachevsky commented.

"No, don't say that! I've taught school among them for five years, but now I've had to run away from them because they wanted to beat me too. It's their old-time hatred for the gentry, no matter who they may be. They've plundered everyone about us.... If it had been rich people only.... But take our neighbour, a poor old widow. One of her sons is in Siberia and the other in prison. She had not a thing in the world, but her old cottage and orchard. They've destroyed everything. They've pulled the house log from log, cut down the orchard and torn up the books of her sons. She refused to plead with them as the others did. Yes, some of the others came out to meet the crowd with icons in their hands and little children and stood kneeling in the mud for hours, begging for mercy and kissing their hands. The mob did nothing to them."

"How horrible!" *Pani* Natalya said mechanically. She still sat very upright and tense, as though expecting something.

"Shush!" she hissed suddenly.

There were distant shouts. Everyone grew still, turning to the windows.

The noise seemed to be coming nearer. It was like an oncoming tornado or the distant roaring of beasts. "Ah.... Ah.... Ah..." rolled the echo from wall to wall. Then there was a swift rush of feet over the cobble-stones outside.

"The scoundrels! I'm going out!" Chubinsky came

to life and darted about the room as though searching for something.

Everybody pounced upon him at once, urging him in strange altered voices not to dare to go out, because it was him the mob was looking for. He would do no good, and would only desert his wife and children. The *pani* insisted she would die if left alone.

Meanwhile the noise was subsiding.

The frightened children stood sobbing in a corner.

"Varvara," *Pan* Valerian ordered, "take the children to the next room and keep them quiet somehow."

Varvara entered, broad and placid, her reddish arms bare to the elbows. A word or two from her quietened the children at once. She embraced them with her heavy hands and hustled them away.

Stillness returned.

"You're lucky to have such a nice maid," Tatyana Stepanovna observed.

Pani Natalya was heartened to see that at least one bright spot had been found in all that gloominess.

"My Varvara is really a treasure! She's a true friend. Calm, sensible and loyal. And just think, we pay her only three rubles a month."

"She is very good-natured," *Pan* Valerian added. "She's been with us for four years. We've grown used to her, and she to us. She's fond of the children too."

Dwelling on this topic for a time, the guests arose to leave, when Tatyana Stepanovna suddenly remembered why she had come. It had seemed to her that it would be best for *Pan* Valerian to keep away from home for a while, especially after those speeches he had made at the meetings. He would do better to stay with some reliable neighbours.

But Gorbachevsky objected: on the contrary, it would be best for him to stay at home and never appear in the streets. Their house was not too well known, because they had moved into it but recently. The closed shutters would lead people to think that the house was empty.

"Well, I'll stay home, come what may," said *Pan* Chubinsky as his guests took leave.

Husband and wife were left alone. He was still darting to and fro amid the clouds of cigarette smoke, as though fleeing from anxiety. *Pani* Natalya sat looking at him gloomily until he at last sat down beside her.

"There's no need to worry," he soothed, trying to regain composure. "There's no danger really. They'll shout themselves hoarse and go home."

"I'm not worried any more. Pay no attention to me; it's just my nerves. I, too, think nothing will happen." She could hardly keep from trembling.

"There are not many real rowdies among them, I'm sure!" he soothed. "The people will not be led by them!"

"Yes, they're not rowdies . . ." she faltered.

"Surely, it cannot come to bloodshed."

"Oh no, of course not!"

Anxiety gathered over them like detonating gas now that they were alone in this dark room enveloped by forces unknown and ominous and were trying to conceal their feelings from each other.

What could he do unarmed against the fury of the mob, people who knew not what they were about? She realized it very well.

But what if the mob really came?

Well, they would barricade themselves behind the door and fight to the death.

The bell trilled sharply, startling Chubinsky.

"Don't go! Don't open the door!" *Pani* Natalya pleaded, wringing her hands.

The bell danced and rattled.

Chubinsky rushed to the kitchen.

"Varvara! Varvara!"

"Shush! Don't shout!"

But there was no sign of Varvara. What were they to do? At last, the maid hurried in. "It's the doctor! He's coming through the kitchen!"

The doctor entered the room almost running. A big man, he was waving his arms like a pair of flails, shouting:

"There you are, sitting about without the faintest idea of what is happening. They're killing people! They'll slaughter everybody! They've smashed up the apartments of Dr. Garnier and destroyed his instruments. They've dragged his wife about by the hair and taken Garnier away with them to make him carry the portrait of the tsar at the head of the hooligans; that's one thing."

"Good God!"

"They've dragged Ivanenko from a cab and broken his head; that's what they did. Zalizko was beaten until he swore allegiance to the autocracy; Rashkevich, the obstetrician, was beaten to death more likely than not. There's not a single policeman about. We've been left to the mercy of the drunken mob. We must defend ourselves. We ought to gather at the square near the Duma. Do you hear me? There's no time to lose. We've got to defend ourselves with arms in hand."

The doctor was thundering as if facing thousands of people on the square.

Pani Natalya felt that his voice would break her heart. Not so loudly, not so loudly! her eyes and painful grimace seemed to plead. She kept pressing her hands to her heart, whispering:

"Oh, *Pan* Doctor, *Pan* Doctor, will you be so kind. Oh, dear God!"

But the doctor would not listen.

"Take your revolver and let us go!"

"But I have no revolver!" Chubinsky retorted angrily.

The doctor whistled with astonishment. "How can that be? So it's only speeches we can make, and when it comes to.... No, my dear sir, that won't do. You sit waiting there to be seized like a hen in a coop. I'm going!"

"But where to?" shouted *Pan* Valerian in his turn. "That's sheer madness! You'll accomplish nothing at all."

But the doctor waved his hand and dashed from the room.

Chubinsky was seized with most shameful fear. What was he to do? He did not want to perish in such a wretched, terrible way. Perhaps he ought to hide? But how could he hide the whole family? He looked around the room. His wife sat back moaning, almost unconscious, crushing her head between her hands. Varvara was fussing over the table. Perhaps they ought to run, all of them? But where to? Dozens of schemes struggled in his mind like will-o'-the-wisps and were extinguished as suddenly. No, there was nothing to be done. Fear drove him about the room from door to door. He trembled with his efforts to suppress it. "Don't lose your head!" something seemed to say to him, but his thoughts kept wandering like wild animals in their cages. What was that Varvara was saying?

"Shall I serve breakfast?"

The words sobered him a bit.

"What's that you're saying?"

"Shall I serve breakfast, sir?"

"Breakfast? Of course not. Haven't you heard what is happening?"

"Why, of course! Ha!"

This "ha" stopped him in his tracks. He saw the

maid's features tremble like a still surface under the plash of a fish. One of the ripples had reached him.

"They're killing the gentry," he explained and was surprised to see that her heavy body was shaking, as though with suppressed laughter.

"What is it?"

"I. ... I. ..."

And suddenly it came in a burst:

"Ha-ha-ha! They're beating them! Well, let 'em! Ha-ha-ha! Enough of their lording it! Ha-ha-ha! Thank God that the people have not waited in vain!"

She even crossed herself.

The blood rushed to her face; her eyes were flashing. She stood rocking with laughter as though drunk, her red arms akimbo, her ponderous breasts quivering under her greasy bodice.

She could not stop that bacchanalian roar that boiled up within her, flinging off a froth of words.

"Ha-ha-ha! They ought to wipe them out! Ha-ha-ha! Them and their offsprings! ... Ah-ha-ha!" She even sobbed.

The laughter seemed to whirl about the room and was as painful to behold as a frenzied dance of cold and glittering knives. It was a torrent of laughter, a lightning storm, dreadful and deadly in its peal upon peal.

Chubinsky leaned against the table. The laughter descended upon him like hail. What was that she was saying? Something preposterous, quite senseless.

Pani Natalya was the first to spring from her place.

"Get out of here!" she shrieked. "Get out of here! She'll slaughter my children! Away with her!"

Varvara stopped laughing. Her breasts were still heaving, but her head was bowed. She looked up at the *pani* from under her brows, collected the dishes and trod heavily off to the kitchen.

They could hear her bare feet padding over the floor.

Chubinsky felt that he was stifled. He shook all over, advanced a few steps to follow Varvara, but then halted. But it was preposterous, incomprehensible.... It was a nightmare.

He rushed to the kitchen door, opened it and saw Varvara standing by the table, unafraid of the light, composed, hunched and wilted. She stood wiping some dishes.

"Var...." He could say no more, and just stood staring, his eyes wide, anxious and unusually searching. He took in the whole picture to its smallest details, things he had usually passed like a blind man: the bare feet, red, muddy and chapped, like the feet of a beast, the rags on her shoulders that gave her no warmth, the sallow complexion and the blue lines under her eyes. "We've eaten her out of all the good things of life—together with our dinners." There was the bluish smoke in the kitchen, the hard bench on which she slept amid the slop pails and dirt like an animal in its lair. Life had been sapped from her by others. Hers had been a sad, hazy sort of an existence, a life in a yoke ... without a glimmer of hope ... and all this for the comfort of others ... and he had thought he had a claim to her devotion.

He could not speak. And why should he? Was it not all clear?

He plunged back into the dining-room.

"Have you seen ..." he turned on his wife. "Oh, you haven't? You'd better have a look...."

"Why doesn't she go on strike!" he cried in a strange voice. "Why doesn't she?"

He was driven about the room as if lashed by a whip. He was suffocating.

Dashing to the windows he unthinkingly began to unfasten the bolts. It was done quickly and impatiently.

"What are you doing?" cried the *pani* in despair.

Paying no heed, he tore at the bolt with all his strength. It finally broke loose, striking the shutter with a bang echoed by the high ceiling. The window flew apart, hitting the jambs, and the room was flooded with a yellow hazy light. A puff of cold dust and distant medley of sound came with the autumn wind.

"Why doesn't she go on strike?"

He struggled for breaths of cold air, oblivious of the tumultuous roar rolling down from afar.

It was like the moaning of the street itself.

"A-a-ah!" came the distant thunder as though a dam had burst.

"A-a-ah!" It rolled nearer, gaining articulation in the tinkling of shattered glass, separate cries of agony and the rush of thousands of feet. A cab hurtled over the cobble-stones pursued by the rumbling of its own wheels, while overhead there fled yellowish clouds scudding before the wind.

"A-a-ah.... A-a-ah...."

February 7, 1906
Chernigov

PERSONA GRATA

Lazar loathed the warden, him whom the prisoners called the Mug. Everything was hateful about him: the fat face which could not grow a single hair, the small cruel eyes fastened on nothing but observing everything, and his special gift for torment. The rare moments in which their eyes had accidentally met were memorable to Lazar and invariably stirred his forebodings. Lately, too, he had been particularly uneasy, for the Mug had been scrutinizing him all too often, as though probing his body, arms, legs and heavy stooped shoulders. Lazar would try to be as inconspicuous as possible, wrapping his prison jacket more tightly around him and suppressing his anger as best he could. The gimlet eyes in that creased face would haunt him long afterwards. Things had come to such a pass that meeting Lazar in the yard, the Mug would halt before him, dagger-eyed, moving his lips yet uttering nothing. His orbs would then revert to space and on he would walk. Others, too, had noticed this, and stopped work, the whites of their eyes glinting quizzically from under their grey cloth caps.

The Mug, finally, spoke up one day:

"Well, brother, how do you like the life here?"

Lazar drew his jacket closer about him and grew tense as though expecting an assault. "Can't you leave me alone?" his posture seemed to say. He seemed very small and inanimate at that moment. But the Mug waited for no reply. Touching his elbow with two fingers, his eyes wandering somewhere overhead, he enigmatically pronounced:

"Never mind, brother! Things may improve."

And away he strode in his military step, very gingerly carrying his cube of a head.

Lazar followed him with a lowering stare, the lines of his face showing angry curiosity.

He was summoned to the office on the following day. He was gone for an hour or more and the other grey jackets were agog with conjectures and cynical observations, exchanging knowing winks. When he returned, Lazar was at once beset with questions; the men eyed him curiously. His account was trivial, but there was mystery lurking in his eyes. No one could miss it. It was like a seed that had been planted in him and its first shoots were growing even then.

It might have seemed that everything went on as before, and yet, there was a difference. In the general hubbub, Lazar would suddenly fall silent as if hearkening to an inner voice. In their rare moments of respite, he would sit aloof, his brow in his hands, brooding. There was something astir within him. It was something long forgotten and unpleasant, buried under layers of fresher events and impressions. He tried to dig through it all, gleaning fragments of memory and piecing them together. If he had been able before to recall everything down to the cries of his victims and children's hands raised to protect themselves, if he had remembered the five corpses in an outlying pub, the only obstructions to his plan of robbery, his attention was now focused upon himself. Had he ever really deliberately thought of killing anyone? Had he been frightened then? Perhaps he had thought of killing someone, but only to prevent them from raising a row. Under what circumstances had he killed his first victim? Had the next, the others, been easier? Had he been able to finish them off at once, or had he needed time? Had he or had he not seen their eyes or faces? His memory stirred sluggishly. Goad it as he would, he could not distinctly recollect his actions and sensations. He would return to his memories again and again until his exhausted mind kept slipping round and round like a broken key in its lock and his thoughts wandered away elsewhere. How was it going to be now? Would it be hard? Would he be afraid at first? Would he get used to it? Suddenly he remembered that he had hanged a cat when he was a boy. It was a wretched animal with tail and ears lacerated by the dogs.

There was no time to finish his train of thought, because there was a tub he had to carry, and he tackled the job at once, placid and indifferent, with the same mystery lurking in his eyes. The tub suspended on the pole over his shoulder swayed splashing splotches. He could see a back and a wax-like neck just ahead. The tattered cat suddenly loomed in his mind, struggling at the end of the rope with curling feet and tail, its glowing eyes popping from their orbits. What would it be like? Would the animal struggle long? Or would it close its eyes and drop its paws? His curiosity twitched as wildly as that cat at the end of the rope.

What will it be like now?

He was weary. The thoughts carved his brain like a plough the dry earth. To avoid them, he would begin a quarrel, stupidly, viciously, without rhyme or reason, deafening himself and the others with his vile rhetoric which seemed to contaminate the very air. He was glad of that malice within him, and tried to fan it to fury.

"You there! The two of you!" he cried in falsetto. "You scum! I'd hang you all to the same bough, the lot of you, if only it were strong enough."

This gave huge fun to the grey jackets for a while and smiles spread over their faces like wet spots on a wall.

This infuriated Lazar even more, keying his voice even higher. His motions were like those of a hangman embracing the legs of his victim to hasten death. He thirsted to hang, slash and kill all who were laughing and all who were outside the walls. What was there to it, after all? Like snapping a chicken's neck, nothing more! Yet, there lingered a buzz of a thought, as persistent as a mosquito: what would it really be like?

Somewhat reassured, he would get down to work again, carrying wood and water and sweeping the courtyard as if nothing had happened. He seemed to be contemplating himself. The lips under his abbreviated moustache were tightly pressed. He knew what he knew. As he walked he would at times mutter something in a matter-of-fact way, bending his fingers one by one.

"Twenty-five for one. Fifty for two. Three hundred less fifty for ten. Clothes free."

The rustling of bills and tinkling of coins effaced the prison, the grey jackets, the wretched cat with its spitting agony.

Snatches of the conversation rambled through his mind instead: "Think you could do it, brother?" "No need to worry." And then he remembered the hairless dial of a face, now somewhat less repulsive.

Lazar's life took a sharp turn that night when he was secretly removed from the prison and put in a railway coach. He wore a yellow shirt, a peaked cap and high boots instead of the prison garb. It seemed so queer to him to see his legs encased in boots instead of the ponderous prison shoes. The shirt, too, seemed so light that he was not too happy over the change. But the gendarme on the seat opposite spoke so affably that he gradually grew used to his new position. He had nearly forgotten that he was a convict. He might have passed, after all, for a cabman, or the janitor of a prosperous house, for a free man sitting there casually chatting with this important policeman in his blue uniform with sabre. Who could say it was not so? The policeman grew more talkative and congenial. At first he talked about how hard things had become and then of the people who had caused this. Lazar approved. And when the policeman brought a bottle of vodka and they had a drink together, they were soon shouting, clasping each other's hands, vowing something or other. There was a slight fuzziness in his head. It was so warm and so nice to have this important gendarme in his uniform with sabre clasping his hands and talking to him as to an equal. They travelled all night, all day and arrived by night. After a long ride in a cab, Lazar found himself in a prison again. Though the hour was late, he was received by the warden himself. From the looks and whispers about him, he felt that he, Lazar, was no ordinary man. The short reception over, a lock was clicked back to admit him to a cell. An obliging hand lit a lamp and he saw a high-ceilinged, rather clean room with a window, a well-prepared bed, a table covered with a table-cloth, an icon in the corner: the Saviour extending a blessing hand.

"You may turn in now," the warden said in a shaking, obviously frightened voice. "Call Ivan or Kalenik if you need anything."

When they had gone out, the lock clanked twice, and Lazar stood alone between the clean bed and the table laid with a cloth beneath the icon. He sat down, felt for the quality of the blanket and the pillow. They were made of good soft material of a kind he had never seen. There was a brand-new chair by the table. In the corner there stood a basin and pitcher. It was just as in a gentleman's home. If not for the tall barred window and the night-pot, he could have felt that he was a guest at some gentleman's house. He let his eyes roam over the ceiling, the lamp and the icon, placed his shoulders against the brightly coloured pillow, raised his booted legs and quickly fell asleep dressed as he was, without putting out the light.

In the morning Kalenik brought the tea-kettle and a loaf of bread under his arm. He put them on the table and turned to face the bed with hands clasped across his stomach. He was a short man and, apparently. good-humoured. His moustache, hair and worn uniform all had a droop in them as though they had been soaked in water and only just taken out. His eyes, too, seemed soaked. They settled on Lazar, shifted to his hands, shoulders and legs, until a satisfied smirk crept under his snuff-stained nose. Lazar was sure that this man would have a long, wracking, shrill cough if ever he did cough.

And sure enough, Kalenik soon obliged with a shrill cough, shaking his head kindly, wetly sucking in the air.

"A big fellow you are!" he exclaimed softly, scattering his laughter. "Let's have our tea! It's against the rules to lie down with your boots on, but the rules are made for others, not for you."

"How do you know?" Lazar half rose from his bed.

"But I do know. That's the orders...." There was another splash of his laughter. "You're an official man now," he added earnestly. "You serve the state."

"So there are no rules, eh? What about vodka?"

"It's not forbidden."

"And some cards?"

"Any time you like. You can play with me or with Ivan. It's in the rules."

Still, there were some things that were forbidden after all. It was forbidden to open the window and to leave the room. Those were the orders. He was no longer the free man he had been when coming here, but only a convict as before. His position was even worse in a way than it had been, for in the old prison he could walk about the prison yard, see people; and though the work had been heavy, he was used to it. And now, too, the old question mounted again: what would it be like?

Lazar washed his face hurriedly, because the tea was getting cold and the look of the loaf whetted his appetite. He had not yet finished his tea, when the door opened and something rumbled behind it. A tall thin man dragged a large faded armchair into the room; it was torn at the back. He bumped it over the threshold and pushed it against the wall in the corner, Then came Kalenik, gingerly carrying a portrait of the tsar; it was a little fly-blown.

"Give us a hand, Ivan," he mumbled; it seemed that he was chewing something.

Ivan took the portrait and held it against the wall, while Kalenik took the lump of dough out of his mouth and pasted it on the wall. The room seemed even cosier now. What pains they were taking for his comfort!

The dinner was both good and substantial, including vodka. When it was over, they sat down to cards. Ivan, the loser, grew sulky. Kalenik was luckier. There was flush after flush and every gain was peppered with his laughter, though his playing was not aboveboard, and he ought to have been watched more narrowly.

The days slipped by. Lazar slept as long as he

wished, ate as much as he could, played cards, drank vodka and lolled in his armchair. He was quite a gentleman now and could do anything he liked. The old question of how it was going to be kept worrying him at first when he was alone. He was expecting to be summoned soon. It would be a new sort of work. But time passed and no one troubled him. Life went pleasantly and he thought he had been forgotten. But once, he was roused at night. Half asleep, he thought it was Kalenik, but it was an unknown gendarme. He grumbled, unwilling to get up, and complained of the light of the lamp in his eyes. But get up he did, taking his time with his boots and yellow shirt. The gendarme's spurs tinkled as he offered Lazar a jacket. Dawn was breaking when they came out; the air was fresh and chilly. When the prison gates were behind them, and Lazar caught sight of the carriage and horses his heart sank.

They drove for a long time through deserted streets, passed still houses with sleepy windows. Then they turned into a field. It grew lighter and one could see the wheat, stiff and fresh. The gendarme yawned and made the sign of the cross over his mouth.

"A good crop that ..." he drawled.

The air grew transparent. A strip of woods showed black on the horizon, though cotton wisps of mist clung to the valley below.

When at last they arrived, Lazar saw a post. He descended and approached it, looking dully at the rope suspended from it; the rope was fuzzy and did not seem quite straight.

"Make ready," the gendarme said.

Lazar climbed the scaffold, touched the loop and dumbly watched it swing. He was like a sleep-walker. Everything was fast asleep in him: malice, brain and blood.

"Roll up your sleeves!" came the curt order.

Lazar began to unfasten the buttons at the wrists of his jacket. But suddenly this seemed unnecessary to him; he whipped off the jacket and tossed it aside. Then he began to roll up his sleeves, slowly and importantly, inspecting the bluish knotted veins on his swarthy arms.

The gendarme mounted the scaffold too and touched his bare arm.

"It won't be long now," he commented, looking at his watch. He then lit his cigarette.

Some minutes passed in silence.

Swaying the rope, the morning breeze coldly patted his bare arms. A landrail chirped in the violet field and curls of smoke rose from the gendarme's cigarette.

Suddenly there was a clatter of arms, and a procession came into view. The first was a priest in his long surplice; then came the warden and some others. The black figures of the soldiers followed, leading something white between them. That white blot seemed so queer against the black that Lazar could not take his eyes from it. The first detail he could take in was the flaxen hair. A white kerchief had slipped off on to the shoulder and the yellow strands shone as though of burnished gold. She was a slight girl, frail, and seemed to be walking in such a carefree and even cheerful manner that Lazar now took his eyes from her to search for someone who would have justified the ceremony better.

He peered into every face, but found no one likely.

Could it be this child, he wondered somewhat crestfallen, as though cheated. He waited, arms folded, as they came nearer and placed the girl below the scaffold. Why didn't she weep? Why didn't she scream? Instead, she was looking at him straightforwardly, her yellow hair shining. At a word from the warden, the priest approached and offered her the cross. She waved it aside and said something in a loud clear voice, much like the cry of a sea-gull. The gentlemen and the soldiers stood guiltily by, while she lightly mounted the scaffold. Lazar stood and stared in a daze. He felt neither malice nor curiosity.

"Tie up her hands, you idiot!"

Goaded into action, he descended upon her rudely and clumsily. She crossed her wrists over her chest, waiting patiently, while he was busy with the rope, sweating profusely.

"Where's the sack, you ass?"

He had forgotten about the sack.

The long white sack was brought at last. Lazar fumbled with it hurriedly. His hands trembled as he touched the girl's hair and her soft warm neck. He started back as though scorched by her skin, but still seemed to be asleep. There was something in him that could not wake up. In a stupor, he laid the noose around her neck, adjusted it and kicked the board from under her feet. The rope tightened with a jerk, and the white blot whirled before him, growing longer and broader until it covered the people, the horizon and the world. It was a white wall, but then it shrank together and hung limply in the rising sun. Only then did he notice the fields and the stillness, an extraordinary deadly quiet. In that silence her shoulders kept twitching, the landrail chirping and the watch in the doctor's hand shining.

The warden came up to Lazar, made to pat him on the shoulder, but suddenly drew back his hand.

"Good for you!" he said in a husky voice; he was very pale. Then he turned aside and twirled his moustache. Again there was a clatter of arms, motion, and that was the end.

Lazar drank as much as he could that day. Ivan and Kalenik grew tired of carrying the bottles, but he would not stop drinking and talking on and on, trying to kill that silence and also to recall what she had shouted. He could still hear the voice, the words lay somewhere in a haze, in the fuzziness that had wrapped his brain; his memory was blank. Quite drunk towards evening, he began to fight. Ivan and Kalenik ran away and he collapsed on the bed and fell asleep.

Fragments of an apparition haunted his drunken brain, but gradually the haze melted away and he distinctly heard those proud words; he could not understand what they meant, nor did he care to. He distinctly saw the golden strands, the small hands, like those of a child, once more felt the soft neck, which made his body tingle all over. He saw all her movements now: the expression of her eyes, the pale face, the lines on her forehead, a patch of her dress as she walked. He remembered every trifle, her soft figure reminding him of a fluffy bird. He saw her twitching under the shroud, her head bent, her pointed shoes thrust back like a swallow's tail. In his uneasy dream he inspected his hands, to see if they were sticky.

Roused quite often now, he got up in the dead of night and went to his work lethargically. What would it be like was a question that no longer troubled him. There was no need to fan his malice, as he had done when in the other prison. There was even something pleasant about it all, for he could see the fields, the new rye, the clouds scudding overhead in the noisy wind, the sunrise.

He had to deal with various people. There were some who were bold and proud, flaunting vehement words. Others were as pale as corpses, barely able to move their feet, almost fainting so that they had to be carried up. There were still others who swore and fought furiously. He had to twist their arms and struggle with them for a long time, sweating from every pore. He had to handle both men and women, the aged and those in their prime. Some were big and some small as children. Some were gentry and some plain folk. When he was lucky the job was clean. But there were times, too, when the noose slipped and twisted the head round. The white sack would dance about for a long time then and, to put an end to it, Lazar would have to throw his weight on to the victim's feet. On one occasion, the rope snapped and he had had to begin anew. On another occasion, the rope proved too long, and when Lazar kicked loose the board, the falling weight of the body tore its head off, setting it bouncing away like a kite, copiously spattering the shroud with red. The warden had scolded him then and he had had to wash the shroud himself.

Each of his "clients" gave him some small keepsake in his last moments: a peculiar glance, voice, colour of hair, twist of neck, gesture or word. He could not rid himself of these keepsakes and they lived on within him myste-riously. They were the only vital things left of the hanged. Curiously enough, he saw them only in his dreams, never awake. In the day-time he slouched about irritable and cantankerous. He sent Kalenik and Ivan about on errands, throwing his boots at them when they were slow about it, swearing and drinking heavily as always. The fumes played havoc with his brain, begetting apparitions and exciting the wildest of cravings. He would shout, pound on his door and annoy everyone.

One morning Ivan brought him his tea as usual, but he would not touch it. "Bring the samovar!" Ivan remon-strated, but Lazar snatched the kettle and threw it at him. Ivan was scalded and some plates were broken. The sen-ior warder came in shouting, but Lazar kept pounding the table and bellowing: "Bring me the samovar!" The warder withdrew and the samovar was brought in. Sens-ing his power, Lazar made more and more demands. In addition to his vodka, he demanded beer and this too was brought to him daily. He was served with choice meals, and his room was covered with carpets. The guards grumbled, shrugged their shoulders, but continued to obey. This went to Lazar's head.

"You swine!" he roared, exulting in his power. "Do as I say, because I'm your lord and master!"

The obedience of the guards and their warden stimulated his craving to inflict torment. His misty consciousness kept inventing more and more humiliations and annoyances for them. He would summon Kalenik and gruffly order him to cough.

Kalenik smiled and kept uncertainly silent.

"Cough, damn you!"

Kalenik shifted his weight from foot to foot, winced and began to cough softly.

"Can't you do it louder, you idiot?"

Kalenik did his best and his artificial coughing soon turned into the real thing, filling the room with its shrill chatter until he wheezed and gasped for breath.

In a few minutes Lazar would call him again.

"Cough!"

When in his cups, he imagined that he was a count or a grand personage visiting the prison to put it in order and protect the prisoners from injustice. He would begin with an inspection of Ivan and Kalenik. Lolling in his chair, he would extend his legs encased in his long boots. He wore his usual yellow shirt and sitting there proudly would wrinkle his flushed splotchy face. His shifty yellow moustache made him look much like a dog.

"What's your name? Ivan? You're a liar! I know that they call you the Hooker. I can see through and through you, you scamp! Why do you torture people? Do you think a convict is not a human, you pig face. Perhaps he's even better than the likes of you. He's suffering for his sins, while you are being paid for them. Take care! If anything comes to my ears ... in twenty-four hours...."

"Now I'll deal with the second one. What's your name? Kalenik? So be it, the devil take you! Make your report!

Is that the way to stand? D'you know who I am? Have you been stealing again? Feeding the men with wormy soup? Slapping them around? Why are their shirts so dirty? You lousy rat, slippery rat! There's disorder everywhere. I'll teach you a thing or two. Call the warden!"

The warden was not called and Lazar would begin to fight. The guards went off to complain, and the warden appeared at last, very timidly, but apparently trying to pull himself together. He never blustered, but did his best to soothe the man, pleading with him, shaming him and smiling his sickly smile.

Lazar felt their fawning and knew again that nothing was forbidden for a man as important as himself.

He would resume his tricks, inventing new ones.

At times, however, he would grow suddenly afraid. Everything seemed hostile then and conspiring against him. Everything lay stealthily in ambush for him.

Sometimes he imagined that Ivan's eyes were upon him. He would feel them resting quietly on his neck or back, probing for a weak spot. Lazar would stiffen and suddenly wheel round. But the eyes always slipped away in time, laughing in Ivan's face and telling him what they had seen.

Lazar would fly into a rage, shouting: "Stop looking at me. Take your eyes off me, or I'll knock them out!"

But the eyes returned, stealing over his face, neck and chest, gently tickling him or piercing him somewhere to get in. He would rage and storm until he was tired. Things were bad with him and he was sick of everything, of the walls, the vodka, Ivan and Kalenik. The first prison had been better. It was easier to carry the barrels or water or sweep the yard. There had been sunshine, movement and people there. He never thought about his new work by day, but at night his fingers felt the soft neck and hair. Eyes loomed in the darkness—all sorts of eyes: brown, grey, blue, all of them speaking of life and death,

Splendid words burst into blossom, while curses drooped like thistles in the dust. The keepsakes of death were jealously cherished in his memory. They led their separate mysterious lives in his mind until he grew will-less and limp.

Again and again he was torn from his dreams. He had to gather new keepsakes, though the old ones would not leave him be. Hoisting himself humbly from his bed, he dressed grumbling.

Then came another day of drunken stupor and cantankerous pranks.

Such was the procession of days and nights.

Still, the nights were better.

One night, he was visited by one who had presented him with the keepsake of his eyes. Seating himself at the foot of the bed, he began to talk.

HE: Why did you kill me?

LAZAR: How do I know? I was told to.

HE: That's a lie. How can anyone make one man kill another? Better tell the truth. You killed for money.

LAZAR: But I killed five before!

HE: Say frankly! What did you do it for?

LAZAR: They were screaming, and I was afraid the people would come and seize me.

HE: Go on!

LAZAR: I don't know how I came to do it. I didn't mean to. I didn't want to.

HE: There you are! You didn't want to! It was fear that made you sin, and for this there was retribution and your redemption. You were just defending yourself. But now? Why do you kill now? For vodka, for money? What have all those people done to you?

LAZAR: Don't look at me that way! Take your eyes back, do you hear?

HE: Never more! My eyes will be fixed on your breast until they pierce your heart. Still, you're a better man than

those who tempted and made you kill. You are unknow-
ing and have taken to this from need alone. But they are
book-wise and wealthy!

LAZAR: Do you think I find it easy? I'm so tired...
in body and soul. There's something eating at my heart.
Don't look at me that way! Take your eyes back, do you
hear?

But the eyes would not go. In all their horrifying lustre and plea for life, they floated through the air and settled on his chest. Lazar felt them piercing him deeper
and deeper.

He awoke with a heavy head and a wild hankering.
The cell was stuffy, drab and narrow. His numb muscles
would not obey him. He did not even care for the vodka
he drank. The taste was atrocious, somewhat watery and
bitter, the smell evil. It refused to intoxicate him. Again
he began his shouting and his pranks with Ivan and Kalenik. He wanted the cell filled with a hubbub of outcries
and commotion. He wanted the walls to tremble, the window to rattle. He smashed the plates, pounded the door
and banged the table with his fist. But the silence was
still there, hovering over him on the ceiling and grinning
from every corner. It had won.

He fell silent himself, lay down on the bed and closed
his eyes, wondering if his visitor of last night would come
again. He did not. Arising again, Lazar trod heavily to
and fro, colliding with the walls. He pressed himself
against the cold stone, needled by his thoughts and winc-
ing. "The swine!" He resumed his pacing, weaving a web
of impressions and still hissing: "The swine!"

He clenched his fists.

At night he was visited again, not by him whom he
expected, but by the first, the fair-headed one. She too
sat down at the foot of his bed and at once demanded:

"Why do you kill?"

He did not know. He could not answer, but desperately wanted her to keep talking, to explain. Very well, so be it! In that voice still living in his ears, she told him that she had left an old mother now in mourning. She had not wanted to die, but he had killed because he had been paid. Had he needed the money so badly? Had it brought him comfort, health and happiness? He had taken a life and was rewarded with prison, vodka and the weight of sin. Was he better off now? A few strands of gold shone over her brow as she spoke.

He wanted her to go on, to tell him something he did not dare to ask, and the girl, as frail as a mist, seemed to divine his thought.

"Still you are better than those who make you kill. It is not the axe that kills, but the hand that wields it."

Something moved in Lazar's heart. Was it joy or compassion? For her or for himself?

Now he craved to know what words were those she had cried out before dying.

But the girl half smiled and said with reproach: "Why didn't you listen?"

. . . .

Ivan and Kalenik decided that Lazar had been drinking too much of late. They inferred this from his strange behaviour. He was too quiet and kept brooding. He would walk about and suddenly extend his hand for no visible reason, inspect his fingers and then hide them in his pocket. He would then pace the cell again and whenever he thought himself unseen would extract his hand, examine and hide it again. Why was he doing this?

This new habit of his was especially conspicuous when they were playing cards. He would sometimes drop the cards, careless of whether they saw them or not, and hide his hands under the table. When it seemed to him that

Ivan and Kalenik were looking at his hands, he would stop playing and thrust them into his pockets or behind his back. His lowering wrath then drove them from the room.

He ate very little now. Kalenik remarked to Ivan that Lazar seemed to be afraid of bread. He had seen him reach for it once and shrink back gasping: "But bread is a sacred thing!"

"He's turning into a hermit! Ha-ha! Into a hermit, haw-haw!" they bawled.

The gendarme did not come for him for several days, but Lazar never forgot him when he went to bed. Who was it that sent the gendarme to him, the warden? No, he too was an axe in someone else's hand. Who was it then? What sort of people were they? Was it one or many? He would have liked to see those people who were worse even than himself, those people who were ashamed of the sun, because they always called him before dawn. But where were they to be found? Who would show them to him? How would he recognize them? His mind struggled with this like a fly in a glass, round and round until it fell. But there was something rising within him like dough in an oven, fermenting like yeast. He was so chock-full of thoughts that he gasped for air. He would climb the table and open the window though it was forbidden. Dampness and quiet seeped through the bars and his eyes fastened on everything they could. It was a free and tranquil world out there. There were the dark tall trees with blue between them, a blue as deep as an overflowing lake filled with starry goldfish. The heavy black cloud dozing overhead flickered now and then in distant lightning. Beneath, there were glowing windows, and there was calmness everywhere.

Calm for all except Lazar—for Kalenik would come in at once to shut the window. They were afraid that someone would catch sight of him by chance.

So that is how it was! They were hiding him away. They were ashamed to have him seen. Now, who were those people?

*   *   *

"Lazar! Get up!"

He had had a dream. The words crawled over his body like caterpillars. He would have liked to brush them away, but could not. They continued to crawl, furry and irritating, on his shoulders.

"Lazar! Get up!"

He opened his eyes and saw the gendarme bent over him.

He got up and felt his feet hit the floor.

He sat still for a minute, blinking at the light, and then lay down.

"Well?"

"I won't go."

Ha-ha-ha. That was so funny! He wouldn't go indeed! The gendarme laughed to the accompaniment of his rattling sabre.

"Stop playing the fool! It's time to go."

But Lazar was not playing the fool.

"I won't go," he reiterated morosely. The determination in his voice made the gendarme angry.

He would not go! But the superiors were waiting. Everything was ready. What did he think after all? Who did he think he was? A fine gentleman or important chief? But why waste words on a wretched hangman! Hadn't he heard his orders?

Lazar lurched up so suddenly that the gendarme shrank back before the vision of a new and strange face wrought with anger, of two wolfish eyes and the broad hairy chest and naked fists. It was a monstrous figure descending on him, hot and breathing hard.

170

"So you're better than I, eh? You don't do the hanging yourself, you swine!"

His huge body swayed on his bare feet, breathing ire from the pits of hell.

"Show me your hands! Think they're clean, eh? So you think I alone am the executioner. If that's so, then why curry favour with the executioner, you swine?"

Before the gendarme realized what was happening, Lazar seized the chair and dashed it to the floor. Squealing, it was splayed four-footedly.

"Damn!"

"He's drunk!" the gendarme shouted. "Tie him up!"

That was not so easy. Lazar threshed about the room like a wounded bear, smashing everything that came his way, dragging down the carpets, ripping them asunder and trampling upon them.

"That for you!"

It seemed as though it were the inanimate objects in the room that roused his fury rather than people.

There were clouds of dust, a great clatter and much grunting. He fought off until beaten up and firmly bound.

The warden came, remonstrating and pleading. How could Lazar do such a thing? They were doing their best for him, taking all manner of care of him. What convict enjoyed such rights and privileges? He should not drink so much. That's what it came from.

Tightly bound, Lazar lay amid the debris of the room. He was breathing hard after his struggle, but was maliciously gleeful because he knew that there would be no execution that day, that those unknowns who had the right to kill depended entirely on the executioner.

But then he seemed to grow resigned, grew quiet and no longer argued when he was awakened at night. He went to do his work as he would do any other humdrum job. But there was a hidden something lurking in his eyes.

He was mostly silent now, gave up his old caprices and did as he was bid.

Kalenik and Ivan could not praise him enough. They even relaxed their watch over him. He had had his lesson, they decided, and had learned the strength of the authorities. It was about the authorities that he spoke to them mostly now. Take the warden or the gendarme. They didn't do things on their own. There were some who were above them no doubt. But those, too, had their superiors. And beyond them there must have been still someone who said: let it be thus and thus. And everyone did his bidding from top to bottom.

This "he," so distant and mysterious, about whom Ivan and Kalenik could tell him so little, was his chief interest now. He had only to say: "Kill!" and the gallows were made ready.

The victim would then be led away, and the gendarme would come to fetch Lazar and he would put on the noose. "He," up there, was a huge spider ogling his prey. In the narrow chamber of the executioner's brain the thoughts had lain hopelessly entangled, but now they had been unravelled and tidily wound into a ball. He was sure that the evil lay concentrated in one spot alone, spreading its tentacles to all sides. If only he could approach it, lay his grip on it and crush it until the tentacles limply fell. The gendarme would stop waking him at night then.

Lazar was thinking about "him" all the time. Who was "he"? What was "he" like? Where could "he" be found? Perhaps he looked like the Mug, a fat, hairless snout and little cruel eyes. Lazar imagined himself advancing to his very snout and saying: "You are the evil." And bang, bang. "You are grief, you are injustice!" Bang, bang. "It's you who are shedding blood."

Then he would hang him. Not like the others, but without a shroud so that all could see his face, and its anguish, the twitchings of his shoulders until the face grew livid and the piggish eyes were extinguished. He knew how to do this, for he had been taught.

Overcoming his habitual fatigue and lethargy and forgetting his aversion for his work, he for the first time knew the joy of murder.

He knew hatred in his heart and the luxury of agony.

June 20, 1907
Chernigov

INTERMEZZO

Dedicated to Kononovka Fields

PERSONAE DRAMATIS

My weariness	A cuckoo
Fields in June	The larks
The sun	The iron hand of the town
Three white shepherd dogs	Grief

Now I had only to do the packing, but that was only one of my numberless "had to's" which both exhausted me and deprived me of sleep. A paltry "have to" or not, it demanded attention not as a thing which I could control, but rather as one which controlled me. I was indeed a slave of this hydra-headed monster. If only I could have got rid of it for a time to forget myself and have a rest. I was tired.

Life had been sweeping over me as ruthlessly as the thundering surf. And not only my life, but life in general. After all, how should one know where one's own life ends and another's begins. I can feel someone else's existence entering mine like air the windows and the doors, like the tributaries their rivers. I cannot part ways with man, cannot be alone. I must confess that I sincerely envy the planets, for each of them has its own orbit and there is nothing to obstruct them. As for me, I always find man in my path.

Yes, you will stand in my way, won't you? Making claims upon me! You are everywhere I go. You have clad the globe in steel and concrete and breathe your fumes through your countless thousands of yawning windows. You have lacerated the sacred silence of the earth with the clang of your factories and the rattling of your wheels. You have polluted the air with smoke and dust. You are howling like a beast from joy, malice and pain. I meet your glance everywhere. Your greedy prodding eyes are searching me and the pupils of my eyes too catch you in all your varieties and shapes. I cannot part ways with you. I cannot be alone. It is not only that you walk at my side, but you try to penetrate my innards. You heap your pain and anguish, frustrated hopes and despairs, cruelty and predatory instincts, the horror and filth of your existence into my soul as if it were a repository of your very own. What care you if you torment me! You want to be my master, to take complete possession of me ... of my hands, mind, will and heart. You would sap my blood like a vampire, and you are doing it. I live not as I would, but as you compel me to with your innumerable "have to's" and "musts."

I am tired.

I am tired of people. I refuse to be the courtyard of an inn where all jostle, shout and quarrel. Throw open the windows! Let there be air! Get rid of the garbage and the makers of it. Let there be cleanliness and tranquillity.

What will bring me the joy of loneliness? Death?

Sleep?

How I long for both!

But even when the beautiful brother of death took me into his arms, even then was I waylaid! People wove their lives with mine into one fantastic design and tried to fill my heart and ears with that which tormented them. Hear me! So here too you have brought me your sufferings and your filth. But remember that my heart is brim-full! Give me a rest!

That is what the nights were like.

By day I shuddered whenever I felt the shadow of man behind me and listened with loathing to the current of human speech clattering towards me through all the streets of the city like runaway horses.

The train rushed past full of the din of humans. It was like the city's iron hand spread out to seize me, putting me in an annoying flutter of uncertainty. Would the hand relax its iron claws and let me go? Would I ever get away from pandemonium to the green solitudes? Perhaps the fields would at last cover my retreat and frustrate the clanging grip, would at last envelop me with their silence.

When it did come about, it happened so imperceptibly that I failed to define the quiet: it was torn by words as paltry and superfluous as shavings and wisps of straw in the floods of spring.

...I knew a lady who had that heart trouble for fifteen years.... Click, clack, click.... Our division was then stationed.... Where are you going?... Click, clack, click.... Tickets please!... Click, clack-click, clack-click.

The green chaos about me seized the carriage by the wheels. There was so much sky that one's eyes sank into it as in an ocean with nothing to hold on to. They were helpless.

Finally we arrived. The white walls brought me to consciousness. A cuckoo called when the carriage rolled into the yard. It was then that I grew aware of the vast stillness It lay over the yard, lurked in the trees and fell away in the deep blue spaces. It was so quiet that I was ashamed of the beating of my heart.

The ten rooms were filled to the ceilings with darkness. They surrounded my room. I shut the door, afraid that the light of my lamp would seep away through the crevices. I was now alone. I knew there was no one around, but still I could sense a presence behind the wall. It was troubling me. What was it? I sensed the hard shapes of the furniture steeped in the darkness and the floor creaking under its weight. Well then, let the furniture pieces stand where they were and have a good rest! That was nothing for me to trouble my head with. I would do better to lie down. Better put out the lamp and sink into oblivion, perhaps turn into an inanimate object, into nothingness. How good it would be to be nothing, voiceless, undisturbed, composed. But surely there was something behind that wall! I was certain that if I entered the dark room and struck a match, everything would leap into place—the chairs, sofas, window-frames and even the cornices. But who could say that I might not catch a glimpse of people as unsubstantial and pale as those on ancient tapestry, all those who had left their reflections in the mirrors, their voices in the crevices, their shapes on the soft mattresses, and their shadows over the walls? Who can define the goings-on in places one cannot see?

What nonsense! You wanted solitude and peace and now you have got both. But why shake your head? Don't you believe in solitude?

I know nothing. How can I.... How can I be sure that one of those doors will not come half open—just like that —with a faint squeak. And people then will come out of the endless darkness. There shall be many whom I have never seen before, but who are in me because they have stored their hopes, wrath, anguish and savage cruelties in my heart as in a repository of their own. They are those with whom I cannot part ways, those of whom I am so tired. It is no wonder that they would come once again. Oh-ho, how many of you there are! You are those whose blood seeped out through little holes made by soldiers' bullets. You are those who swung in your shrouds for a

while and were dumped into shallow graves, an easy prey
for the dogs. You are looking at me with reproach and are
quite right. You know, I once read about how the lot of
you were hanged, the twelve of you, and it only made me
yawn. On another occasion I sweetened a report made on
a number of shrouds with a ripe plum. It was this way:
I picked a delicious plum, put it in my mouth and had a
pleasant sensation. As you see, I am not ashamed. My
face is as white as yours, because the horror froze my
blood just like yours. There is not a drop of warm blood
in me to spare for those living corpses among whom you
march as bespattered ghosts. Go away! I am tired.

But even more of them come: one after the other without end—allies and enemies, friends and strangers. They
keep shouting things into my ear about life and death.
The heels of every one of them leave marks on my soul.
I might lock my ears and shut my heart and shout: "No
entry here!"

I opened my eyes and saw the blue sky and the
branches of birch-trees through the windows. A cuckoo
was calling, as though striking a crystal bell with a little
mallet: "Cuckoo, cuckoo!—and sowing stillness in the
grass. The green yard had penetrated my room. I jumped
up, put my head out of the window, shouting: "Good day!"

There was plenty of everything: sky, sun and jolly
greenery.

I ran into the yard and heard a rustling of chains: they
were being tugged by the dogs, big white shepherd dogs
rearing bear-like with fluttering shaggy hides. "What is
it, doggy? What do they call you? Well, yes, enough—I
know! Your name is Overko." He did not seem to hear
or even see me. His red eyes were bouncing about, like
his broad head and hairy white trousers.

Fanged fury strained between his jaws, but could not
get at me. He could only tumble his shaggy fur about.
"What's the matter, Overko? Why are your eyes on fire?

Why have fear and hatred been molten in them? I am neither your enemy nor afraid of you. At your very worst you could only tear a piece from my body or sink your teeth into my calves. That would be only a trifle, hardly worth your while. Now be quiet. I know what is troubling you. It is the chain. Perhaps you are more angry with it than with me. It is because of the chain that your forepaws can dash only at the air. It throttles you and dams your fiery wrath. Wait a bit! You'll be free in a minute. What will you do to me then, I wonder? Now stand still while I remove the chain. Off you go, but where to? Ha-ha-ha, what a silly dog!" He closed his eyes, and rushed blindly forward head down, pawing at the grass, scratching it away and dashing on with flying hair. "But what about me? Have you forgotten your revenge?"

That was a fine somersault! Let's have another! You dear animal! Your freedom is worth more to you than the gratification of malice.

Next, I introduced myself to Pava, a sedate matron, and her second son, the terrible Trepov. If Overko was altogether sanguine and attacked everything blindly as though there were a rosy mist over his eyes, Trepov was ponderously deliberate. Very deliberately he could sink his teeth into a man's throat. Even then every movement of his as he stood on your chest would be full of dignity.

Even when lying still, gnawing at the flees on his rosy belly, his abbreviated ears were alertly pricked, his big head preoccupied and wet tongue lolling from the jaws in a dignified way.

I spent my days in the steppes, in the valleys filled with green wheat. Numerous secluded paths obviously intended for the initiated led me across the fields, through the green waves tumbling to the horizon. I had a world of my own now; it was like the shell of a great oyster. One of its folds was green and the other blue, and between them they held the sun like a pearl. As for me, I was looking only for a place to rest and kept walking pursued by a cloud of gnats as though I were a planet and they a mass of satellites. The sky was being carved by the wings of a raven, which made the heavens seem even bluer and the feathers blacker.

The sun stood in the sky and I in the fields and besides us there was nothing. Walking, I now and then stroked the sable fur of ripening barley, the silk of the undulating wave of it. The wind filled my ears with shreds of sound, a tangled, many-patterned noise. How hot the wind was and how impatient! It set the silver-haired oats aboil. They were kept astir everywhere. The flax, on the other hand, flowed in quiet blue rivers amid green banks so soothingly that one could have wished to set sail upon it. Somewhat beyond, the barley was drooping and weaving green muslin with its tendrils. It was still weaving as I went on; the muslin was swaying. The paths wound through the rye so that it was my feet rather than my eyes that found them. The corn-flowers were looking at the sky. They wanted to be like the sky and were. Then came the wheat. The stiff ears slashed at my hands and the stalks tried to trip me. I went on and on, but found no end to the wheat. Where were its limits? Its streaming waves shone in the sun and scudded before the wind like so many foxes. And I walked on and on as alone as the sun and the sky. How glad I was that there were no intruders! The surf of the wheat rolled past me into the unknown.

I halted finally. I could not go on because of the white foam of buckwheat, fragrant and airy, thoroughly whipped by the wings of the bees. There it lay like a vast harp alive in every string.

I was filled with this wondrous harmony of the fields, this silky rustle as tireless as the rush of water or the pouring of grain. My eyes were filled with light, for every stalk offered me a glint stolen from the sun.

But it was dying! Everything! Darkness! Shadows! Where from? An intruder? No, it was just a cloud, only an instant of grief yielding to smiles on the right and the left until the golden fields spread their wings to the ends of the earth. As though preparing to soar aloft. It was then only that I perceived its warm and living might in all its infinity. The oats, wheat and barley blended into one swelling wave carrying all before it. Youthful power vibrated in every stalk. The juices within seethed with hope and that great yearning known as fertility. Suddenly, I saw a village, a cluster of dishevelled thatched roofs. It was hardly visible at first. It lay clasped in the green hands clinging to the very huts. It had got entangled in the fields like a gnat in a web. What were those huts before the assault of the fields? Nothing! The green would close over them and they would be gone. What was man compared with those waves? Nothing! A white speck showed for an instant. Had it been shouting, singing or making gestures? It vanished in silent infinity. Even its tracks were obliterated like the paths and the roads. There were only green waves as far as one could see. A rhythmic throb dominated everything as steadily and unwaveringly as the pulse of eternity, as the wings of the mills waving far away. They described complete circles languidly and continuously, as though to say: This is how it has been and ever will be ... *in saecula saeculorum ... in saecula saeculorum.*

I would come home long after dark, winnowed by the breath of the fields like a wild flower. I brought their aroma in the folds of my clothes like the Biblical Esau. Soothed and alone, I would sit on a step of the empty house, watching the creation of night from airy columns behung with a net of shadows from the quivering walls of black to the starry cupola when its supports were sufficiently solid.

I could go to sleep in peace now, for its stout walls would rise between me and the world. I wished the fields a good night and another to the cuckoo. On the morrow the cuckoo's contralto would flood the room with the first rays of the rising sun. This greeting would at once put me in good spirits, for that bird had become a dear friend.

Trepov, Overko, Pava! I put four fingers in my mouth and emitted a robber's whistle. They came trotting at once, like three white bears. Would they come to attack me, or just to accept my invitation for a stroll in the fields. Ho-ho! Overko was fond of his jokes and gambolled about like a silly calf looking at me through the corners of his red eyes. Trepov carried his fur proudly, setting his feet down like white columns, his abbreviated ears twitching. Pava, too, was advancing importantly with a certain sadness and kept somewhat behind. I followed them, keeping my eyes on their heaving backs, so soft, fluffy and strong.

The hot sun in which their white fur grew dazzling was not to their taste. I was grateful for its warmth, however, and walked straight towards it. Never would I turn my back on it, I decided. That would be downright ingratitude. I was happy to meet it here where no one could come between us, and so I said to it: "How grateful I am to you, O Sun! You are sowing gold within my soul. Who can say what shall sprout from it. Perhaps there will be fire.

"I love you because ... listen ... I came into this world from the black of the unknown. My first breath was taken in the darkness of the womb, a darkness which prevails over me until this day; throughout the nights, through half of my life, it has stood between you and me. Its handmaidens are the clouds, the hills and the

182

dungeons that try so zealously to conceal you. All three of us know that the time must come when I shall be dissolved in darkness as salt in water. You are just a visitor in my existence, O Sun! When you go away, I cling to you, try to catch your last ray in the clouds, to re-create you in a camp-fire, in a lamp, in fireworks. I strive to collect what there is of you from the flowers, a child's laughter and the eyes of my beloved. When you fade and flee, I create your image in the shape of my ideal. I put it in my heart then where it shall shine.

"Gaze upon me, O Sun, and scorch my soul as you have my body to make it impervious to the gnats."

I caught myself addressing the sun like a living being. Could this mean that I missed the society of man?

We were strolling through the fields—three white dogs and I. The faint whispers hovered about us—the breath of the young ears in a blue haze. A landrail piped coolly somewhere on one side. A cricket plucked its silvery string somewhere in the rye. The air was quivering with the heat and the distant lindens were dancing in a veil. There was wideness here, quiet and comfort.

The dogs were suffocating. They lay down on a path between fields like three heaps of wool, their tongues lolling and their sides heaving. I sat down near them. Only our breaths were audible. It was very still.

Had time stood still? Perhaps we ought to go home? We got up lazily and cautiously carried our repose back to the house. As we passed some land that had been ploughed to lie fallow, the dark odours of damp earth, an atmosphere replete with quiet hope, enveloped us. My greetings! Rest quietly under the sun, for you are as tired as I. My soul too lies dark and fallow.

Never before had I felt myself linked with the earth as now. The earth of the cities is clad in stone and iron, but here it lay open to the hand. I, too, was the first to break the slumber of the well. The empty pail fell on the water's breast which would sigh down below and let the liquid in. For a while it trembled then, shimmering in the sun. I drank it, fresh, cold and still full of dreams, splashing my face.

After this came the milk, a white aromatic liquid foaming in my glass. Putting it to my lips I knew that I was imbibing vetch as soft as a child's hair, the vetch that only yesterday attracted a host of butterflies. It was the essence of the meadows that I was drinking.

Or the black bread made of whole-wheat flour, the bread that had such a nice rustic smell. It was as dear to me as a child grown up in my presence. It had sprung from the rye which rolled wave upon wave through the fields, like a shaggy beast in flight, and from the mills which stood like fanged traps at the edge of the fields to grind the grains to flour. I saw it all and my kinship with the land was direct and simple.

I felt rich though I had nothing. For the earth belonged to me apart from any political parties and programmes. It lay within me—vast, luxurious and already created. But I had created it anew and felt, therefore, that I had even more rights to it.

Lying on my back, staring at the sky and harking to the chorus of silence from the fields about, it occurred to me that there was something of the heavens in this quiet.

It was as though someone were tooling metal in the sky, letting the shavings fall to earth. The bustling fields on all sides prevented me from hearing it distinctly. I tried to dismiss all sounds but those of the rain of heavenly shavings. And then I recognized them for what they were—the larks! Invisibly, they were drilling the sky with their songs, resonant, metallic and so capricious that the ear could not keep with their moods. Perhaps they were singing, perhaps laughing, perhaps sobbing.

If I sat up and closed my eyes I might hear better. Sharp piercing sounds punctuated the darkness. It was laughter falling like small shot on a metal surface. I should have liked to hold it in my memory but could not. Here, I had caught it: twee, twee, twee. But no, it was nothing like that. Twoo, twoo, twoo! No, that was wrong too.

How did they do it, I wondered. Had they struck the disc of the sun with their beaks? Or perhaps they had plucked at its rays as at strings? Or perhaps they had sieved their melody to sow the fields?

I opened my eyes and understood that the seeds they had sown had sprouted and grown into silver oats, into barely bending and flashing like sabres, and wheat streaming by like swift rivers.

Meanwhile, they continued to spill and spill those seeds from above. They were tinkling their bells to exhaustion, planing planks of silver, drilling through steel, and sobbing and wailing and shaking their laughter through closely-meshed sieves. A spark of melody was then ignited and fell to earth like a meteor. I could not bear it any longer. There was something evil in that chorus. It kindled cravings. The more one listened, the more one wanted to listen. The harder one tried to catch it, the more elusive it became.

I walked about the fields for hours hearing the orchestras and choirs of the heavens.

I started up at night and listened intently, for something was drilling my mind, stinging my heart and throbbing elusively about my ears.

Twee, twee, twee! No, that was not it.

But how did they do it?

I had a peep at it at last.

A little grey bird, much like a crumb of earth, hung overhead. With flapping wings it was carrying the end of an invisible string aloft from the earth. The string vibrated for a while, then fell, and the bird dived to pick up another. It was thus that it linked the earth with the skies and played its field symphony on the resulting harp.

And so my unsullied intermezzo passed in quiet and solitude. Blessed was I between the golden sun and the green earth. Blessed was the tranquillity of my soul! A fresh page had been turned in the old book of my life. How could I forbear from looking to see what was written there. Could it be that I would never again tremble at a man's shadow, that I would no longer be troubled by the thought that human grief lurked somewhere?

If this miracle should ever come to be, it will be your work, you rustling silver fields, and yours, cuckoo. Your music that washed away my weariness was as copious as the sap of the birch.

But we did meet after all: man and I. We stood together for a moment. He was an ordinary peasant. I cannot say what he thought of me, but it was thanks to him that I caught sight of a cluster of black thatched roofs hemmed in by the fields, of girls returning in clouds of dust from other fields—dirty, ugly, with hanging breasts and bony backs, pale women in skirts of ragged black, bent over the flax like shadows, syphilitic children and mangy dogs, all the things I had never noticed before. He was like the conductor's baton which summons forth a host of sounds.

But I did not run away. On the contrary, we talked like old friends.

In a simple and casual manner, much like the lark pouring down its song, he spoke of things that filled me with horror. Something throbbed within me as I stood listening.

And so I had been overtaken by human grief after all,

but I did not flee. The strings of grief were taut again and could be played on as before.

Say on, say on!

But what else had he to say? He owned a droplet in this green sea. God had taken pity on some whose children had been carried off by the fever, but as for himself, he had five mouths to feed, each like a windmill claiming its share of grist.

For some reason, the fever had spared his five hungry children.

Say on, say on!

The people had wanted to take the land with their naked hands, but found only dank graves or hard labour in Siberia. He had been lucky himself. He had fed the lice in prison for a year so that now he had only to put up with the gendarme who struck him in the face at least once a week.

He was struck in the face at least once a week.

Say on, say on!

Other people went to church on Sunday, but he to the gendarme. Even so, the gendarme was easier to bear than his own folk. He was afraid to say a word, because even a friend could betray. A word torn from the heart might be thrown by him to the dogs.

One's nearest of kin can betray.

Say on, say on!

He walked among people as among wolves. The chief thing was to beware.

There were ears everywhere and outstretched hands. One beggar might steal the shirt hung on a fence to dry by another. Neighbour might steal from neighbour, father from son.

It was among people as among wolves.

Say on, say on!

Syphilis, need and vodka were devouring the people,

and the people were devouring each other. How could the sun still shine? How could one live on like that?

Say on, say on! Melt the heavens with your wrath! Darken the sky with the clouds of your grief! Let the thunderstorm break and freshen the earth with its torrents. Put out the sun and kindle another! Say on, say on!

The city's iron hand was reaching for me in the green fields. I delivered myself to it, but even as it clanged away with me, I once more took in the tranquillity of the plains and the bluish haze of the spaces. Farewell, kind fields! Let your sun-kissed waves roll and rustle on. Perhaps you will do as much good to someone else as you did to me. And farewell to you, cuckoo, perched on the birch-tree. You too helped to tune the strings of my soul. They had grown loose, because plucked by rude hands, but now they are taut again! Do you hear? Here is the first chord! Farewell! I'm going back to man. My soul is healed and well attuned and playing.

1908
Chernigov

WHAT WAS WRIT IN THE BOOK
OF LIFE

The old woman had to get off the oven, because her sick granddaughter needed warmth. As there was no room on the benches in the crowded cottage, she had to make her bed on the floor. Her son and his wife seemed not to notice this; and so there she stayed.

Everything looked unusual from her corner between the door and the dish racks where she lay on the floor, an old mother forgotten by death. She had lain on top of the oven for years and had been accustomed to view everything from above. Her grandchildren had seemed very small from up there, and her dimming eyes either rested on their fair heads or caught glimpses of the harassed angry faces of her son and daughter-in-law as they floated by from door to oven. She could hear their voices but indistinctly.

Now, everything had grown all at once. She looked up at the children when they came near the dish shelves, dropping bread crumbs and other litter on her. Her son's old frozen boots, as ponderous as the hills, and the bare legs of her daughter-in-law came by her face blotting out the world. She saw the furious fire in the oven which devoured fuel, yet died of hunger, and the gaping black corners breathing musty dampness under the benches. When the door opened the vapours rushed in over the floor, a great mist, and it seemed to her that death must be even so: hazy, eyeless and like the cold on her legs.

But where was he? Why didn't he come? Call as she would, she got no answer. He was simply roaming about, oblivious of her. He had carried off her husband and seven of her children and was now preparing to seize her granddaughter. He had mowed them all down, the sheaf of them, but had quite forgotten her. It was strange and terrifying to find it so difficult to die.

She would lie very still for long days and nights when the mice scampered over the rotten potatoes and her body and the roaches kept rustling near as if she were nothing more than an old rag. A plaintive sigh escaped her withered chest now and again—a whine like that of a blind puppy.

"Oh-oh-oh! Where can death be hiding himself?"

"I wish you were really dead! We can't sleep!" her daughter-in-law would grumble on her creaking bench.

"I wish I were!" the old woman would moan, running her tongue over her gums and dry lips.

She would have liked to eat something sour: cabbage or a sip of the water in which the cucumbers had been pickled. Her dreams would blend with reality: snatches of fairy-tales, Our Father and the ponderous boots of her son which left wet traces behind.

Suddenly the dream would vanish as though wiped away and she would be fully conscious of her body which felt hard and cold on the thin mat on the floor in the damp corner.

What was the good of her? Who needed her? Life had eaten the strength out of her and had tossed her aside like a bit of potato peeling. Still, her soul clung to that wretched shell, unwilling to part with it.

Though she occupied very little space, she was constantly in the way, and though she ate only a few morsels, these too were precious in their poverty.

"Oh, death of mine! Where can you be keeping!" her voice would crackle like dry leaves.

Still, the body made its claims. Fantastic, incredible desires sometimes grew out of this bag of bones, utterly clouding her reason.

"Give me some milk!"

The daughter-in-law would be seized with a fit of laughter. She would say nothing, but her face, breasts and stomach kept shaking with the paroxysm, her teeth white between bared lips. The old woman would be offended then. They did not want to give her a drop of milk.

She would screw up her face and grumble. She desperately wanted a drop of milk, though she knew that there was none even for her sick granddaughter.

Her daughter-in-law, finally, would take to the broom and send clouds of dust floating over her.

"Move your legs or I'll cast you away with the filth."

The old woman would shift her legs and cough unseen under the bench for a long time.

In the day-time her grandchildren would surround her like five yellow-beaked sparrows. They formed a circle of eyes staring at her mouth.

"Tell us a story!"

Her mouth would open like an empty purse and she would hiss forth words about a tsarevich, gold and costly feasts. Then she would lick her lips as though to wash away what she had begun and tell a story about the horse's head or the Tsarevna Frog. Old-fashioned words would occur in her speech, words which the children could not understand. They were bored.

"Granny, when will you die?"

They would try to smooth the lines on her neck as though they were folds of an old boot. They would explore her empty withered breasts with the golden cross between them and touch her legs which were dry and black, much like the bark with which Mother kindled the oven.

They were curious to see how her soul would fly from her body.

"Granny, will your soul fly away like a bird?"

Then they would reach for the dish shelves, treading on her chest with their bare feet and spilling crumbs into her eyes.

Her daughter-in-law would talk about her death loudly and angrily, as though it were a tax long overdue.

"What are we to bury her with when she dies?"

To which her son merely snorted, glaring at her corner. At such moments the old woman was afraid to call death: what if he came and there would be no money for the funeral? The priest had to be paid, the boards were dear and there would be people eating and drinking a great deal in memory of her.

She had only one consolation. When they forgot to close the door sometimes, a speckled hen would dart in from the passage and make straight for her. The bird would crane its neck, cock its head and raise an anticipating foot. When the old woman extended her dry palm containing a few crumbs, it would peck at her hand, pricking it now and then.

The hen would pay dearly for this, for when caught in the room it would be kicked cruelly about and then tossed into the passage crouching.

"Wish you'd croak!" they scolded.

The old woman would have preferred to be scolded instead. Perhaps she would die sooner then.

She had been pondering of late. By day and night, very secretly and all to herself. Her lips kept smacking and her eyes seemed to look inwards. Her mouth at times formed some words, but at once grew numb. She would whisper: "Son!" and then keep quiet, afraid that he might have heard her. Her weak arms and legs would grow moist with perspiration and she would lie like a corpse.

But at last she mustered her courage.

"Sonny!"

He was mending something and did not hear.

"Potap!"

"Yes?"

"Come here!"

"What is it?"

"Sit down, next to me!"

He got up unwillingly and took a seat on the bench under the shelves.

One of his huge boots stood before her, casting a shadow over her face.

"It's time to die."

"Shall I call the priest again? You said the same thing last time and I had to pay him for nothing."

Potap was angry and avoided her eyes.

"Ekh, Granny—Mother!" he exclaimed in a softer tone.

The line deepened between his mouth and chin, containing something unspoken.

"There's no need of the priest! God will forgive without him. The trouble is that I just can't die."

"You've said that before."

"Death has forgotten me, and there's just no end. Perhaps you could help me?"

She stirred on her mat. He heard the knee joints crack and the piping of her lungs. His anguish wrung an exclamation from him:

"Well?"

But she lay still, muttering as in a dream:

" 'The son took the sledge, put the old one on it and drew it to a gully....' "

Potap raised his brows.

"What's that you say?"

The old woman grew afraid.

"I've just been saying.... Nobody needs me. I'm just encumbering the earth and occupying this corner.... I'm eating the bread the children need. It's hard for everyone and for me too. Take me to the woods."

He did not understand, but stared at her wondering.

"Help me, my son. Take me to the woods. It is winter now and I'll freeze in a moment. It won't take much for an old body like mine. I'll take a breath or two and that will be enough."

The strange words stirred something in him, a memory of a long-forgotten dream, which only touched his consciousness and flew away.

He hated to listen, but could not help it.

"There's no sin in it. The forest is clean and white and the trees stand like candles in church. I'll just fall asleep, and when I awake I'll say: 'Mother of God, don't judge my son for this, but blame the poverty of the people!' Don't listen to what people say. They will not help you when in trouble; they'll leave you to die alone."

His mother's words sank into his mind like seeds in a well-ploughed field. He was well aware of this, and it provoked insincere anger.

He got up, finally, and shouted at himself rather than at her:

"Enough of this! God gave you life, and he will bring you death. Go to sleep."

When the light was put out and they had all laid themselves to rest for the night, his thoughts tossed about the room, disordered and dark as a storm-cloud. A clear patch shone only from time to time.

God?

Was he looking down? Well then, let him!

The bright flashes too were angry and cold.

Sin?

The whole world was sinful. Wasn't his hunger the sin of the sated?

He banished the thoughts, especially the ones brought up by the old woman, but even as he thwarted them there stood up in his mind a half-forgotten memory, a thing that he had heard long ago from mother or grandmother —that the children, long, long ago, had killed their parents. They had carried them to the fields and left them there to die. Of what good was life to the old? Old must die and young must live. That's the way things were. The old leaves fell and were replaced by the new. When spring came, winter perished. The seed disintegrated in the soil to bring up a shoot. That's how things had been as long as anyone could remember.

The old woman had lived too long, but could not die. She asked for death, but God withheld it. Where was the sin in helping her?

Again something intangible arose within him like the vapour over the rotting marshes, erasing his thoughts, benumbing his body and covering his forehead with burning beads of sweat.

"Ugh, how awful! To think of dragging my old mother out of the cottage alive!"

The night bore down upon him with all its weight, suffocating him, and thought again curled in his brain and then oozed about.

The devil take it! Come what may! What would people say? They would condemn him of course. When a man was starving with his little children, was howling like a dog, when fate was tearing him limb from limb, there was not a soul of them about! What could be more terrible than that solitude they called people?

Potap could not fall asleep. He tossed about, now and then raising his head to listen to the breathing from the corner under the shelves. He could not hear a sound. Suddenly it seemed to him that it was all over. His mother was already in the forest, and there were no groans, no extra mouth to feed, no harrying thought about where to get the money for the funeral. He felt easier of heart even.

But suddenly he heard the scratching of mice

somewhere under the shelves and then the dreary piping voice so familiar:

"Oh, death of mine, why don't you come?"

He got up rather late the next morning.

It was a still, oppressive day. The grey sky rested heavily on the earth, and wisps of cloud roamed by like lost souls.

It was time to cart away the manure. Trudging by the sledge, he was himself as grey as the mist, intent upon something within himself, something that had hardened in the night.

He stopped working earlier than usual for some reason, when there was still light, entered the cottage, stood shifting from foot to foot for a while and then turned and went out. He came back and stood by the door keeping his eyes from that corner. He wanted to say something, but could not find the words.

His mother said nothing.

"Have you come to your senses?" he blurted awkwardly and angrily.

"What's that you say?"

"Have you forgotten your chatter of yesterday?"

"Oh no, help me, my son."

"So you're still at it?"

"Take me to the woods."

He leaned forward, bringing his face closer to hers, so close that she could feel his hot breath.

"Do you mean to say that that's what you want?" he hissed.

"Yes."

"Think well! Do you really want that?"

"Yes."

He unbent and sat down by the table. He was about to cut a slice of bread, but changed his mind and put the knife down.

He looked at none of the others, though he knew very well that they all understood. He was not at all surprised when his wife calmly said:

"We ought to warm some water."

So grandmother was to be laid out at once.

He indifferently watched the fuss they were making. He saw them fill the oven with straw, the children whispering in the corner as though glad that Papa would take Granny to the woods at last, and the old woman stretching a hand from under the shelves.

"Get a fresh shirt!"

"But we have no candle!" shrilled his wife.

He reached beneath the icon where the Palm Sunday candle was kept. It was not seemly for him to watch the procedure and he went out. Everything was finished when he returned. She lay there as dry and small as a plucked hen. A cross lay on her chest, and her clean heels peeped beneath the black woollen skirt like at a proper funeral.

"Have you finished?" he meant to ask, but did not, because all were waiting for him. He drew near the bench on which she lay.

"But perhaps you'd rather...."

She shook her worn face on which a fresh shadow lay.

Then he came to her determinedly, kissed her hands and lips and let her bless him with those same hands as dry as the twigs in autumn.

The wife and children approached her for the same.

The old woman moaned with pleasure at the feel of the warm lips.

Her daughter-in-law even sobbed, but grew quiet as soon as Potap asked her to give him a rug.

"What for?"

"I want to cover her."

"Mind that you bring it back."

Potap gently lifted his mother and carried her to the

door which opened, admitting a cold gust of air. The dark passage rang with the weeping of the children.

There was some hay in the cart that Potap arranged under her sides as he covered her with the rug.

"Are you comfortable, Granny?" he said, taking up the reins.

"I've called her Granny again," he thought, but did not correct himself.

"Mind you don't forget to bring back the rug!" his wife once more admonished as he got on the sledge.

The old nag's rump moved and Granny sailed forth.

For three versts they had to travel over the fields which began directly outside the cottage.

Night fell suddenly, engulfing the sunset. Only the nearest snow-drifts could be seen, while the mist dressed the trees in hoarfrost for the night.

They kept silent. What could they say to each other? Firstly, constant need had long sealed his lips and it was only his heart that spoke. Secondly, something inexplicable and disturbing had arisen between himself and the living body that he carried in the sledge, something he dared not chase away with words.

He kept his eyes fixed on the mare trailing her shaggy tail already covered with hoar, thought of the forthcoming straw carting and calculated when he had best take his straw to the cutting machines. Perhaps he ought to do it today, when he returned, or tomorrow? Then it occurred to him that he had forgot his gloves and also to wash his hands of the manure which covered them like bark.

It seemed to him that the old woman was muttering something.

"What is it?" he shouted, turning.

With some difficulty he understood her to be asking whether or not they were driving through Nikita's field.

"Nikita? Why, he's been dead long ago. His sons sold the field."

"To whom?"

"It's a long story."

He grew animated and turned shouting so that his mother could hear him, rapped the sides of the sledge with the handle of his whip and waved his arms. He was glad that his loud talk could drive away that troublesome mysterious something that lay between them.

The sledge swept along over the hardened road, swaying on the bumps, while he kept one leg hanging over the side to steady the vehicle on the uneven parts of the road when necessary, as he always did when he carted manure. He lashed the horse. "Gee!" he shouted, and then turned in his seat.

Both were glad to be doing something together as of old when she had been younger and could walk about.

The old woman seized upon the news greedily. She knew nothing. What could one know, lying under the dish shelves? And this Nikita had once meant to marry her. He-he!

They hardly noticed how the forest enveloped them.

Potap reined the horse.

"Are you very cold?" he asked, approaching her.

"No."

"Well, we've arrived."

She tried to rise, but fell back.

"Just wait a bit. Lie there for a little while."

Breaking through the deep snow, he went to look for a suitable spot.

"This is the best place," he said aloud, choosing a higher spot under an oak.

Then he looked around.

In the deep silence the trees interwove their white branches as though trying to cast a net over the ocean of sky where the stars shimmered like the scales of golden fish.

"It's nicer even than in church," he thought.

He brought some hay to the spot, prepared a couch and laid the old woman upon it on her back. He wanted to cover her legs with the rug, but she would not have it.

"Don't! Take it home. It's a useful thing."

"It is," he thought and laid it aside. But then he changed his mind and covered her with it to the chin.

She put her hands out over the rug obediently and he crossed them on her chest like those of one deceased. He lit the candle and placed it between her fingers.

"What else should I do?" he thought.

He knelt in the snow, his face against the hands of his mother.

The warm wax which trickled down stirred something bitter and vague in his breast, something that had no name. Clinging to her calloused hands which would soon testify to their toil berofe God, he wanted to say something about his life, about the injuries he had suffered in this stillness where the trees stood like the candles in church. Instead he merely said:

"Forgive me, Mother."

"God will forgive you," she granted.

"God will forgive me," he murmured.

He wanted to get up and be finished with it, when he heard a whisper.

He glanced at her face which seemed to be melting like the wax of the yellow candle.

She was sucking her lips as old women do, twisting her mouth so that the old bluish gums were visible.

"Don't butcher the speckled hen!" came her moan. "She'll lay eggs."

A tear rolled from her dimming eye.

He promised. Why did she think he would butcher that hen? Hen was no food for a peasant's table.

Was that all? He got up, bowed and strode away over the snow.

He fell heavily on to the sledge and lashed the horse. The mare kicked up its rear and plunged off slamming the sledge against the trees and jolting it over the bumps.

When he managed, in spite of the shaking, to turn round, he saw the candle burning in a soft and even light, like a star which had descended with the hoar and had come to rest on the snow.

He felt easier of heart suddenly. The burden had fallen from his shoulders. He took a deep breath of the icy air and feeling a void in his chest filled it with a wild shout:

"Gee! You damned nag!"

He rocked in his seat as if drunk, as if he were returning from a fair with many drinks below the belt. He was indifferent to everything and unafraid as if even the sea were knee-deep to him.

The trotting horse wearied in the fields and slowed to a walk.

But suddenly he recalled a day of his childhood.

It was on a Sunday and the cottage was filled with light. He was eager to run off and join the other boys and hated to waste time changing his shirt. But Mother caught him and, weep though he did, thrust a clean, cold, white shirt over him, brushed his hair, caught him once again at the doorway and shoved a fat slice of warm pie into his bosom. The pie was so hot that it hurt his chest, but he took it out only when he had joined the boys. It made him gleeful to see the others watching him nibbling at the pie and poking the filling out of it with his finger.

That was all he could remember.

It was a memorable day too when Father died. There had been a great funeral feast then, at which the guests ate cabbage and honey cakes with black raisins in them shining like flies.

He had stuffed himself as much as he could then.

The sledge carried farther and farther over the fields
The horse was so white that it blended with the snow, but
the sky above was purely black.

"Nikita's field indeed! Nikita wanted to marry her
he-he!"

A lone white cloudlet roamed the dark like the wing of
a dove.

He took his eyes from the white wisp and drew his
shoulders in. A coldness gripped his chest. Perhaps it was
not a cloudlet, but his mother's soul?

His thoughts turned back. She must be lying there on
her freezing couch like a wounded bird, looking at the
cold sky through her tears. There was only the candle to
cry over her, and the hot wax was dripping on her dry
folded hands.

He should not have done it. She had wanted it so herself, but things could have been otherwise. It might be
otherwise.

He held his breath, seeing neither the field, the sky,
nor the horse. Only one scene stood before him crowd-
ing out all else.

They had just brought Mother to the graveyard with
icons and a priest in a good Christian way. The cottage
was filled with people and there was steaming food.
"Drink about, dear brother-in-law, to the soul of the deceased!" "May God rest her soul!" The vodka scalded
throats and stomachs, and there was a great hubbub.
There was warmth from the honest folk and the hot meat
in the plates. "Let's drink another!" "She was a good
woman!" There was a rattling of spoons and smacking
of fatty lips. All bellies were full. The soul seemed afloat
then, open for all to see, and one wanted either to cry or
sing. "What can be sadder than...." "Let us drink, sister-
in-law, to the soul of the deceased!"

He was suffocating.

"I could mortgage half of the vegetable patch," he said aloud and shuddered.

Whose voice was that?

He looked about. The horse was barely moving and the mists from nowhere covered the sky with their tops and the earth with their bottoms, seeming to sow gloom and despondency.

He had to fight down that temptation. He tried to remember snatches of the priest's sermon in church, or what people generally said to one another in polite condolence. He thought of sin, the soul, the prayers and the Christian customs. "Obey thy father and mother." But it was all so cold and melted so easily in the warmth of the pictures which his brain conjured.

"We have only one mother and one death," he said to himself. And then he thought he heard the words: "Have some food, sister-in-law! Let's drink to the soul of the dear departed." He felt himself submerged in the noise and warmth of voices, tasting the rich food and the festive joy of the living.

He could see the cottages by now.

Then he arose, looked ahead, then back, and sharply turned his horse.

"Gee, you brute!"

He tore into the mist once more and through the snow kicked up by the mare—to fetch back the old woman.

November 26. 1910

THE DREAM

Every day was the same. His feet, as though they had nothing to do with him, seemed to find the old paths by themselves, and his eyes, as though not really his own, took in all the dull old scenes. The houses of the little town just floated by until they vanished. The people whom he met were as familiar as the drab furniture one can see for years without seeing. Equally familiar was the park lane lined with bare poplars looming whitely against the autumn sky like the bones of fish. The alley through which he passed every day was known to him in every one of its hollows and every stone over which he stumbled; it was as familiar as the figure of the treasury clerk who was now approaching to meet him, sauntering unhurriedly in his black coat fastened to the bottom. There was a flash of dyed side-whiskers as he raised his hat over a colourless face.

This figure did not enter into conversation nowadays as before. And why should he? Anton knew everything that he could possibly say. He would hear only the hollow voice croaking from the depths of his tightly fastened chest; and through the dyed side-whiskers would come the story of his last game of slam at the club or some complaint about his stomach catarrh.

The figure had passed and was indeed far behind when Anton grew aware that he himself was moving in his usual saunter, the walk of a treasury clerk.

The alley was deserted again. The newly planted trees with most of their branches broken pricked the sky, stout posts with shreds of bark hanging about them. Mud oozed from the benches on which someone had evidently piled some earth. An indeterminate odour came from a heap of leaves and the autumn sky seemed to exude boredom. All this grey slippery wretchedness lay enmeshed in great flocks of fluttering rooks and was filled with their raucous cawing.

Anton reached the end of the alley and turned back. The desolation through which he had just come faced him again and he found himself toying with the question as to what his wife's dream had really meant?

She dropped her feet to the floor—they were white and bare like hunks of lard—and told him with animation, though still hoarse with sleep, that she had dreamed of milking a cow. When she had pulled at the udders, the thin stream hitting the bottom of the bucket turned out to be not milk but ordinary water. What could that have meant? Just ordinary water!

He could not find the answer in the morning and forgot about it in the afternoon, but now he found himself worrying over this preposterous question as though he were trying to scrape some tar loose from his boots. What could the water have meant? This question completely engrossed him in the park lane under the skeleton trees etched against the grey in that filthy trough of an alley. It occurred to him that if he could only get away from this path, this scene would surely be extinguished amid the cawing of the rooks.

He left the park lane and emerged on the town square with its great puddle in the middle. There was no need to look at the town. He could just bend over the puddle and see the whole picture: the clumsy white church hatted with a green dome, the brick box of the council house and the yellow walls of the court house. There was room for it all in that one puddle.

A calf stood on the pavement. Three figures with three same faces, all in blue trousers, *à la* student, were trying to drive it into the puddle. But the calf would not go, flourishing its tail and staring with terrified eyes. When they succeeded at last in forcing it into the water so that its four slender legs struggling in the mud broke up the reflections of the church, council and court, their idiotic laughter seemed to freeze in the grey mist and plump into the puddle as well.

Then they began to vie in spitting, trying to see who could spit all the way across. Anton did not care to wait for the results.

A sediment had settled on his heart. It had begun at home and continued like a rusty chain, here in this colourless boredom of the town. Nothing ever happened and one day was like another. His life was reflected in every passing day like the town in that pool.

While still abed in the morning he listened to his wife's dreams, as prosaic and dull as reality. Then he drank a hurried glass of tea at the table still covered with crumbs and the wet rings of the glasses from the night before and rushed off to his classes at school. Then he had his dinner always at the same hour and with the same exclamation: "So there is green *borshch* today!" Then followed his wife's usual complaints about the kitchen maid. His wife usually went to sleep after dinner, while he went out for a stroll in the forlorn hope of seeing something new, but returned to his evening lights with the same boredom.

His wife's friends would sometimes come to play cards of an evening and not for money, but for the sheer fun of it. Sick of all this and tired, he would retire to his room then, smoking prodigiously and writing something for himself, just to satisfy some inner craving.

At times, too, there would be news. It was either that the wood fuel had been brought and he had to receive it, or that a child had fallen ill. But it was soon over and life trickled on through its old ditch.

Anton wandered aimlessly through the desolate streets. There was something sticky and black that clotted his heart; and yet a certain freshness struggled through this crust, something young and yet untrodden, a craving for something new and beautiful.

He passed some girls, provincial little goats with limpid eyes, oval faces and lithe bodies. Something lingered behind them like the refreshing calm after a storm in spring. He wanted to experience something poignant and magnificent, something like a storm at sea, like the breath of spring—a new fairy-tale of life. He wanted to give voice to the song that slept in his breast with folded wings. He would find new words for that song, not like those of the autumn leaves rustling underfoot, but rich, weighty and sonorous words.

But everything faded in the autumn bleakness and he walked on past the wet fences with the bare branches slumbering behind them.

It was growing dark, but Anton slouched on from block to block. He saw the trees sink into the bluish mists, silhouetted against the sky like veins in mother of pearl. A milky haze hung over the crossing behind which gleamed something distant and infinite. The fine drizzle touched his face like a caress.

Lights sprang up here and there. The shining pavements reflected the shadows of the trees. The dripping from the roofs, walls and rain pipes swelled to a drubbing. The drops tinkled and played, changing the time, timbre and key until the whole street was filled with this symphony of drops. The lantern-lighter emerged from the mist distributing burning dots, a myriad of reddish lights shimmering and dissolving in the twilight. The lantern-man's legs were black, but there was a light swinging over him. The crescendo of the drops grew livelier; there were sad bars and joyful ones, some sluggish, some brilliant, some muffled and some resounding. A window-pane flashed in the distance; an invisible hand was closing a shutter. It is thus that an eyelid falls to in sleep.

Anton's hunger for beauty drove him to search for it everywhere, but reality was so stingy! True, once he had been to distant lands where the sun and the sea had vied in beauty, but that was ever so long ago and humdrum existence had long spread its dry sands over the embers of his memory. It was only in his dreams that a fragment of them sometimes occurred, igniting anxiety. He was fond of his dreams. When asleep it seemed to him that he was roving the seas of a night, black and unknown. What adventures he would meet before the dark waves tossed him ashore to the light of day!

But it was time to go home. The picture he would see already stood before his eyes. All the rooms would be dark, except for the dining-room ablaze with light. The children would be sitting about the coughing samovar drinking their tea with milk, while his wife would be plying her hooked knitting-needle. He knew the familiar whiffs he would catch in the dining-room: that of tea and milk, his over-heated wife, the cat eternally lolling on the sofa—a human lair, the sated comfort that irritated him like a whiff from a rotting marsh in the summer, but which was deeply gratifying to his spouse.

It was all there, just as he had imagined it.

"You've come just in time!"

Martha met him calmly, in a matter-of-fact way. Harassed by her eternal cares, she had unfastened her blouse, revealing her broad throat and bare arms.

"The glazier's been here today. It's time to put the window-panes in order for the winter, but I could not decide...."

She poured him a cup of tea and moved the bread plate to him.

Ah, how many cares she had!

A barrel had to be bought for pickling the cucumbers. Or perhaps they had better order one made? What did he think? True, that would be more expensive, but more satisfactory on the whole.

In great detail they discussed how the new barrel ought to be soaked first, if the cucumbers were not to have a tang. It would be best to pickle less cabbage this year. They ate very little of it. More cotton wool had to go into the warm blankets.

Martha grew flushed again and languidly hot. Her broad collar and wide sleeves seemed to exude warmth.

She pursued him to his room and while he stooped to remove her dresses from the chairs, clothing which still preserved the warmth and shape of her body, she took them from his hands absently with her mechanical: "Oh, excuse me."

She had not finished. She wanted to know what he thought of the new material and the cut of the children's vests, the family's supply of beets and hundreds of other household matters. He listened in a daze, noting how her chin lept at every word, and thought: "Did we expect that after twelve years of married life we'd have no other topics and that these words would come between us and fall to the ground like so much litter?"

The rest of the house was quiet. The lamp burned evenly and wreaths of tobacco smoke hung over its milky light.

And she kept on and on rather for her own benefit than for his, convinced that her husband was a helpless unpractical man of little use for anything.

The tenor of their life was as calm and steady as always. Even the strongest wave would fail to stir this sluggish puddle. Anton was so irritated that he could have shouted, thrown something about or broken one of the windows if only to admit a breath of fresh air through the shattered glass.

He awoke one morning in a curious frame of mind, as though harking to an internal voice. On that morning he could not for the life of him have said whether or not his wife had told him her dreams, whether or not he had seen her white calves as her feet groped lazily for her slippers. All this escaped him on that day. There was something new, youthful and disturbing in his movements and gait.

With his unfinished tea before him, he sat sucking at his extinguished cigarette with unseeing eyes. He got up then, pacing the room uneasily.

He was late for dinner, but entered the room with springy steps, squaring his shoulders, somehow oblivious of his surroundings.

Martha could not help noticing the change.

"What's the matter with you today?"

She was troubled by the look of him.

"Has anything happened?"

She repeated her question, but he briefly said again that nothing had happened, which was something she could hardly believe. The green *borshch* brought no response from him. He ate little and answered her questions at random.

"What are you saying? Don't you know where you are? Wake up!"

Guiltily he then made an effort to be very attentive,

to ponder every word he said, but his absent air of concentration withheld something.

Her curiosity mounted when Anton, after his usual walk, went not to the dining-room, but to his own room. She heard his measured steps which seemed to be beating time to his thoughts and also the frequent scratch of his matches as he lit his cigarettes. His closed door allured her all the more for being closed. She could not resist opening it finally.

"May I?"

He nodded.

"What's the matter with you, Anton?"

He was evidently in two minds. He would have liked to tell her himself, but at the same time hungered to have her wrest it from him.

"There's nothing the matter."

But these words were tossed off too lightly to be convincing. She felt that it would not be difficult to overcome him.

"Now then, get it off your heart!"

Anton paused, glanced at his wife and after a moment's hesitation blurted:

"I had a dream!"

"So that's it!" Martha sighed with relief. She was even chagrined. Still, she nestled more cosily in her chair and made the kittenish grimace which had once suited her so well.

"Was it a nice dream? Tell me about it."

She was fond of dreams.

But he had suddenly wilted. He was reluctant to tell her. Would she understand? There was no distinction between reality and the dream for him. Didn't he see, laugh, suffer and feel in a dream? Didn't reality, too, fade away like a dream? Wasn't the whole of life a flitting dream? And a dream life?

Anton paced the room feeling that all he had lived through last night was surging within him, ready to brim over.

"I was back again in that distant warm country," he said mysteriously at last.

His wife's eyes grew puzzled and round and he had to remind her of the country through which his life had flitted once as in a dream.

"I stood on an island surrounded by the sea in the morning. It was a tall proud island, and the old continent seemed to be sinking in the blue sea. I thought that this island had torn itself away from the mainland in its youthful ardour and had sailed forth to create a life and beauty of its own. The sea was smooth and blue, a taut screen on which the sky was projected. There was so much azure there! There was the whole of the sea in the sky and the whole of the sky in the sea. Everything was blue, warm and spacious in my soul as in the spaces. I was drunk with the fragrance of the wild wormwood which covered the rocks and filled the air. Even by day the silver of the wormwood shimmered as though touched by the moon. Overhanging the cliffs it looked like a shaggy faun shaking his beard over the sea.

"The mirror of the sea was webbed with paths of light. 'For whom are they intended?' I thought, looking at them. 'Who is destined to walk upon them?' They had covered the sea with hieroglyphs, but who would be able to read them? I, myself, had turned into a song, a chord of sorrow blending with the song of the sea, the sun and the rocks.

"Suddenly, I heard a voice, clear and harmonious as though sprung from the azure warmth.

" 'Can you tell me what those strange ciphers mean?'

"I turned and saw a woman with a pale face framed in gold. She extended a hand to the sea and the wormwood embroidered her black dress with designs of silver, while a torch of poppies flamed in her other hand.

"She and I were troubled by the same question, and so I said:

" 'These are the ciphers of happiness.'

"She looked at me.

" 'They may be. A breeze will obliterate these ciphers of happiness before we can read them.'

"And she brought the gold of her hair to me, the burnished silver of the wormwood, the torch of poppies and also her eyes, the pools of sea water."

"Is that so?" smiled Martha.

"Please don't interrupt me. We sat like old friends on a warm stone bench. Even without looking at her I was aware of the strands of her hair trembling over her forehead like tiny tongues of fire, and of the warm blue playing in her eyes.

"In silence we looked at the sea. There were white sails dotting it like moths, or a solitary boat would appear from nowhere moving its oars back and forth, like an ant crawling over the table-cloth. Then suddenly, a sail would burst into its white like a flower from a bud. The flower would then sink to one side and flutter against the blue.

"A warm breeze touched our faces. . . . That was the breeze awakening, the breeze that obliterated the paths. The sea began to burn by the shore.

" 'Don't you think,' asked my neighbour, 'that the sea is like the blue bird of happiness which has buried its head in the blue mists, fanning its peacock's tail by the rocks, with every eye in it aflame with blue and green? Just look!'

"We leaned over the precipice, and when our vision penetrated the chaos of shattered rocks and wild plants we saw the sea caught in a net of shining dimples, in a net made of strands that were blue, green and pink. We could also distinguish the mosaics that lay under this net. There were violet blots of dense weeds, blue gleams from underwater sand, old bronze and deep blue enamel —and all these had been blended into a single fiery alloy.

" 'And don't you notice,' I said to her, pointing to the sea and white, sun-drenched villas, 'don't you notice that we are afloat? The island has submerged its tentacles like an octopus, seizing the bottom as though eager to stop its drift; but stop it cannot. It is afloat, eternally drifting, and knows not where amid the sunshine and the blue. Our island is laughing, baring its teeth in the shape of the rows of white houses.' "

Anton mopped his forehead and went on in a quieter tone.

"I don't know whether we conversed in words or in silences, but we were drifting through the great spaces, shoulder to shoulder, saturated with the sea air, the fragrance of its salt, wormwood and the sun. We were pure and as strong as the cables of a ship. Perhaps we exuded light.

" 'To the sea! To the shore! Hurry!'

"She commanded as if she had power over me, and clapped her hands so that some petals of the wild poppies fell on her dress. One of them fluttered to my hand coldly.

"We descended to the seashore.

"The rocks towered over us now, warm, even hot, as if there were blood coursing through their stony veins. The gold of genista shone in the mosaics of folds and twists. The wormwood splashed silver and the myrtle rose in its wedding attire. But then a bare rock would fasten our eyes, the naked chest of a giant offering repose from the orgy of colours. But how glad we were when we noticed a tiny blue flower which clung to the boulder. It, too, seemed to have settled there for a moment's rest. On what did it live? Probably it drank the blue mists of the sea every morning. I did not know its name and this made it seem even dearer.

" 'Isn't that a cluster of amethyst on the grey rock?'

"And so it was.

"On our right a rivulet of poppies ran to the sea with us, and the sea smiled at every turn of our path. The broken rocks in the distance were fringed with green, reminding one of worn velvet.

"The heat increased. The rocks, the road, the dust underfoot, the sea and the air seemed to be burning and we too gave off warmth.

"Lizards crossed our path now and then and the baked rocks seemed to quiver with their movements. The tiny creatures would flash the colours of their motley backs or sharp tales and vanish. Then they would appear again on their crooked legs bent with fear. They would halt, rearing their heads and cocking their round circled eyes. We could see their hearts throbbing under the thin skin. But no sooner was there a shadow or a rustle than they vanished into invisible crevices becoming one with the stones. One of us remarked that they were the souls of the stones, the throbbing pulse of those inert and heavy masses.

"Finally, there was a sigh from the sea and we too took deep breaths. The sirocco had begun, it seemed.

" 'Here's the shore at last.' My companion sighed with relief when she saw the grey sand. As she ran forward to it, I admired the gold of her hair shining against the blue water.

"The sea rolled its waves shoreward, flinging them off one by one with the motion of a habitual card-player.

"There were people bathing at Piccola Marina. We passed their sunny laughter, the splashing of their bodies sparkling greenly in the water, and sat down to rest in a solitary spot. The sea was blinding. It was abloom in silver and though the life of every blossom lasted but an instant there were hundreds of others instantly to take its place. Each flower would twinkle but once. A new star would appear in the azure.

"We could see the whole of the island from top to bottom. The waves burst on the tall cliffs of Monte Solaro and Faragloni. The island sizzled like a heated stone thrown into the water.

"We sat dissolving in the azure and listening to the sea.

" 'What are you thinking of?' I asked finally.

"She embraced me with a glance reflecting the sea and sky from horizon to horizon.

" 'I am looking at the South, at the infinite sea,' she answered softly. 'The sirocco brings me the sultriness of Africa and the aromas of Egypt. I am dreaming of the land of white sands and black people, of cactuses, palms and pyramids. These waves have come from Africa to kiss these rocks in brotherly greeting. And the very wave that washed the feet of an Arab may now be playing about my own—a symbol of communion.' "

"What a wonderful story!" said Martha, interrupting.

Anton fell silent, aware of his wife only now. So she was here! He looked with astonishment at the light of the lamp, his wife's puzzled eyes, an unfastened button on her blouse, a wreath of tobacco smoke over the bookcase and the cold black windows on which the rain was strumming a dreary tune.

Anton shrugged his shoulders as though to rid himself of something. Then he rapidly began to pace the room again.

"We parted and I did not know whether it was for a time or for ever.

"It was dinner-time and when I entered the dining-hall of my hotel the first gong reverberated over the snow-white tables as yet unoccupied. I went to my place. The sea lay about in individual seascapes framed between the columns of the terrace serving as a restaurant. A yacht on the horizon flowered in its sails. The sun set behind the dozing Castiglione and curled the mountain girdled with olive trees as with a dark Turkish belt. The vineyards sparkled in it like precious stones of green. There was hardly anyone about, but I already saw the familiar unchanging scene. A gentleman in a black coat and white trousers was methodically carving a dish of half-raw meat, while the lady at his side was studying a red-covered Baedeker. There was a hum of voices, a rattle of plates, ripples of laughter, the bubbling of beverages, the vigorous rumble of the sea, while the gentleman in black and white continued mechanically to carve the half-cooked meat and the English lady in white was engrossed in her red book. The first to appear in numbers were the Germans who filed noisily between the tables, ladies and gentlemen in a row of geese. They occupied a separate table and at once clinked their glasses. They had isolated their table from the others with the ring of their broad backs, fringed the white cloth with their ruddy faces and accompanied their loud speech and laughter with the clattering of plates.

" '*Ja-ja! Ja-ja!*' came the shattered approval over the table while their dusty shoes under heavy woollen calves thundered beneath it. Their plain freckled ladies tossed their bony shoulders about in badly fitted blouses and repeated the words they heard like talking dolls:

" '*Ach! Wunderschön!*'

" '*Ja-ja ... ja-ja!*' the men hacked.

" '*Kolossal!...*' the ladies resounded, piling generous helpings on their plates.

"A solitary Russian sat eating at a separate table, looking fearfully about like a wolf at bay.

"The waiters in black moved about noiselessly, their faces dignified as always. The silver glistened, the vines crept up the columns, the palms rustled beyond, and still farther there was the voice of the sea.

" '*Ach! Wunderschön!*'

" '*Kolossal!*'

"And then the familiar crown of gold appeared once more against the blue, her sea-coloured eyes gazing at me and her white face nodding recognition. She was a little late."

"So she's turned up again!" Martha exclaimed, but at once felt awkward. "Excuse me! I won't interrupt again." Her face reddened and there was a glint of suspicion in her eyes. She arose, picked up the clothes, bending over them, and began to jab some piece of apparel nervously with a needle.

But Anton was not to be hampered and plunged on with his story.

"How strange it was that we seemed to be conversing even when silent. Our thoughts were attuned like the strings of a single instrument. When I looked at a cloud, she at once saw that its shadow was dancing in the sea. Whenever I saw a puff of white over a rock, she would remark: 'That's a kiss of the sky!' Even more surprising was that a supreme silence seemed to have grown up about us, as though there were no one else about in the world. It was then that I saw that her lips were deeply red."

Martha put down her sewing, sat upright as though grown in stature, her lowered eyes fixed on one spot.

"You ought to have married a blonde!"

"Do you think so?" Anton said absently, puffing at his cigarette.

He could not help continuing his story and told how when the boulders had grown more dazzling in the heat and their breasts had intaken the air as hot as molten lava, they had wandered about the deserted streets past the wild olive trees which seemed to stand with bent knees and wiry hands—like petrified slaves kneeling amid the blood of the poppies. The heated air seemed to be dancing a tarantella over the rocks and the cicadas played their castanets in the grey olive coppices. They had walked past some walls of roughly hewn grey stone adorned with wan ferns. Other walls rose behind —of opuntia with round leaves as roughly hewn as the stone. There was something wild about this plant, something incongruous, shapeless—a frightened flock of prickly leaves. They seemed to be crawling over one another, these lobsters of vegetation, and their spines stood on end as if in mortal horror. There was the braying of an ass, a shout that struggled amid the opuntia and seemed as prickly as they. At times the two had had to stop to make way for the women ascending the stairs with the water splashing in the glazed white pitchers which seemed to have grown to their heads. They formed a long line of immobile faces and scrawny necks; their breath came gaspingly quick like that of dogs in hot pursuit. Their feet of a luscious brown seemed to cling to the ground at every step. And the two went on over the pebbles rolling away beneath their feet, over the carpets of genista, golden and fragrant and upon which the trees shed green tears. Suddenly they would stop, dazzled by the sea. It appeared unexpectedly gladdening their hearts with its joyous colours, its bluish haze over which Vesuvius floated like a great jelly-fish. Then came the grey dust again, the shark jaws of the agaves, the boulders and the genista that were like the brushes which had combed the sun and captured a few of its golden strands.

Anton saw it all so clearly as he told his story. Martha listened in a daze, carried away by the beauty of his words. She followed him like a superfluous shadow, yet marvelling at this power which she could not overcome. As though enchanted, she wandered after him through the narrow sleepy lanes, parting the vineyards and lemon groves which were white in the sun and grey in the shadows. It seemed as if some swift waters had once rushed from here, leaving only their stony beds and the shining lizards as grey as the souls of the rocks, creatures that wound their ways quickly and silently. Then they came upon an obstacle: a great mass of prickly hay, filling the street from wall to wall, was carried slowly upwards on the head of a woman. For an instant they saw her chin, the tip of her straight nose, the flash of her dark eyes, and then the bed of the dead stream lay empty and desolate as before. The slow footfall of the peasant woman was muffled in the sultry air. Once more the sharp tails of the lizards flashed against the mosaics of the walls. Once more the vines cringed within the shadows and the yellow lemons shone like the breasts of women.

"We came into the mountains, into the shadows of the great boulders, the petrified tragedy of the giants. Something terrible must have happened here long, long ago, when the earth was young and hot. Their eternal immobility had been disrupted then. The rocky masses had screamed and the world had come tumbling down. The rocks had cast their disobedient children away. And they had stood ever since, a petrified scene of horror, staring frozen-eyed at their giant parents and their jaws gaping in a silent cry for ever.

"We climbed higher, to the very summits, and what a scene confronted us there! The wind brought the fragrance of the wormwood and genista from the valleys; the bushes shone in maidenly freshness; the sun was wandering between the rocks, changing the sorrow of shadow to the joy of light. The sea played with fire, spreading its silk from its seething depths to the horizon.

"I sat on the grass, while she lay on a warm rock. Her body seemed to imbibe the warmth of her couch of stone. She told me the story of her life, while the wind played with the gold of her hair and her eyes reflected both sky and sea.

"She had sprung from the Caucasus, it seemed. Or at least, she told me that she had fought against the soldiers during the revolution there. She had lain in ambush in the hills, had taken part in hard campaigns as tirelessly as the bravest youth and no less fearless of death. She had crossed the rapid Kura on inflated wineskins by night to bring ammunition to her comrades-in-arms. She was wounded by a Cossack and unfastened her sleeve to show me the scar. I bent over it.

"We were alone in these spaces under the high sky, and the island floated on with us as a great cloud. I felt fresh and pure. I was young then, you see. I was neither conscious of my years, my body, nor the filthy sediment of life. I was winged then. Do you know what it means to be young and pure? Have you not forgotten?"

Anton did not notice that he was shouting.

Martha sat crushed and guilty. She sat embracing her knees, her head bent, her face lost in the sad shadows of her hair.

He grew aware of her mood at last and spoke gentlier.

Uncertain that he had seen everything he had told her in his dream, he was seized with a craving for creation, for a draught from the spring which he had himself struck forth from a rock like Moses.

With dreamy eyes, he told her softly about their evenings together. The tops of the rocks were still white in the sun, but the shadows had already traced violet silhouettes on the sea, as sharply etched as battlements against the sky. The evening sun had already wrought silver pedestals for the lonely rocks in the sea, which seemed as light and transparent as though they had dissolved in the heat. When the evening at last flung its rose and violet capes over the boulders, they had got up and gone to Piaza to admire the sunset. Ischia already stood gilded like a ripe fruit. Monte-Michele was dressed in red basalt, and Vesuvius seemed to have hoisted a two-coloured pennants blue and pink. Naples, Puzzuoli, Procida and the islands showed pearly-grey against the burning sky. The sun was setting. Ischia was waiting for it darkly in the golden mists like a Moorish face under a veil. The sun's scarlet hand reached for the earth for the last time. The tops of the almond-trees were stained with rose and the vines undulated in high menacing waves. The gory disc of the sun had already touched the hill.

Then Ischia cast off her veil and swallowed the sun as she always did, eternal sun-eater that she was. And then it was all over. The earth had returned to humdrum dress. The gardens bloomed no more, while Ischia digested her supper.

The island was grey and dreary after the sunset, its colours had run together like those of a wet water-colour. And yet, the twilight seemed to be hemming the distant island with faded silk, the island which lay beneath the steely sky like a piece of old tapestry.

When the shadows grew deeper, the calm bay was adorned with a necklace of lights and the Catholic chapels shone softly amid the grey walls.

It was getting late. The sleepy kitchen-maid thrust her head through the door for the third time, complaining that the supper was getting cold.

Martha got up, outwardly calm.

"Let's have our supper," she said indifferently.

The lamp in the dining-room had been turned down. The meat lay black on its cold plate. The children were asleep.

Supper was eaten in silence. Martha mechanically drew a dish closer to her husband, choosing the best portions for him. He ate quickly, but without pleasure as though he were hurried on by the rain drubbing the window-panes.

Their bedroom was very still when they retired. He asked her about something, but did so with such indifference that he never noticed whether she answered or not.

Martha pretended to be sleeping, while he leafed through a book with which he covered his face, though it was obvious that he was not reading.

Martha's heart turned to ice. The man who was dearest to her in the world had gone so far away from her. The few paces between their beds had turned into a cold infinite distance. She would have liked to see his face, but could not: the covers of the book concealed his features, and his fingers, rosy in the light, were fumbling with the pages.

Martha waited tensely. Perhaps he would be the first to speak and melt the ice? But no. The rustling of the pages ceased a little later; his arms unbent and the book fell to the bed. He had gone to sleep without turning off the light.

She got up and approached his bed with bated breath. She took up the book and laid it on the table. About to put out the candle, she paused. Her night-dress was slipping from her shoulder, and she was afraid he might wake up. Keen curiosity fastened her eyes upon this stranger. Sleep had already cast its shadow over his features. Was he asleep? What was he dreaming now? What did his soul say to him now that it was freed from the daily cares? How could she know? She felt very lonely, as if isolated from the whole of the world She looked at her body. Had she grown old? But then she thought bitterly: "What is the body anyway?" She wanted to weep. Anton had thrust a bare leg from under the cover, and she covered it carefully. "Why should I care about a body?" she said scornfully and extinguished the candle.

But her thoughts kept her awake. It was the eternal care for the body. She had cared about his body for years, had wanted him to have enough food, to be comfortable and in good health. She had spared neither effort nor time. It had been her duty and had seemed so natural that it was no longer difficult. Their life together had floated peacefully on and she had had no reason to complain. They had never quarrelled, were respected and were not even in debt. She was proud that her husband never played cards and even boasted of it to others.

But today he had broken it all, had filled her with alarm. He had become a problem requiring solution. He had seemed comprehensible until that day. She had known everything about him and had been able to put everything in its proper place. And suddenly.... She was insulted. He had deceived her. He had withheld a treasure to which she too had claims. It was only her body that he had shared for years. They had abandoned themselves to crude joys, anxieties, petty worries, remaining alien in spirit. Perhaps it was her fault? Perhaps it was a curse of life?

The words she had heard today, the beauty of them which could be sensed only by a susceptible soul had awakened something old and familiar within her. "Do you know what it means to be young and pure? Have you not forgotten?" Yes, she remembered, though, to be truthful, she had almost forgotten. When they had just married there had been other words between them, but the millstones of life had ground them to dust, and this

Anton who had preserved them through some miracle seemed very mysterious to Martha.

Anton was tossing on his bed. Martha raised her head, listening. She was drawn to him by curiosity: even his breathing seemed different that night. She could not see him in the dark, but this only whetted her imagination. She still saw him pacing the room with that face which had grown suddenly younger. She was impatient for the new day to begin, the day unknown yet attractive.

In the morning Anton met Martha only for an instant as he left the house. There was something challenging in her glance, something provocative, but he paid no heed.

It was a bleak grey day. There was something hopeless about the listless drizzle.

When he was coming home for dinner, he met Martha in a new blue suit very becoming. Sparks of rain quivered on her hat and there was something fresh and light about her.

"Where were you?" Anton was surprised.

"I went out to buy a few things."

She flushed deeply, for there was nothing in her hands. She must have come out especially to meet him, for she turned and walked by his side.

There was a pause until she said timidly that everything seemed to have faded in the rain—the pavements, the streets, the houses, the glistening roofs, the wet horses and people, the carriages, trees and shop windows. It seemed as if the rain had meant to wash away all colours and contours. Wasn't it so?

A girl in a broad-brimmed hat came from the opposite direction. She was just passing, swaying on her rubber heels, when Martha's cheeks grew very red. "I hate fair hair," she observed as if to herself.

They went on, now silent, now talking, but Anton noticed that his wife sought to intercept his glances and looked carefully at those who seemed to have caught his attention.

Dinner was ready when they reached home. The table was laid with the Sunday table-cloth and fresh roses stood in the crystal vase. This was a real surprise. Anton was not accustomed to such things.

He stared at her, wondering what to make of it? She evaded the question, lowering her eyes and flitting away to the kitchen.

Evening came.

Anton found that he wanted Martha to come, and yet did not. He was divided in his desire. He would have liked to go on with his story and yet felt like retaining it as something precious and comprehensible to himself alone.

But Martha came, merry, a little excited and with shining eyes.

"Here I am!" She sat down very upright and looked at him.

"I've come to hear the end of your dream."

He was in two minds.

"But you didn't tell me the name of your blonde," she said, trying to draw him on.

"My blonde?"

"Yes, ha-ha! Your blonde."

"I really don't know. I did not ask her."

"I don't believe you. Weren't you together all the time?"

"What of it? I was not interested. When we met our eyes fed on the splendour of the sun and the sea and that was enough. We drank of this beauty together from a green cup brimming with the richness of grapes, lemons and oranges, and it was this that linked us. What else can I say?"

He stood thinking for a moment.

"We usually met in the morning, took a boat and put out to sea. Sometimes the sky seemed bluer than the sea, sometimes the sea bluer than the sky. One could have thought they were envious of each other. The white sails in the distance fluttered like the wings of white doves. We sailed by the grey rocks encrusted with coloured molluscs. When the heaving sea withdrew from the rocks they bared their rosy gums. Coming back, the sea closed their fresh healthy mouths with the gentleness of a kiss.

"The sea gave us a better view of our island. The sun turned even ordinary rock into marble, compelling it to nourish its plants. It seemed to be trembling with crea-tive effort. The orgy of sunshine and colours subsided only now and then, when a cloud passed overhead. Such lulls were momentary, however.

"We could now understand something of the eternal encroachments of the sea storming the island. Whatever its mood, it kept beating against the rocks, grinding them down, burying them beneath the water. As we sailed over them, we saw the subdued monsters lying on the bottom, humbled and vanquished, letting them-selves be enveloped in amber seaweeds. The pebbles that had once been stones lay heaped on the shore, and where they had been ground into white sand the waves played in blue fire of triumph. The boulders towering over the sea gave way at last: the sea had eaten its way into them, leaving deep grottos. No, not so much grot-tos as castles of fantasy. We drifted into them, lying on the bottom of our boat, and found ourselves in a fairy-land. There were wonders about us that seemed unbelievable. The water seemed afire with emeralds, and the froth and foam shone in all hues of rose. The walls glowed mysteriously, in green hues and blue. The water coloured our boat, oars and hands with silver. The multicoloured molluscs decorated the walls with their bodies. There was the scintillating of rainbows, the sparkle of diamonds and other precious stones.

"The sea swept through the blue grottos, pouring itself into them. Our guide caught up the chain to direct our boat and the crest of a wave carried us through a narrow passage. Our craft flew through the spray and foam, creaking and bumping against the rocky sides until she finally steadied and stood swaying like a swan. The first thing I noticed when I sat up was the white teeth of my companion. It was her joy over all this azure that had prompted her to show them. My teeth too perhaps flashed. I'm sure they did. What words shall I find to describe that grotto. If you were to cast a vault of silver and fuse it with precious turquoise, make it play in the maddest lights throwing blue shadows on the walls, and then gather all the azure of all the sea and sky to saturate the air about you, you would achieve only a feeble semblance of that grotto. How one's body shone in that water! It seemed to radiate blue flame. We sat swaying in the boat as though rocking in the sky. We cupped the water in our hands, scattering it in trickles of gems. The silver waves now and then brought other boats into the grotto, so that the teeth of others flashed as ours had done in that blue light.

"We went fishing sometimes for a change. We cast our lines into the depths and felt them tremble like a pulse when the fish bit. We drew them into the sun, those exotic fish which looked more like flowers, those tricoloured viols, red devils and cardinals, dogfish and kingfish. We plucked a whole bouquet of them.

"We returned scorched by the sun, winnowed by the winds and salted by the sea.

"But it happened sometimes that my companion failed to come and then. . . ."

Anton sprang up and paced the room again, as

though intent on trampling his memories with heavy step.

"And then?" Martha prompted.

Their glances clashed like flint and steel.

"Then?" Anton echoed. "Then I wandered alone ... as mute as a violin whose strings had been cut, as inarticulate as a man who had lost his voice. I called to her, my unknown friend, called her to read the book of beauty with me, for it was tightly shut without her. I could look, but not see. I called to her, but she did not come."

It seemed to Martha that Anton had sighed.

"It was the moonlight that brought us together again. I was sitting somewhere on a rock. The moon had not risen and the dry grass was filled with the chorus of the cicadas. One of them seemed especially vibrant, weaving a silver string of notes from sea to sky.

" 'Are you sad?' I heard a familiar voice—and then saw her behind the boulder. 'I too am sad!' it said. 'We both belong to the species of the lonely, just as this island.'

"She sat down next to me and pointed to the sea.

" 'Just look! It's still afloat, lonely as ever in the spaces of the sea splashing upon it. And the roads from it lead nowhere, except perhaps to the gold bridge built by the moon to link the island with something distant and unknown. But this bridge is so frail and airy that only dreams can pass over it and drift away in their inaudible steps.'

"I heard her voice and was no longer the inarticulate stringless violin. My voice came back to me and my eyes regained their vision. I saw the moon rising and the sea casting a golden carpet before it, while the palms extended their fans and seemed to cry: 'Hosanna!' Now I perceived again how the warm waves of air woven of moonbeams, the fragrance of the sea and wild grass breathed amid the olive-trees and swept our faces in scented surges. I saw the wrinkles of Monte Solaro which never grow older—those wild rocks which rose like an amphitheatre of antiquity, watching the mystery of the moon enacted on the sea."

Anton paused. He tried to remember, but could not.

"There is a gap in my dream here," he said guiltily. "A chasm. I seemed to have vanished from the face of the earth with the island, sea and her. Everything sank into this chasm.

"I cannot remember just how it came to be that I found myself in a boat, that is, not myself alone, but both of us. The moon still hung over the sea and the distant rocks seemed to have come nearer, frowning in violet folds. They seemed to be bending over the sea with a maternal solicitude. There was a tenderness that linked the earth and the sea—agreement and sorrow. And when the moon rose higher and grew paler, the rocks grew paler too. The peaks grew sharper, each boulder distinct and alone as it turned into carved shining marble, and the island now looked like a cathedral of Milan behung with a bridge of gold spun by the moon.

"Our oars were splashing softly, scattering hosts of tiny sparks, green and blue like the fire-flies at the end of June.

"We guided our boat towards the shadows on purpose. The sparks were brighter there. Our oars seemed to plow up the treasures hidden in the sea. She unfastened her sleeve, rolled it shoulder-high and thrust her arm, blue in the moonlight, into the water.

" 'Look!' she cried, combing the merry sparks with her fingers.

" 'We are like the gods now!' she laughed. 'We ought to shout: "Let there be light!" '

" 'Let there be light!' I repeated her words, plunging my own arm into the water.

"We bent over the side and our heads were so close together that we felt the soft mingling of our hair and the warmth of our cheeks. We watched the sparks trickle through our fingers gliding through the mysterious depths.

"I then withdrew my streaming arm, took to the oars and set the boat in motion, scattering cataracts of sparks.

"Sometimes we passed the boat of a fisherman. Its reddish lamp lit up the sea, its gunwales, rigging and the good-humoured weather-beaten face.

" 'Good luck!' she nodded to the fishermen.

" 'Let the Madonna bring you happiness too!' a deep voice would respond, while a black hat gracefully swept the light.

"We returned to the grotto which was now raven black. No sooner had we intruded upon it than it was broken with sheaves of sparks turning the surface of the water into a starry night.

"We were seized with mystic horror in the Grotto of Saints. We had seen this marine tomb by day. The floating rocks within had resembled reclining figures, and these people of stone were still asleep. One lay like a woman wrapped in a sheet with a moonbeam stealing over her shroud and knees. A white patriarch lay plunged in sleep, his hands clutching his temples in deepest grief. The lights of invisible lamp shimmered under the Gothic vaults and it seemed that they were being swayed by the wind. Through the green moon-drenched water we saw a naked woman with a child on her lap, her thigh caught in a ray of light. Green stars swam in the darker corners and were extinguished.

"Then we headed for the sea. The lights of the fishing vessels shone in the distance. Swaying to the rhythm of the sea, we sat shoulder to shoulder, trembling as one. I saw her lips so near, and they were so red that even the night...."

Martha did not wait until he finished. She arose, pale and severe.

"You kissed her, I suppose?"

Her question gave its own answer. She looked at him as though she wanted to drink the poison floating in his eyes. She supported herself with a hand on the table.

Anton sprang up too. The blood had rushed to his head.

"Yes, I did!" he thrust, as vindictive as a knife.

"I kissed the lips that spoke to my heart in the language of my soul. Were they not worthy of it? You would like me to be as insensible as the rocks, but I'm still alive! Do you hear?"

He felt that he was wounding her with every word and cruelly rejoiced.

Martha covered her face and subsided into a chair sobbing. He felt relieved at first, watching her shaking figure, but then rushed to her side.

"What is it, my dear Martha? Please don't! It was just a dream."

But Martha shrank from him and stamped her foot.

"Keep away from me!"

"But, Martha!" pleaded Anton, trying to remove her hand. "Can't you see that it was just a dream."

But she sobbed even more and would not listen.

"You kissed her!"

He kneeled at her side, trying to soothe her, and felt annoyed at the same time.

"Now don't be a child, Martha! Understand that this is nonsense and no one is responsible for his dreams."

She seemed to regain her composure, wiped her eyes, removed his hands and rose to her feet.

"I know it was just a dream, but you're not incapable of doing just that in reality."

She made for the door, but Anton intercepted her.

No, if it had come to that, it was time to have it out to the end. It was possible that she was right, that he had been himself in his dream and was quite capable of doing just that when awake, and no one else was to blame for it but she.

She? Ha-ha-ha!

Yes, she! She did not know how to revere life and preserve beauty. She had littered his life with all sorts of trifles and petty chores until it had become a cesspool. Poetry could not live in a cesspool and life without poetry was a crime!

Martha was seething with rage.

And what about him? He had isolated himself from her, concealing the live stream of his soul like a miser who was afraid that someone else might see his riches. Why was she alone to blame?

No, he had been a different man at first, but one could not rear flowers on arid land. They would wither. He realized, of course, that life was inconceivable without prose, but let the froth keep only to the surface. The depths must sparkle like pure wine, and she who had diluted it had spoilt it.

The bleak autumn wept outside, and the battle of the two dissatisfied souls raged on in this stuffy, smoky room, the sleepy realm of the children's beds.

They reproached each other for even their tiniest faults before the holy spirit, accusing each other of indifference and blaming each other for loneliness in the slough of daily cares.

"You're covered with trivialities like a tree with its bark!" shouted Anton.

"You were just a lodger!" she retorted.

They were suffocating. Anton unfastened his collar and rushed about the room dishevelled, as if trying to widen the house with his shoulders, his streaming hair pursuing him.

Martha stood flushed, mopping her neck, her eyes blazing.

"Like Circe you would have turned me into a swine!"

"Go and kiss whomever you like! I don't care!"

Their quarrel was complete.

* * *

Their quarrels flared up often now—passionate argument which cut across their lives like strokes of lightning, their lives which had been so calm, unchanging and happy, as Martha had thought. But the tempests abated, Martha's heart bathed in her tears, grew younger and flowered again. She was happy when she was able to find a common language with Anton if even for a moment.

She was jealous. It was a stubborn, secret, burning jealousy of everybody and everything. She was jealous of the women who passed, of nature, of the evenings which he spent locked in his room, of his thoughts and dreams. She wanted to possess him entirely. She was no longer sure of him. Her eternal anxieties lent him the freshness of a new acquaintance. He no longer saw the bare legs of his wife in the morning, no longer heard her dull prosaic dreams, no longer had to gather scattered clothing. There was something young and maidenly about her now, something which had shaken her peace, that peace she had so recently craved. This urge to recapture something she had acquired long ago harboured a fresh attraction, an echo of her spring. She was not sure that she would be strong enough, that the time would come when the tempests would be laid for ever, but meanwhile, the roses flamed forth on her table more and more often.

May 28, 1911
Chernigov

THE HORSES ARE NOT TO BLAME

"Savka, where's the eau-de-Cologne?"

Arkady Petrovich Malina thrust his head through the window, shouting angrily at his servant who was helping to unharness the lathery horses from the cabriolet.

Wet all over with perspiration, he stood by the window in his shirt alone, unfastened at the chest, impatiently watching Savka running across the yard in his gold-braided livery.

The flask turned out to be on the bed-stand, but had somehow escaped his attention.

"You're always mislaying things," he grumbled, accepting the flask from the servant's hand. Stripping off his shirt, he began to rub down his body sallow with age.

"That feels good!" He rubbed his silver-haired chest, toyed with the pits of his arms and copiously sprinkled his bald head and long, flabby, though dry-fingered hands. He then drew a fresh shirt from his clothes closet.

He was in best spirits apparently, his usual frame of mind after a meeting with the peasants of his village. He was pleased that he, the former general whom his neighbours regarded as a radical and suspicious, had always been true to himself. Even in these troubled times he held that the land should belong to those who tilled it. "It's time we got rid of our gentility!" thought Arkady Petrovich, fastening his right cuff after he had done the same with the left. His ears still tingled with the joyous hubbub at the meeting with the peasants when he had explained why the people had a right to the land.

Such occasions never failed to stimulate him, giving fresh keenness to his appetite and zest to life.

The door creaked as he was tucking his shirt-tails into his trousers and his pet dog Myshka, a pedigree fox-terrier, came prancing to him.

"Where've you been, you rogue?" Arkady Petrovich bent over the little bitch. "Where've you been?" He fondly caressed her head and ears, and she caught a lap at his face, her nose wrinkling and stumpy tail wagging. "Where've you been trapesing about, you little devil?"

The midday sunshine poured through the windows commanding a view of a sea of green fields—nine hundred dessiatines of his land undulating from gully to gully.

Arkady Petrovich carefully parted his hair, combed his moustache to its yellow tips and then stood admiring his dry high forehead and aristocratic features reflected in the bluish mirror of his toilet set.

His grey, somewhat cold eyes had lost their lustre and their whites were veined with red. This rather troubled him. Perhaps a poultice would help, he thought. Then, there was a small pimple on the side of his nose. At once, he extracted a jar of cold cream from his toilet set, daubed it cautiously and powdered it.

"I'm hungry!"

He was as hungry as a young man of twenty-five, and this sharpened his pleasure too. What a fuss they would make when they learned that he was hungry! His old busy-body of a Sonya would break into "ahs" and "ohs," and Savka would spring about with redoubled alacrity and all eyes would be fixed on his mouth. It was so rarely that he had an appetite these days!

But where was Savka, to say that dinner was ready?

Arkady Petrovich opened a drawer of his dresser and extracted a neatly folded blouse of grey wool, à la Tolstoi.

His body still tingling and refreshed, he drew on the shirt conscious that he was a democrat and a friend of the people whom he need never fear. The peasants had grown fond of him ever since he left the ministry and retired to this village. And why not? It was he who stood godfather to their children and gave away the bride at wedding parties, forgave trespassing and offered advice so that they all came to call him father.

He was thinking of this with pleasure and also of the meadow mushrooms which would be served at dinner, for he had noticed them in Palashka's apron as she was carrying them to the kitchen.

It was just then that Savka thrust his white-gloved hands through the door and respectfully announced that dinner was served.

Arkady Petrovich entered the dining-room looking somewhat like a church bell in his great blouse.

There was a shuffling of chairs as his children kissed his hands. On the one side there was his son Antosha with already thinning hair, and on the other, blonde Lida, his daughter and a widow at twenty-five. They had not yet met today, for Antosha had just arrived from the farm and Lida had been in bed until noon.

Sophia Petrovna, or Sonya, wore a new summer dressing-gown and brandished a silver ladle over the tureen of hot *borshch*. The table was set for nine.

Arkady Petrovich subsided into a wide armchair at the head of the table and slapped the seat of the chair beside him.

"Myshka, up with you!"

The fox-terrier squinted unenthusiastically, made the jump and sat on end.

"But where's Jean? Call him!" he said to no one in particular.

The door opened at this moment and blind Jean, his wife's brother and retired admiral, came in supported by his minesweeper, as he called his servant. Big unshaven Jean, as stately as a mainmast, was tapping the floor with his crude cane, hardly daring to bend his knees and turn for his blindness.

He was brought to his chair with great ado, and the minesweeper posted himself respectfully at his elbow.

"Good morning, Jean," Arkady Petrovich greeted him from his place of honour. "What did you dream last night?"

Everybody smiled at this long-standing quip, but Jean fastened his unseeing eyes on the wall and earnestly began to tell his story.

"I saw a city in my dreams, only not one made up of those ugly boxes now called houses. It was not a pile of filth and litter, nor a den of poverty. In short, it wasn't what you'd call a city."

He even winced.

"It was a glorious, unheard-of city, containing everything that has been created in architecture, all the masterpieces of the past, present and future. It was a marriage of beauty and comfort, a palace worthy of man. It is only that your descendants...."

"Jean! Your *borshch* is growing cold!"

"Ah, excuse me, Sonya. Well then, minesweeper number seventeen, tie up my napkin!"

"Yes, sir!" minesweeper seventeen (Jean often changed his servants and numbered them as he did) promptly complied. He had stood ready with the napkin for some time.

"It seems to me that ..." Lida said somewhat benevolently with her golden madonna-like head slightly tilted.

"Have they begun with the carting of the hay, Anto-sha?" asked Arkady Petrovich.

Antosha could not hear him, for he was engaged at that moment, putting some bones on to the plate before his dog Neptune who sat on a chair by his side. He was bent over so that only his thinning pate could be seen above the table.

To avoid looking at Jean who was eating somewhat slovenly, leaving bits of beet on his moustache, Sophia Petrovna addressed her son:

"Your father is asking you about the hay, Antosha!"

"Oh, I'm sorry." He raised his sun-tanned face. "They brought away ten instead of twelve carts," he lisped. "Artyom made two trips and then said that his Ksenka had hurt her leg with a rake and he had to fetch the doctor. He's lying of course. As for Bondarishin, he took the money in the winter and is now stringing me along."

Antosha sat flushed with the hot *borshch* he was eating as well as with his cares. Beads of perspiration stood on his white forehead and his eyes seemed glazed.

He knew everything that went on in the village. He had fathered the greater part of a dozen of children with various village girls and had more than once measured strength with the sturdiest of young fellows there, despite his officer's rank.

"They're all like him." Sophia Petrovna sighed angrily and stroked a dachshund who sat on the next chair, its amber chest protruding much like a waistcoat.

"You're too critical, my children!" Arkady Petrovich remonstrated good-naturedly, almost finished with his *borshch*. "The peasant has his own needs just as we poor sinners."

He was still in good spirits after his meeting with the people.

"It seems to me that Father...."

Lida tilted her madonna-like head again, primly widening the line of her lips.

But this made Antosha angry. There went Lida again. Those radical students had wound her up like a gramophone and she repeated all the nonsense she had heard.

"A peasant will be a peasant, no matter what you say. You treat him with honey, and he...."

The admiral (the "battleship," as he called himself) at once sensed the charged atmosphere and began to relate his second dream, while Savka gathered the plates from masters and dogs with expert white-gloved gestures.

He had been at a concert and heard the music of a future generation, the most incredible combination of sounds, entirely dwarfing Bach, Haydn and Beethoven.

Antosha was bored. He had heard more than enough of his uncle's dreams and preferred to give his attention to Neptune.

He laid a slice of bread on the dog's nose.

"Now don't you dare!"

Neptune sat up importantly, but squinting displeasure.

There was silence for a moment.

"Take it now!"

Only Lida extended her long neck politely to her uncle.

But her little Milton, a poodle shorn of everything but a frill around the neck like that of a dowager, put a tentative paw on her arm, pleading for food. Whereupon Lida turned and adjusted the bow on the animal's nape; it was blue like the colour of her dress. She gave him a buttered slice of toast.

The thoughts of the mistress of the house were concentrated on the forthcoming second course.

"Now I think that reality can be more surprising than

any dream," she said with a toss of her shoulders and looked absently over the heads of the company.

"That's very true," Antosha agreed. "Sometimes it's hard to guess the end of things that happen. They say that yesterday the peasants seized and ploughed up Baron Kleinberg's land. The whole village of them just went into the fields with their ploughs and drove away the farm-hands."

"You mean they've actually done it?"

"Gone just like that!" Antosha whistled with a gesture. "Gone is the land of the baron, and he had to run too, for fear they'd kill him. Awful things have been happening and here's Papa with his liberalism!"

"How awful!" sighed the mistress of the house.

"Well we have no need to run away!" Arkady Petrovich laughed. "They won't trouble us, I'm sure. What do you think, Myshka? They won't trouble us, will they?" He stroked the dog's muzzle and she responded with a playful bite at his finger and a wag of the stumpy tail. "You know very well what I think." He withdrew his finger and held it some distance from Myshka's teeth. "The peasants have every right to the land. It's not we who till it, but they. That's what I've always said."

"Arkady!... *Laissez donc.... Le domestique écoute!*"

Sophia Petrovna was so frightened that her voice fell by an octave, but Arkady Petrovich was not to be quelled.

"You want to be gentry for ever, my heart? That won't do. Others too must have their chance. Never fear! They'll not take all the land. They'll leave us some, about five dessiatines or so. I'll turn vegetable-gardener in my old age. I'll wear a broad-brimmed hat and a beard down to my belt. I'll do the planting, you the harvesting and Antosha the carting to town. Ha-ha-ha!"

"A fine time you've picked for joking!"

Sophia Petrovna angrily eyed the family and the four dogs. Only Antosha sympathized with her.

As a token of protest, he poured himself a glass of vodka, gulped it down and leaned back with his hands thrust deep in his officer's trousers. Jean continued to munch his meat unconcernedly under the wing of his minesweeper. Savka wore an air denoting that he was not present in the room at all, while Lida's lip-line widened even more as she bent to her father.

"I was sure that. ..."

"It's all right to joke at home," Antosha interrupted her, "but why should Father preach it to the peasants? Their mood is such now that there's no telling what to expect."

"But I'm not joking. It's time to rid ourselves of our prejudices. 'He who does not work, neither shall he eat,' my darling. That's it."

Cheerfully, he proceeded to evolve his ideas, helping himself to a huge pile of salad, oblivious of poor Myshka licking her chops, wagging her stump of a tail and looking up greedily.

"Lida there, in her pretty frock which, by the way, suits her very well, will drive the cow to graze and do the milking in the evening with her dress tucked up! Ha-ha-ha!"

"As for me, I. ..."

"That's the spirit!"

The dessert was served. With tinkling spoons, Savka thrust his white-gloved hands between the elbows of the masters and muzzles of the dogs. The minesweeper was wiping away a bit of sour cream that Jean had let fall on his admiral's uniform. Sophia Petrovna's dachshund was licking its plate, while little Milton was softly whining, forgetful of propriety. to catch attention.

"Will you have some more cream, Arkady?"

"Yes, *ma cherie*! I'm hungry today."

He really felt unusually vigorous today after having so staunchly stood up for the rights of the people.

"Blessed is he who has mercy upon the animals in the field!" quoth Jean to himself, his unshaven face illuminated by his blind whites. "Minesweeper, a cigarette please!"

"Yes, sir!"

"Good for you, Jean!" Arkady Petrovich laughed. "That goes for animals, and for people too."

"There goes the Bible again!" Antosha could not abide quotations.

He tossed his crumpled handkerchief into a corner of the room to see Neptune jump up and bring it back. It was funny to see the dog as he approached flap-eared with the white cloth under his black cold nose.

"Here, Neptune!"

He had just recovered the handkerchief from the dog's wet mouth, when the animal stiffened and barked twice. The other dogs too grew uneasy and Myshka bounced to the door with her piping version of a bark, her stubby tail down.

"Who's there? Go and see, Savka."

Savka returned and reported that the peasants had come.

"Ah, the peasants? Tell them to come here."

"Perhaps you'd better finish dinner first, they can wait?"

But Arkady Petrovich insisted that they come in; he had already finished his meal.

The peasants entered and stopped in a group at the door. Bondarishin, the one who had taken the money in the winter and now failed to cart the hay, was also among them.

"What have you to say, my good people?"

They shifted uncertainly, looking somewhat like sheep in their white flax-woven clothes. They looked at the glittering table surrounded by the gentlefolk and their dogs.

"What can I do for you?"

The red-haired Panas winked to the grey-headed Marko and the latter in turn nudged Ivan. But Ivan held that Bondarishin would be the best spokesman and they all looked to him in sign of their agreement. Not daring to emerge from the group, Bondarishin bowed from the waist to the benevolent *pan*.

"We have come to the *pan* to talk about the land."

"That's very nice. About what land?"

Bondarishin looked at Ivan, his relative by christening.

"About your lordship's land, if you please," Ivan came to the rescue.

"Such are the times now," added Marko.

"And the *pan* said so himself," blurted Panas.

"And so," continued Bondarishin, "the village has decided to take the land from the *pan*."

"What?" Arkady Petrovich suddenly shouted. He bounced from his chair and approached them, napkin in hand.

The crowd of them, however, looked calm and as matter of fact as if they had come to talk of some ordinary farming matters.

"We do not want to offend the *pan*. Let there be peace! God's way!" the grey-headed Marko mumbled toothlessly with a deep bow.

"Keep quiet! Let Bondarishin talk!" The red-haired Panas waved the old man back with his hand.

Now the whole family, Sophia Petrovna, Antosha and Lida, sprang up and stood behind the master of the house. Only the blind admiral kept his seat, turning the whites of his eyes on the dogs licking the plates.

"Of course we don't!" Bondarishin went on humbly and with seeming indifference. "We'll leave the *pan* a bit of land, something in which to grow onions for his soup and a bit for playing croquet."

"How awful!" Sophia Petrovna's head swam, and Lida had to bring her a glass of water.

"The scoundrels!" Antosha hissed, his hands deep in the trousers of his uniform.

"We'll do this, because the *pan* has always been kind to us and we are grateful!" Bondarishin bowed again and again.

"Of course! It would be a sin to say it wasn't so. Don't we call the *pan* our father!" the crowd murmured.

"Very well then," said Arkady Petrovich repressing his resentment. "I won't go back on my word. If the village has decided...." His words were as ice.

"Arkady! What are you talking about!" Sophia Petrovna cried. "How dare you!" she turned upon the group.

Antosha was on the point of saying something, the blue veins pulsating at his temples.

"So that's how things stand, *Pans*.... We'll divide the land in two days, next holiday, and let the *pan* choose his plot. Near the house or near the fields."

"It would be better near the house, of course. There's more manure about, and it's better to have it close at hand," the red-haired Panas said helpfully.

"The *pan* will think it over himself in the next two days. We shan't hurry him. He's been a kind *pan*, and we're grateful to him and the *pani*. They've always remembered us."

"They were always helpful with powders and ointments, God keep them!"

All stood very still while the peasants were leaving. Only Arkady Petrovich toyed with his napkin.

Sophia Petrovna was the first to recover.

"Arkady! You're mad! What right have you to give away your land? You have children!"

"We can't leave it at that! We've got to take measures!" Antosha raged, kicking Neptune who whimpered with pain.

Lida alone was still tilting her head sympathetically with her pale lips drawn in a wide smile.

"Ah, leave me alone!" Arkady Petrovich said irritably. "Try to understand that I can't do otherwise!"

He crumpled his napkin, tossed it on the table and rushed from the room. The hubbub that followed was suppressed by Jean's stentorian voice.

"Well, minesweeper, it's time you got your steam up. We're off on a long journey."

"Yes, sir!" The minesweeper stood at attention.

But the journey was not fated to take place. A family council was to be held instead, and the admiral was invited to join.

To dispense with the servants, they took him by the arms and led him into the next room, followed by the dogs.

Myshka, however, had chosen to vanish some place.

• • •

She at last pattered to her master in his study. He stood facing the glass door of the porch, watching a fly buzzing persistently against the pane. She nosed one of his boots, but he gave her no attention. Then she made several leaps to catch the fly, but soon grew tired and curled up on her cushion in the corner.

The white colonnade of the veranda and the flower-beds beyond could be seen through the glass doors. The poppies had bloomed and the gillyflowers were just about to blossom. Arkady Petrovich had seen these beds day after day, but hardly ever noticed them before. He opened the door, exposing his bald head to the sun. Then he strode down the steps towards the beds and bent over them.

This could not occupy him long. There was a heaviness in his heart, and he did not dare to confess to himself that it was resentment. The land was theirs by right, of course. He had always thought so, and had never been afraid to say so. But to take the land from him. . . Fine neighbourly relations! He recalled how often he had advised and helped them, how he had stood godfather to their children and had given away their brides. If his memory served him correctly, he was godfather to the child of this very Bondarishin. And now it had all been forgotten.

"For a plot of onions and another for croquet. Ha-ha-ha!"

The sun was baking his bald head. Unhampered and incessantly, it scorched the flower-beds and the fields rolling from hill to hill as far as one could see.

He returned to the house, put on his hat and, instead of his usual after-dinner nap on the sofa, went into the grassy yard. The coachman was fussing about the carriage with Savka's help. They were probably discussing the news. Arkady Petrovich would have liked them to saddle his horse, but said nothing, feeling, strangely enough, that this was not his own farm. He passed them in silence and went into the fields. The rye was ripe. The golden anthers rocked on their stalks, their imperceptible coats of pollen glittering in the sun. The children's eyes of the corn-flowers peeped through the rye. Myshka rustled among the stalks and suddenly scampered ahead. The fields now descended to a small valley, now rose to gentle slopes, as though the earth were luxuriously languishing before him.

Abandoning himself to the green waves, Arkady Petrovich tried to dismiss all thoughts, staring into the mysterious depths of the green rye and aware of the tender softness of the path underfoot. True, it seemed to him that some voices came from it, saying something that he did not want to hear. He wanted only rest and solitude. But the farther afield he went, the most distinctly did he hear them, soft, tempting and arguing. For the first time in his life, he sensed with all his being that this was the earth itself talking to him, the earth to which he was as accustomed as to his wife, daughter and son. He remembered now that his father and grandfather had walked here before him, and it was their voices, the voices of all the Malynas, that he heard. He now knew that everything he prided himself on and appreciated in himself, his educated, cultivated tastes and even his ideas, had been nurtured by these fields.

But Arkady Petrovich's own ridicule caught up with him on time. "Ha-ha-ha! It runs in the blood, doesn't it!"

He dismissed his thoughts with an effort and wandered on.

The wheat terminated in a moist valley on his left where the meadows began. He could see the grazing cows and calves. Fedka, the little herdsman, whipped off his cap when he saw the *pan* and stood respectfully still, barefooted and some bags over his shoulder.

"Put your hat on!" shouted Arkady Petrovich.

The boy must have misunderstood, for he ran to meet him.

The cows strayed over the meadow, as richly fat as the grass they grazed upon. The colts raised their heads and looked at their master, their sinuous necks showing that they were ready to prance away on their slender resilient legs at any moment.

He approached his pet Vaska and began to stroke his mane. Vaska, in turn, put his head over Arkady Petrovich's shoulder and dreamily veiled the fear in his eyes. And thus they stood for a long time feeling some animal sympathy between them. They were both happy, the one because he could stroke the strong neck, and the other because the caress was pleasant.

"They will take him too!" thought Arkady Petrovich bitterly, and went on. He strode through the damp fresh grass in the hollows. The horse sorrel and thistle were shot with green light perpetrated by the sun.

There was something as fascinating about the land today as the features of a deceased whom he had known all his life and with whom he was now to part for ever. He noticed flowers and other plants which had hitherto been inconspicuous, soft contours, the aromas of grass and earth and dear familiar vistas.

Tall willows rustled over a gully and the sky between them was like blue enamel. He sprang over a ditch bathed in wormwood and wild marjoram and found the path again. The rye fell away on one side and a clay cliff yellowed on the other, bestrewn with poppies. How glorious it all was! He could hardly believe that he had ever been here before. Could it be that all this was someone else's? No, indeed, he was treading his own land. He was astonished at how little he had known his own land. The flowers were noisy with their insect suitors. Myshka had dug a hole in the clay and was sniffing at it. The path led uphill, losing itself here and there in the burdock. The field seemed to broaden its shoulders and spread its garments; and when he reached the summit of the hill, he had a full and splendid view of his fields, the green stain of the water-meadow and deeper stain of woods. Up here, at the hub of his land, he sensed rather than thought that he would yield it to no one.

"I'll shoot them down if they come!" he said aloud.

This astonished him so completely that he looked round. Could those words have come from him?

But there was no one around—only the fields spreading from hill to hill.

He was ashamed. What a pig he had turned out to be! He lifted his hat and mopped his perspiration. Could he go to such lengths? Of course not! Surely, he could not go against himself, against his outspoken credo. He and his kind were only a handful and of no significance in the grand process of life. They represented only a few withered leaves in the verdure of spring. It was obvious to him, however, that he would not be able to support himself on a plot of onions and would have to accept a post somewhere in his old age. That would mean two small rooms in the suburbs of the city. His wife would have to cook his meals, and he himself would go to market with a basket. Would you put up the samovar, Arkady? Did he really know how? It was something he would have to learn. Antosha and Lida would earn their livings easily enough, because they were young. And you, Myshka, would have to forget all about creams and delicious bones.

Foolish little Myshka seemed cheerful at the prospect. She jumped upon him and soiled his trouser cuffs. But what did the trousers matter. He enjoyed imagining himself as an impoverished victim, one destroyed by the grand process of life. He was the martyr who had taken up his cross willingly.

He felt his body tingle with perspiration. He breathed lighter and his self-pity sharpened his appetite. It was such a young and healthy appetite that he was truly surprised.

He hoped that there would be meadow mushrooms for supper just the way he liked them: cooked whole with abundant cream and sprinkled with green onions.

He ought to have told Motrya. These affairs always quickened his blood, setting it curiously afire. But what had happened when all was said and done? There had just been some preposterous boasting and stupid threats. They would melt away the moment he spoke to the peasants, and everything would go on as of old, quietly and peacefully. The idea! Someone thinking of taking the land from him! Ha-ha-ha!

"*Avanti*, Myshka!"

But at home no one seemed even to have thought of supper.

As soon as she saw him on the porch, Sophia Petrovna pounced upon him before he had time to remove his hat:

"Arkady, you have children!" Her eyes were deeply lined.

"Well, what if I have!"

"This is serious. You should go to the governor at once!"

Arkady Petrovich shrugged his shoulders and turned away.

"We should ask him to send the Cossacks immediately."

"Excuse me, Sonya, but you are talking nonsense."

"Are we to wait until the peasants take our land? Is that it?"

"Let them. The land is theirs."

"Your liberal notions have turned your head! If you're so stubborn, I'll call them myself."

"I won't have the Cossacks here."

"We can't do without them!"

"I'll do something you'll be sorry for! I'll go to prison, to Siberia!"

"Arkady, my dear...."

"I'd rather go to hard labour than receive the Cossacks!"

"Understand, my dear, that...."

But he refused to understand anything and kept fuming like a samovar about to boil. Very red and sweating, he stamped his feet and waved his arms about, as though facing not his wife, but one of the hated Cossacks.

This exchange thus ended in nothing, except that his supper was spoiled, especially since they had forgotten to prepare the mushrooms.

"But where is Antosha?"

Antosha did not turn up at supper and he could gather that something was being concealed from him by the uneasy evasions of Sophia Petrovna and the grim line of Lida's lips.

He preferred to say nothing.

He awoke in the blackest of moods on the next morning. It seemed to him that there was something disrespectful in the way Savka brought him his morning's water, set it on the wash-stand with a bang and slammed the door as he went out.

"The scoundrel knows that the peasants mean to take the land. Why should he stand on ceremony with a pauper?"

He ate his breakfast listlessly and then set out to make the rounds of the farm. He stopped at the orchard, the locked barns near which Motrya was feeding the ducks, her skirt tucked up, and the empty sheds which smelled so pungently at the crevices. His coachman was washing the carriage in the yard.

Then he had a look at the stables. The horses stood munching their oats, and a pile of dried manure lay by the door with a moist hand-barrow near by, its shafts buried in the grass.

"Rake the manure into the stables, Ferapont! Why should it be exhibited here before the doors?"

The coachman unbent with the moist rag in his red hands.

"Yes, sir."

"But then why should I care?" thought Arkady Petrovich. "But what's done is done!"

Bondarishin passed the house and bowed when he saw the *pan.*

"He hardly lifted his cap!" Arkady Petrovich raged. "Well, what am I to them now? Nothing at all! The scoundrels!" he hissed, looking after Bondarishin.

The blind admiral supported by his minesweeper set off on his usual "journey." They passed by without noticing him.

"Even the minesweeper behaves differently today," thought Arkady Petrovich. "He's glad there'll be no more *pans.*"

He went to the fields again, but aimlessly somehow. A cloud was coming over and he anxiously remembered that they were still carting the hay. A few great drops fell on his peaked cap, then on his hands and face. He caught a whiff of the rye fields. He should have returned to the house, but did not. The warm torrent poured generously over the fields from the heights of the clouds, but soon the sun kindled a rainbow and the shower stopped. Heavy drops clung to the ears of wheat and a vapour hung over the fields. He too felt as though he were steaming, and was not even glad that the rain had stopped. He wanted more clouds and rain: the devil take the hay!

He returned to the courtyard as aimlessly as before. The coachman was still fussing over the carriage. The heap of manure, now black with moisture, still lay by the door of the stable, steaming after the rain.

Arkady Petrovich shook with anger.

"Ferapont! What did I tell you? Do I have to tell you again? Rake that manure away this very minute!"

He raised his cane, shaking it, pointing at the stable and at the offensive heap, while the surprised coachman leisurely reached for a rake.

"He's deliberately slow!" thought Arkady Petrovich. "Well tomorrow's tomorrow, but today I'm the master here!"

He regained his composure in his study, took off his coat and lay down on the sofa in his shirt sleeves.

"How absurd! Why should I be so troubled about it? What difference does it make where that heap lies?"

He was a little ashamed of the scene he had made before Ferapont.

He lay very still for some time with his eyes tightly shut.

"But what's going to be the end of this?"

He opened his eyes and saw the ceiling. There was no answer. The sun had thrust a broad shaft through the Venetian window. He could see the threads of dust playing in it and hear the clatter of dishes in the dining-room. They were setting the table. He could not help hearing the click of heels, the shifting of the chairs and tinkling of glass. Nothing had changed, and life was taking its usual humdrum course. How strange to think that there might be a change! But it was bound to come. It was this which split his mood. His mind once more gleaned the alarming details, the impertinent manner of Savka, the stubbornness of Ferapont and disrespect shown him by the passing peasants. How he wished that tomorrow could come at once and begin its dangerous game. How would he react? Would he defend himself and even shoot? Or would he let the land go resignedly. He did not know. It was in this uncertainty—apart from all other considerations—that his curiosity over the morrow lurked.

He looked at his watch.

"Ten to twelve," he said. "So there's less than twenty-four hours left!" he thought.

Tomorrow.... He imagined the morning. The whole village of them would crowd into his yard. The women would be screaming and bickering over the different scraps of land. The children would peer through the windows and scamper about the veranda as though at home.

He looked at his watch again. Four minutes had passed.

"Ugh!"

He hoisted himself on to his weary old legs and went to the window. The fields were stirring in the winds to the very horizon, indifferent as to who would own them; they were accustomed to the peasants' hands.

Antosha was not to be seen at dinner either.

Again Arkady Petrovich returned to his study. Again his aristocratic blood pressed its demands, and his reason argued, and his conscience writhed—each in its own way. But his chief feeling was keenest curiosity as to what would happen and how. He filled the room with the smoke of his cigar, trod the floor all over, lengthwise and crosswise, saturated the air with his thoughts, but the morrow continued to rankle in him like a bullet which could not be removed without cutting the flesh.

At last he saw Antosha gallop into the yard on a foam-flecked horse, and then heard him striding straight to Sophia Petrovna's rooms.

Meanwhile, they were setting the table for Antosha.

"There was little time left now. Only the night and a few hours!" Arkady Petrovich kept consulting his watch.

The shadows grew longer and the sun was about to set behind the stables. The herd had been driven home. The cows were swaying importantly in with their ruddy udders and steep horns. The colts were frolicking about the grassy yard.

"Can it possibly be that all this will not belong to me tomorrow?" Arkady Petrovich sadly thought when he suddenly heard Lida's voice:

"I hope you won't mind, Papa, but. . . ."

"What's the matter?" He wheeled to face her.

She stood in the doorway with her madonna's pallor, her lips drooping at the corners in the usual melancholy way.

"There's no need to worry too much. The Cossacks have come."

"What?. . . The Cossacks?"

"The governor's sent them. They're on the road."

Arkady Petrovich winced. The blood ran to his face colouring his bald head and everything but his yellow tipped moustache; his angry grey eyes stood out amid that conflagration like a pair of frozen lakes.

"What's the meaning of this? Did I ask for them? It's a conspiracy against me! I won't have it, damn you!

Call Antosha!" He even raised his white, dry aristocratic hand as though he meant to strike his son.

"Well, it seems to me that ..." stammered Lida.

She would have liked to add something to soothe him, but he was darting about the room like a fighting-cock with flapping wings and craning neck before a decisive battle.

"Bring that Antosha here!"

Dusty and perspiring, Antosha fairly staggered into the room on his legs weary from riding. His anxious mother peeped over his shoulder.

"Was it you who brought the Cossacks?"

"It doesn't matter whether it was I or someone else, Father!" Antosha lisped, spreading his legs in his officer's breeches.

"It doesn't matter, does it? I'll show you whether it matters or not! I'll drive them away immediately. Let me get out of here!" he roared, though no one had made to detain him, and rushed about the room as though he had lost his head.

"Arkady, compose yourself!" Sophia Petrovna pleaded, spreading her arms in the doorway. "It's night-time already and those men are tired and hungry. The peasants would not put them up. How could you think of such a thing?"

"The men! Fine men they are! I'm supposed to harbour Cossacks, of all people! Don't you dare to hold me any longer!"

"But, Father, it seems to me that ..." Lida broke in.

"There's nothing easier than to drive them away!" Antosha interrupted. "But what will happen then? There's no fodder in the village, and the peasants would not hand it out of their own accord anyway. The Cossacks would have to take it by force. If that's what you're after, then drive them away."

"Poor horses!" Lida sighed. "Are they to blame!"

"What did you say?" Arkady Petrovich halted before her with raised eyebrows.

"I said, Papa, that the horses are not to blame."

"They could be put up in the sheds near the stables," Antosha agreed.

"We can give them some oats. That won't make us any poorer," Sophia Petrovna added.

"Keep your advice to yourselves! I didn't ask for any!"

Arkady Petrovich kept lunging about the room, clasping his temples. "I know that the horses are not to blame!" He paused before his daughter. "That's true enough! The horses have nothing to do with it! But what of that?"

But there was an uncertainty in his tone. He seemed to have shrunken somehow. The blood fled from his face until it was the colour of his moustache, and his eyes had lost their icy hardness. There was something guilty and humble about them as he looked at his son.

"Have we enough oats?" he asked unexpectedly.

"I'll see that there's enough, and we have plenty of fresh hay too."

Antosha vanished through the hallway without more ado.

"The idea of bringing the Cossacks here!" Arkady Petrovich raised his shoulders and began to pace the room again. "The Cossacks and I? Who could believe it?"

But his movements lost something of their abruptness.

His wrath had collapsed like an ocean wave, breaking upon the shore in its green fury and hissing into foam over the sand.

The neighing of the hungry horses clattering through the yard and the rattle of the Cossack sabres came through the open windows.

There was nothing terrible about the beginning of to-morrow. The sparrows were skipping about and chirping outside and the sun shone so gayly that the windows, the walls and even Arkady Petrovich's bed seemed to be laughing. As yet undressed he hurried to the window. The warm air caressed his chest and he caught sight of the long line of the shining horses' rumps. Wearing only their coloured shirts, the sturdy Cossacks were currying their animals, the sun playing on their muscles bared to the elbows, on their tanned necks and the puddles of water they had splashed about. He looked at the sun and his fields and the hoofs of the horses and the boots of the Cossacks heavily tramping the earth. The singing of the birds, the snorting of the animals and the crude oaths of the men impinged his consciousness, when suddenly he knew that he was hungry.

"Savka!" he roared. "Serve the coffee!" With this, he plunged back to bed to let his old body luxuriate yet a bit.

When Savka brought the coffee, he ogled the steaming cup lovingly, sniffed at the yet warm bread and chided his servant because the cream, it seemed to him, was not sufficiently rich. Myshka lay fast asleep curled up at his feet.

March 2-15, 1912
Capri, "Villa Serafina"